Hooked on You

Center Point
Large Print

Also by Kathleen Fuller and available from
Center Point Large Print:

An Unbroken Heart
Written in Love
The Promise of a Letter
Words from the Heart
The Teacher's Bride
The Farmer's Bride
A Love Made New
The Innkeeper's Bride

Hooked on You

A MAPLE FALLS ROMANCE

KATHLEEN FULLER

CENTER POINT LARGE PRINT
THORNDIKE, MAINE

To my bosom buddy Eddie. We started out as fellow authors and ended up closer than sisters. I miss your smile, your hugs, your wisdom, your contagious laughter, your cooking adventures, your generous heart . . . I miss everything. There's never been a stronger woman than you.

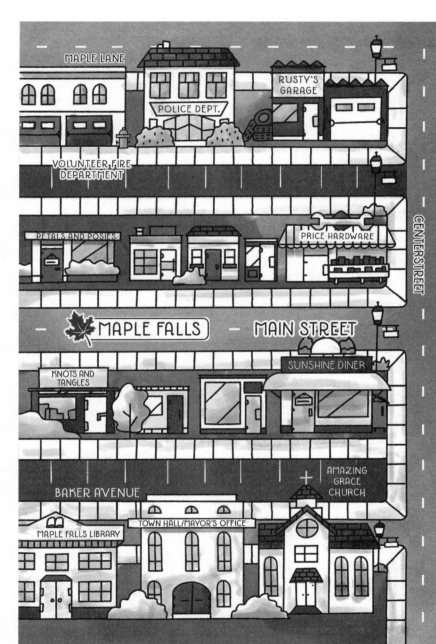

Hooked on You

Chapter 1

A riot of colors, textures, and fibers filled the canvas in front of Riley McAllister. She tilted her head to the right. To the left. Then, with careful precision and pointed tweezers, she started to apply a hair-thin golden thread to the narrow bead of glue on the peacock feather in the center, the final touch to a project that had taken over three months to complete.

"Riley! Your Mimi called!"

Riley flinched and the tweezers pierced through the canvas, marring the multilayered feather. She started to mutter a curse but bit her tongue. She couldn't afford foul language, not when she had almost zero dollars in her bank account. Besides, she was determined to win the cash in the cuss jar at the end of the month. There had to be over three hundred dollars in it already.

"Oops, my bad."

She turned around and glared at her roommate. Melody had entered her bedroom–art studio–living room in the apartment they shared, a silver headband pushing back her short, curly black hair. Then Melody's words hit her. The torn canvas and gold thread forgotten, she jumped up from her chair. *Mimi.*

"Is she okay?" Riley asked, panicked.

"She's fine, but she sounds a bit cranky. She said she must have called five times before I answered." Melody took a sip of coffee out of her brand-new *Probably Wine* mug. The purchase was courtesy of her winning the cuss jar bounty last month. "You really should put your phone on vibrate at least. It's a good thing I saw it light up on the kitchen counter."

Dread filled Riley. "What did she say?" Her grandmother was no spring chicken, and as the years passed, she worried the next call would be *the one*. She grabbed her cell out of Melody's hand.

"For you to call her. You're welcome, by the way." Melody scowled. "Geez, calm down. She's not at death's door, if that's what you're worried about."

Riley turned her back to Melody and tapped Mimi's number on the phone screen. "How would you know?"

"Because she said, 'Tell Riley I'm not at death's door.'"

Riley turned back around as she put the phone to her ear, relief flooding her. "I'm sorry. You know how I get when she calls."

"You get crazy," Melody said with a grin. At Riley's pointed look, she added, "Crazy with worry, I mean."

True. She tended to expect the worst when

12

Mimi called, despite telling herself she was being ridiculous. But she couldn't help it. *If anything ever happened to Mimi* . . . She drew in a deep breath as her grandmother answered.

"Hi." Riley forced a cheerful tone. "I'm sorry I missed your—" She looked at her roommate.

Five, Melody mouthed, holding up her hand.

"Five calls." Riley winced. "Is everything okay?"

"Oh yes, sugar. Just the usual goin' on here." Mimi's lilting Southern drawl filled Riley's ear, triggering the tiniest spark of homesickness, which always surprised her. After nine years of living in New York City, she should be over it, but every time she heard Mimi's voice, it came back again. Riley's life in Maple Falls had been a big disappointment, but that wasn't Mimi's fault.

"The *usual* required five calls in a row?"

"If you had picked up the phone, there only would have been one."

"You could have left a message, you know." Riley plopped onto the pull-out sofa that was also her bed.

"I could have, but then I wouldn't have heard Melody's sweet voice. She's a peach."

Riley smiled and glanced at Melody, spying her friend's frown as she inspected the ruined canvas. Her stomach lurched. With some time and precision, the artwork could be fixed. Still, Riley would always know it was imperfect. She had planned to put it in her show next week, but that was impossible now. The work was too flawed to display in public.

"Riley? You still with me, hon?"

"Yes, sorry." She turned away from the canvas and focused on her grandmother, her prior concern rising to the surface. "How are you? Is everything all right?"

"I called because I haven't heard from you in three weeks. According to your social media, you've been a busy young lady." She sniffed. "Apparently too busy to call your decrepit old grandmother."

"You're *not* decrepit." Erma McAllister was far from feeble, but she was seventy-two, and Riley didn't like thinking about her getting older. She also didn't want to point out that her social media wasn't exactly a reflection of her life. She kept it going with carefully curated pictures of her works in progress, hoping to catch the eye of someone in the art business. A far-flung idea, but it didn't take much effort to post a picture and write a caption. "You're also too classy for guilt trips."

"It was worth a shot." Mimi sighed. "I guess I better get to the point. I need you to come home. ASAP."

Riley pressed her hand against her chest, feeling her heart rate speeding up. "Why? Are you sick? Are you in the hospital?"

"No, I'm not sick . . . or in the hospital. At least not anymore."

Riley sat up. "You were in the hospital and you didn't tell me?"

"There wasn't time. I broke my leg—"

"You broke your leg?" Her voice choked in her throat, and Melody rushed to sit down next to her. "When? How?"

"If I can get a word in edgewise, I'll tell you."

Mimi's quiet, composed tone immediately calmed Riley, as it had for so many years. After an unstable childhood, she'd moved in with her grandmother when she was thirteen. Mimi had been her rock ever since. "I'm listening."

"Put her on speaker," Melody said.

Riley tapped the screen. "You're on speaker now. Melody wants to know what's going on too."

"Oh, hello again, sugar. As I was saying, I broke my leg when I slid into third base last Sunday."

Riley and Melody stared at each other.

"What?" Riley finally said.

"You see, the young man playing third was blocking the base, so I had to slide. Myrtle hit a lousy outside pitch straight to the first baseman, who clearly should have been riding the bench instead of playing the infield. He flubbed the ball, and I thought I'd made it to third, until everyone started yelling at me to go back to second. I was already committed, so down I went. I was safe, by the way."

"Is she serious?" Melody whispered.

Rolling her eyes, Riley nodded. Softball was one of her grandmother's favorite sports, and she had dragged Riley to many a community game until Riley was seventeen. Then the community games had stopped.

"Mimi, you shouldn't have been playing softball in the first place."

"I don't need a lecture from you, young lady," Mimi grumbled. "I need you to come home and take over Knots and Tangles while I convalesce."

"Oh no," Riley said, getting up from the couch. She shook her head. "I'm not falling for this again."

"Falling for what?"

Her grandmother sounded so innocent Riley almost believed her. "Like I've said a million times before, I'm not moving back to Maple Falls, and I'm definitely not taking over the yarn shop for you." She walked over to the painting and scowled at the hole in the canvas. "I am impressed, though. You spun a good yarn, pun intended."

"I'm not spinnin' anything." Mimi's tone was sharp. "It's the truth. Myrtle and I joined the new church softball team a few weeks ago, and we just had our second game. Now I'm out for the

16

season, so stop what you're doing and get back here. Pronto."

Riley spun around and met Melody's stunned gaze. Her grandmother rarely used a commanding tone with her, and not once since Riley moved away had she been insistent about her returning to Maple Falls. Until now. While she had asked Riley to visit around the holidays, she never pressured her and even visited New York a few times. She understood how important Riley's career was to her and had always supported it 100 percent. Riley was banking that she still did.

"Mimi, I'm sorry you broke your leg—"

"Thank you. Now, about your return—"

"And I would love to come help you." Which she would, if it didn't mean going back to Arkansas. "But I can't exactly drop everything here at the last minute. I have a jo—" She hadn't told Mimi she was working part-time for a food delivery service. She had to pay her bills somehow, since her art wasn't making any money. "I, um, have a show coming up." At least that part was true. *Mostly.*

"Oh?" Excitement entered her voice. "I didn't know that. Where is it so I can tell everyone about my famous granddaughter?"

She wouldn't exactly be bragging about her one and only granddaughter, the supposed artistic rage of New York City, if she knew her art show was at the local flea market. It wasn't even a show, really. Just a place to sell some of her work so she could make her part of the rent. Telling herself it was an art show made it easier to swallow.

"The details aren't worked out yet."

"So it's something you can postpone? Sugar, you know I wouldn't ask you to come if I wasn't desperate. Myrtle's going on a three-week cruise again, so I can't count on her."

Guilt hammered Riley, but she stood fast. "What about one of the other Bosom Buddies?" she asked, referring to the small group of ladies that met weekly at the yarn shop for coffee, knitting or crocheting, and copious amounts of gossip.

"I suppose one or two of them could help," Mimi muttered. "But they're *awfully* busy."

Riley pressed her fingertip against her temple, feeling her pulse throb. She had vowed not to return to Maple Falls until she made it big in New York—or at least could say she wasn't living from hand to mouth, and she was barely doing that. She knew the Bosom Buddies wouldn't hesitate to help her grandmother if Mimi asked. Most of the seven women had been friends since grade school, except for two who had been folded into the group over the years.

"I . . ."

She turned and looked at Melody, whose thin brown arms were crossed over her chest, her dark eyes peering over bright-green square glasses. Riley knew that reproving look, and she didn't like being on the receiving end of it.

In truth she didn't need Melody to prod her. Riley couldn't refuse the woman who had practically raised her after her mother abandoned Riley for God knew where. If Mimi needed her, Riley would be there—just like Mimi had always been there for her.

"I'll get the next flight out," Riley said, holding back a sigh. The expense would almost max out her one credit card, but she'd worry about that later.

"Oh, Riley, thank you! Thank you!" Mimi gushed. "I can't tell you how much this means to me. I know the shop will be in good hands with you while I recuperate. I won't keep you. Once you've made your reservation, text me your flight info, and I'll have someone pick you up from the airport."

"I'll just get an Uber," Riley said.

"Nonsense. The airport is over an hour away. That would cost way too much money. Don't you worry, sugar. I'll make all the arrangements to get you back home."

Home? Maple Falls had never felt like home.

"Love you, sweetie," Mimi added before Riley could say anything else. "Talk to you soon!"

She stared at the phone after Mimi hung up. A few seconds later, she glanced at Melody, who had sat back down on their lumpy, secondhand couch and was now grinning at her.

"I knew you wouldn't let her down."

Riley trudged over to the couch and sank onto it again, her phone still in her hand. She continued staring at the black screen. "I don't know about this."

"What's the big deal? You're taking care of Mimi, who means a lot to you."

"But that also means going back to Maple Falls."

"So? You're overdue for a visit home, Riley. I've been back to Minnesota three times this year alone. When was the last time you were in Arkansas?"

Nearly ten years ago, when she first moved to New York. She wasn't about to tell Melody that. The two of them had become good friends over the last two years since they became roommates. But there were things Riley didn't want to share with her—or anyone else, for that matter. Like her reasons for staying away from Maple Falls.

Shifting the subject, she said, "You're right. I need to focus on taking care of Mimi. That's what matters. I'll make sure she's following doctor's orders." She smirked as she set her phone on the coffee table. "She has a tendency to think she's invincible."

"No way." Melody chuckled. "Imagine that."

"I can't believe she slid into third base," Riley

20

said. "Or that she is even playing softball at her age. Then again, Mimi has been in sports all her life. She and Myrtle were on the first girls' softball team in Maple Falls, and they were both excellent. She still plays tennis with Gwen too." Riley looked at her slightly pudgy tummy, the result of cheap food, a few too many glasses of wine alone in her apartment, and more than a little stress. She didn't doubt her grandmother was in better shape at seventy-two than Riley was right now.

"I had no idea Erma was so athletic," Melody said.

"I shouldn't be surprised she's on the team. Well, maybe a little because of her age. Whoever is coaching ought to be smacked upside the head for letting her do something so ridiculous."

"You think they could have stopped her?"

"They could have stalled her at second." Riley shook her head and turned to her friend. "Anyway, what's done is done. I'm heading back to Arkansas." A sour lump formed in her stomach at the thought. She would have to quit her job and cancel her upcoming "show." "Don't worry about rent, Melody. I'll still pay my share." *Somehow*.

Melody nodded. "Any idea how long you'll be gone?"

Riley shrugged. "Depends on how fast Mimi's leg heals, I guess. I'll be back as soon as I can, but it could be a while."

Nodding, Melody adjusted her headband, seemingly deep in thought. After a pause, she said, "Would you mind subletting to Charlie?"

"The guy in your acting class?"

"Yeah. He's been couch surfing for the past two months after a bad experience with his last roommate. He's looking for a place to land until he can find something more permanent."

"Are you sure he's . . . safe?"

"That boy's practically got wholesome tattooed on his forehead. I kinda feel sorry for him. He's character actor material and not bad, but he's rough around the edges. I've gotten to know him pretty well over the past year. Trust me, he's safe." Melody gripped Riley's hand. "Thanks for caring, sis."

"Always." Riley held her hand tight, then let it go. She was so grateful for Melody's friendship. She had answered Riley's ad for a new roommate at the local university where she took theater classes. Friendship had never come easy to Riley, but Melody's easygoing and caring personality had eventually pulled her out of her shell.

She was also grateful to the unknown Charlie for taking over the rent for a little while. "Guess I better search online for a flight."

"And I've got to get ready for the exciting world of waitressing. Double shift today. Yay me." Melody got up from the couch and headed for the one bedroom in the apartment. When they first rented the place together, they agreed to change rooms every three months. The arrangement had worked out well, especially since neither of them was big on entertaining visitors. When she wasn't delivering food, Riley was focused on her art, while Melody, a social butterfly who liked being out and about, often spent time with her actor friends at various places around the city. The few times she dragged Riley out of the cave had been torture. Riley was used to being alone, and she liked it that way.

A few moments later, Melody emerged from the bedroom, dressed in the white T-shirt and black pants her job required. Her blue-and-orange-striped drawstring backpack was slung over her shoulders, and her lips glistened with plum lipstick that perfectly complemented her dark skin.

"See you tomorrow," she said, opening the apartment door. "Don't wait up."

Riley waved goodbye as Melody closed the door. She rose from the couch and turned the double locks into place, then glanced at her ruined art. She wasn't in the mood to try to fix it now. Instead, she walked over to the window and gazed at the view of the brick apartment building next door. Not much of a vista, but like every struggling artist trying to make it in the big city, she couldn't afford to be picky. Still, New York was her home.

The window was cracked open, letting in the buzz of city life. When she'd first arrived, she had been awed by the place. Too awed, to the point of culture shock. She wasn't used to the mix of cultures, but she had quickly grown to appreciate the diversity of the people living here. She'd never gotten used to the nightlife, but that was fine. Her focus wasn't on having fun. She was determined to break into the hip art scene that had eluded her for the past ten years.

She might be broke and in serious need of some vitamin D, not to mention shedding a few pounds, but at least she wasn't in Maple Falls. The only way she'd planned to return was after she had proven to herself and everyone else that she was different. Successful. Responsible. And nothing like Tracey. Thanks to her grandmother not acting her age, Riley's plan was now in shambles.

Riley turned and stared at the ruined peacock feather and the golden threads she had painstakingly glued over thick, lifted curls of purple, blue, ochre, and green acrylic paint. Poking through the colorful swirls in what seemed like a random pattern but had taken hours to design were the glossy black-and-white magazine pictures of city life. The comfort of nature's colors clashing with the harshness of human constructs. She loved to explore opposite concepts in her art using unexpected materials—fabric, feathers, a variety of paints, anything with texture, and especially substances that on the surface were easily discarded things yet could be transformed into something beautiful.

A sigh escaped. There'd been a time when she thought her art was unique, and in the unsophisticated town of Maple Falls, it was. But not here. Mixed-media artists were everywhere, and getting herself noticed in a sea of aspiring creatives had been beyond difficult. But she wasn't going to give up. There wasn't time to fix the piece the way she wanted to, but she would tackle it when she returned. Right now she had to go take care of her grandmother, which meant working at Knots and Tangles again.

A car horn sounded below, jolting Riley's thoughts. She'd never imagined she'd be working there again. During her teen years she spent hours in her grandmother's yarn shop. Not only working but practicing her art in the all-purpose room in the back. The old yarn store had been her job and her haven. But even she could see that it was a fifty-year millstone around her grandmother's neck. Mimi needed to sell the store and retire. Riley had mentioned it to her over the years only to be instantly shut down. Maple Falls was in decline when Riley moved away, and from little hints she gathered during conversations with Mimi, things hadn't improved.

Riley thought her grandmother not only needed to sell the store but also needed to put her large house on the market and move in with Myrtle. Or maybe Myrtle could move in with Mimi. Riley wasn't naive enough to think her grandmother would come to New York with her, but Mimi moving in with one of her good friends was a possibility. They were both widows, and paring down expenses would benefit them both. If there was something Riley was an expert at, it was pinching her pennies.

While her brain knew retirement and consolidation were in Mimi's best interest, the thought of the store being in someone else's hands pinched at her heart. She shoved the feeling away, as she normally did when she grew sentimental. It was time her grandmother embraced change. This visit was a prime opportunity for Riley to convince her of that.

She felt an unexpected spark of hope. She had a plan now—help Mimi heal and convince her to sell her shop and the house. All three tasks wouldn't be easy, but she was determined. Once her grandmother unchained herself from the past, Riley could too—and when she left Maple Falls this time, it would be for good.

She crossed the small living room, opened her ancient laptop, and started to search for a flight. As she surfed, another thought popped into her mind. But no—she didn't have to worry about running into *him*. Like her, he'd moved on from Maple Falls. Still, remembering the crush she'd had on him in high school—one he had no idea about—caused a tiny flutter in her stomach. Talk about silly. She hadn't given him a single thought since she left Maple Falls. Okay, maybe one . . . or fifty thoughts since she'd left, but not any recently. And there was no reason for her to think about Hayden Price again now. She put him out of her mind and booked her flight to Arkansas.

"Erma Jean McAllister, you need Jesus."

Erma set her cell phone on the counter and looked at her friend of close to sixty-five years. She tapped her chest with two fingers. "I have Jesus. Right in here."

"Then you need a double portion." Myrtle Benson straightened the business cards on the counter next to the small antique cash register that was just for show. A working adding machine from the eighties was right next to it. "Good thing we have evening service tonight."

Erma wheeled herself from behind the counter, trying not to knock down a display of knitting needles with her outstretched, plaster-covered leg. She was proud that her little store, Knots and Tangles, was one of the original businesses in Maple Falls and at one time had the most yarn and fiber art supplies within a one-hundred-fifty-mile radius. Her mother owned the shop before Erma, and her grandmother had started the business. A woman entrepreneur was almost unheard of back then. Erma had worked here since she was twelve, and very little of the shop had changed since then. The place was full to the brim, and that was the way she liked it.

Her wheelchair, however, did not. "What are you prattling on about?" she said.

Myrtle sighed. "That phone call you just made to Riley. Land sakes, woman, you know I can cancel my trip anytime."

"And let you disappoint Jorge?"

"His name is Javier. And I'm sure he's long gone from the ship anyway. You know those jobs can be temporary."

Erma caught the dreamy look in Myrtle's eyes, the same one she'd had when she came home from her cruise eight months ago after meeting Jorge, er, Javier, the silver-haired—and silver-tongued, apparently—maître d' at one of the fancy restaurants on the cruise ship. Erma couldn't remember the name of the place, but she did remember how Myrtle wouldn't stop talking about the food—and the *service*.

"You've been looking forward to this trip for so long."

"I haven't heard from him since my last letter." Myrtle stuck out her lower lip, covered in a soft pink lipstick that coordinated with her oversize handbag. "I might as well cancel."

"If you cancel, I'm going in your place."

"With a broken leg?"

Erma gave her a pointed look. "In a heartbeat."

"You might just do it too." Myrtle grimaced. "Fine. You win, as usual. But that still doesn't make it right that you acted like it was an emergency and Riley had to come right away."

"It *is* an emergency." She gestured to the overstuffed shelves and baskets in the store. "How am I supposed to maneuver around this place in this thing?" She slammed her hands on the wheelchair armrests, which jolted the chair and made her leg twinge. Uh-oh, that was more than a twinge. "I need a pain pill."

"Right away." Myrtle rushed to get a glass of water from the bathroom sink in the back, then handed it and a pill to Erma. "Bea has already told you she can help out."

Erma swallowed the pill, then leaned back in the wheelchair. Bea was Erma's closest friend, but Myrtle came in second. She was grateful for their offers of help, but she needed to refuse them this time. "It's high time Riley came home for a visit. Nine years is too long."

"So you took advantage of your injury to get her back here." Myrtle gave her a reproving look. "You know why she left."

Erma lifted her chin. "She can have an art career here."

"That's not what I'm talking about."

She knew exactly what Myrtle was referring to—her no-good daughter who hadn't returned since she disappeared fifteen years ago. Riley still carried the burden of that rejection, even if she stuffed it down behind a facade of small-town girl turned big-city artist. "I just want her home, Myrtle. Is that too much to ask?"

Her friend's blue eyes softened, the creases in the corners deepening. "It might be."

Erma didn't want to hear that.

The bell over the door chimed, and both women turned to see Hayden Price walk into the store. If Erma were fifty years younger and hadn't known not only Hayden's parents but also his grandparents and great-grandparents, she wouldn't mind taking a crack at the handsome young man. As it was, she could still appreciate his fine form, which looked even better in a baseball uniform. He wasn't as winsome as her Gus had been in his day, but he was definitely easy on the eyes. *I might be old, but I ain't dead.*

"Hi, Hayden," Myrtle said, casually patting the back of her short gray hair. "What brings you by?"

Erma smirked. Seemed like she wasn't the only senior woman who thought Hayden was the bee's knees.

"I came to check on our center fielder." Hayden walked over to Erma and crouched in front of her. "How's the leg?"

"Tolerable."

"She just took a pain pill," Myrtle blurted.

Erma shot her an annoyed look. "Don't you have a cruise to pack for?"

"I guess I do." She grabbed her pink purse, which looked big enough to house half the contents of the yarn store, and headed for the door. "*Hasta la*, um, whatever."

"You might want to brush up on your Spanish for Jorge," Erma called out.

"It's Javier!" The door shut behind her.

Hayden chuckled. "You two are a mess."

"Sugar, you have no idea."

He stood, still smiling, a shock of his thick blond hair falling over his forehead. Then all traces of humor disappeared. "I'm sorry about what happened."

She waved him off. "Not your fault."

"I was the third base coach. And I'm the head coach. I should have told you to stay on second."

"I wouldn't have listened to you anyway." She looked up at him, smiling as she remembered the split second before her leg ended up going in a direction God never intended. "Did you hear the crowd cheering?"

"They were yelling at you to go back."

"But I was already committed—"

He held up his hand. "Let's not go down that road again. I came by to take you to lunch if you're so inclined. Today's special at the Sunshine Diner is liver and onions."

"Ugh, who likes that?"

"I do." He looked slightly offended.

"You're too young for old people food." Erma tried to move toward him and knocked over a display of T-shirt yarn. "Oh, for goodness' sake."

"I'll fix it."

She watched as he made a valiant attempt to put all the skeins of yarn in the cube she'd knocked over. They had been neatly stacked—one of the few displays that was—but now they were being haphazardly squished into the space.

"There," he said, cramming the last skein of yarn into the box. "No harm done. So, are we on for lunch? I only have forty-five minutes, and then I have to get back to the store."

Erma was about to tell him she wasn't hungry when an idea jumped into her mind. *Erma Jean, you're a genius.* "I'm not all that hungry, but there is something you can do for me."

"Name it."

She wished there were a way to convince him not to feel guilty over what happened. Truth be told, she should have known better than to attempt that slide. The accident brought home the fact that she wasn't as fit as she used to be, which was another reason she wanted Riley back. Although she'd never admit it out loud, Myrtle was right—she was taking advantage of her accident to coax Riley back to the fold. She was worried about her granddaughter. The child had always been a loner, and that tendency hadn't changed since her big move to New York. Riley needed fresh air and companionship. And potential companionship was standing right in front of Erma, wrapped up in a charming and attractive package.

"I need you to pick up someone from the airport for me," she told Hayden. "Either tonight or tomorrow, if you're free."

"Just so happens I am." He grinned. "All you need to do is let me know when."

"I'll send you a text." As the creator and coach of the newly minted church softball team, he had given all the players his cell phone number. For years Erma had been resistant to texting, preferring to pick up the phone and call whoever she wanted to talk to. But she acknowledged that sometimes it was convenient, especially if you wanted to avoid any unwelcome questions.

"That works." He put his hands into the cargo pockets of his shorts. "Are you sure you don't want anything to eat? I can bring you something if you don't feel like going to the diner."

"No, I'm fine."

"All right. Rain check then." He headed for the front of the store, then turned around and looked at her, smiling again—Hayden Price's typical expression. Not only was he handsome but he was unfailingly optimistic and had been since he was a young kid. The perfect contrast to her serious but sweeter than peaches-and-cream granddaughter. He waved at Erma, then left for the diner.

She smiled, steepling her fingers. Erma couldn't believe it—a broken leg might be just the thing she needed to help her granddaughter.

Chapter 2

Hayden walked through the sliding doors at Clinton National Airport and then glanced at his watch: 10:30 p.m. He was a few minutes early. He walked toward a group of tables and chairs near the coffee bar and sat down facing the escalators, waiting for Erma's mystery visitor to appear.

He stretched out his legs and thought about the text Erma sent him earlier that day with the flight details and thanking him for doing this favor for her. If she'd asked him to jump off the top of the Knots and Tangles roof, he probably would have—or at least given it serious thought. She'd told him dozens of times since she broke her leg not to blame himself, but he couldn't help it. He knew the kind of pain an injury like that could cause, and it was probably more intense considering her age. It was his fault she had to deal with it. Why he hadn't stopped a seventy-plus-year-old woman from rounding the bases, he didn't know. Not at the time anyway. He realized later he'd let his competitive nature get the best of him. He needed to work on that. The days of wanting to win at all costs were over—forever.

Picking up someone from the airport hardly

made up for what happened, but he was glad to do it. He just wished she hadn't been so cagey about who he was supposed to bring back to Maple Falls. Erma hadn't given him a name. All she said was the time the flight was supposed to arrive, along with *"You'll recognize the person when you see them."*

Despite her insistence on keeping her visitor a secret, he wondered if he was picking up her granddaughter, Riley. He'd considered asking Erma outright but decided to let the woman have her fun. There was a chance he was picking up someone other than Riley, who hadn't returned to Maple Falls since . . . Actually, he had no idea when Riley had last been in her hometown.

A few minutes later, he saw several people taking the escalator from the gate section of the airport to the lobby, indicating that the plane had landed. It was the last arrival of the night. He rose from the chair and strolled toward the escalator, keeping a good distance but studying everyone who had arrived. He didn't recognize any of the passengers as they walked to the baggage carousels behind him. Hayden moved closer to the escalator, and soon it was empty. Huh. He hoped he hadn't missed Erma's guest.

As soon as he started to head to the gates, he saw someone appear at the top of the escalator.

When she was halfway down, he smiled. Well, well, he was right after all. Riley McAllister had returned.

She pulled a small roller suitcase behind her, and a large red duffel bag was slung over her shoulder. A small brown leather purse was strapped across her torso. She was wearing a white long-sleeved shirt that looked suspiciously like a man's, slim faded jeans, and hippie sandals with big buckles on them. But while her outfit was casual, the tense expression on her face was not. Riley was home, but she didn't look happy about it.

He met her at the bottom of the escalator. "Hey, Riley."

She looked at him, her head tilting and her frown deepening, as if she didn't know who he was. That pricked his ego a bit. Who in Maple Falls and the great central Arkansas area didn't know Hayden Price? The small-town boy who made it big in the minor leagues, then went on to the majors only to blow out his shoulder when he threw the opening pitch of his first professional game. Then again, it had been almost a decade since he'd seen Riley. A lot had happened since then, but he didn't think he'd changed *that* much.

"Hayden?" she finally said.

"That's me."

"What are you doing here?" She dragged

the strap of the duffel higher on her shoulder, sounding a little annoyed.

"I'm your ride. Erma can't exactly drive right now." He pushed away the niggle of guilt. "She asked me to carry you home."

"Oh." She glanced around the airport, which was nearly empty now. "I offered to get an Uber or a taxi, but she said she would take care of it. I didn't think she'd send *you,* though."

Ouch.

"I mean, I figured she'd ask one of her buddies to pick me up." An awkward pause. "I didn't know you two were acquainted with each other."

"Everyone knows Erma." He shifted on his feet. Not wanting to give Riley the opportunity to ask for more specifics, he added, "I'll get your bag from the carousel."

"This is all I brought." She held both the duffel and the suitcase in a death grip.

Obviously, she didn't need or want help. Fine, less work for him, and he pretended not to be put out that she had refused his assistance.

"I'm parked out front," he said. "We don't have to walk far."

She nodded and headed for the sliding door, her gaze straight ahead like she was a woman on a mission, and he was suddenly transported back to high school. To him, Riley McAllister always stood out from the other girls in his high school, not only for her looks, although he'd always thought she was attractive. She was taller than average, with ash-brown hair that was usually pulled back in a ponytail. Her eyes were her most striking feature, large and bright, like blue topaz. Right now they looked just as hard.

He followed her, and when they left the lobby he gestured to the parking spaces in front of them.

"That's my car," he said, pointing to a twenty-year-old Subaru that had been put through its paces and needed a fresh coat of paint but still ran like a dream.

She turned to him, her quizzical gaze apparent under the bright parking lot lights. "I thought you'd have a Lambo or a Porsche or something."

He laughed. "You have to play in more than one major league game to get that." Fortunately he'd received a healthy signing bonus when he joined the Detroit Tigers, and the team let him keep most of it when he was unable to play anymore. After paying off his medical bills, the rest of the money was parked in his savings account, except for a small portion he'd used to buy an old house on the edge of Maple Falls. He'd gotten the house and the surrounding property for a steal and planned to rehab both as soon as he could. But he'd never made enough money to purchase an expensive sports car, even if he'd wanted to.

"This fine automobile was Harrison's old car," he admitted.

"He's your brother, right?" Riley asked.

Hayden opened the trunk. "The oldest one. He lives in Missouri now. Wife and two kids. The boys are cute as can be, but I'm their uncle, so I'm biased." He held out his hand. "Can I put your bags in the trunk?"

She nodded and handed him the duffel and suitcase. After stowing her luggage and shutting the trunk, he went to the passenger side of the car and opened the door for her. Riley stared at him as if she'd never seen anyone open a car door before, then got in. He closed it when she seemed settled.

The ride back to Maple Falls would be an interesting one. He made his way to the driver's side. Riley was still pretty, but he could see that her personality hadn't changed much over the past decade. She'd been a grade ahead of him, a loner who had an art talent he could only envy. She never hung out with the popular girls or any clique at all. She had kept to herself, and in a small-town high school where everyone knew everyone, she was an enigma, and he had been intrigued. He'd also been too busy with baseball to get to know her better. But baseball wasn't standing in his way anymore, and he had to admit Riley still intrigued him.

What is Mimi up to? Riley had been sure one of the Bosom Buddies would pick her up tonight.

Probably Bea, her grandmother's closest friend, followed by Myrtle. The last person she expected to see was Hayden Price.

She'd been so surprised she couldn't speak when she first saw him. She would recognize him anywhere, and not just because he was Maple Falls' most famous resident. In high school all the girls fawned over him, but she had kept her distance. Not because she didn't find him attractive. She absolutely did, and that was the problem.

And because life could be extremely unfair, he managed to be even more handsome at twenty-six than he was at seventeen. He hadn't lost his athletic build, despite his horrible accident a year ago when he'd injured his shoulder so severely pitching in his first major league game that his career had been over before it started. Mimi told her, of course, but what no one knew, not even Melody, was that she had followed Hayden's career through the newspapers and internet. Now she was sitting next to him, looking like trash after a long day and flight, in need of a shower and some sleep, and totally unprepared for riding in a car with him for an hour.

He climbed in the driver's seat, and she caught the scent of his cologne. Wow, he smelled as good as he looked. Great, she'd been in Arkansas a little more than ten minutes and already she was acting like the high school outcast with a secret crush on the most popular jock in school. Which was exactly how it had been back then. She slid down in her seat.

"Comfortable?" he asked, his voice deep and smooth.

Did this man have a single flaw? She doubted it. Despite his popularity, he had always been nice, and that attracted her far more than his sun-bleached blond hair and light-gray eyes. Then there was that body . . . Her face started to heat.

"I can turn on the air conditioner if you're hot—"

"Yes! I mean, that would be fine. I am a bit . . . warm."

"You know how muggy it can get in May." He flipped on the air conditioner, then backed out of the parking spot. "Summer's arrived early this year."

She nodded but didn't say anything. She and Hayden had never had much of a conversation before. He'd been in her art class junior year, but they sat at different tables, and other than him mentioning that her projects were "really good," they hadn't interacted. They lived in different worlds, even though their town was barely a blip on the map. He was small-town royalty, and she was the hermit who stayed to herself with art keeping her company. Riley was the last girl Hayden would notice.

He headed down I-30, and as they passed green interstate signs, she had a weird feeling that time stood still. It was only yesterday that she left for New York, brushing the dust of Maple Falls and Arkansas off the soles of the brand-new sneakers she'd bought just for the trip. She glanced down at the worn Birkenstock sandals on her feet. She'd purchased them with the money from her first and only real art sale five years ago. The money had run out quickly, but at least she'd been smart with her choice of footwear.

"I'm sorry about Erma," Hayden said, jerking her out of her thoughts.

"How is she really?" Riley knew her grandmother downplayed things sometimes.

"Ornery as ever, but she is in pain."

She grimaced. "When I find the idiot who didn't hold her up at second base, I'm going to lay into him."

"Um," he said, his voice quiet. "That idiot was me."

Forgetting she was supposed to be aloof, she turned to face him. "What were you thinking, letting an old woman run the bases like that?"

"I know, I know. I guess I forgot how old she was. She's athletic for her age and has a competitive spirit. If she'd made it home, we would have won our first game. I lost my head for a minute." He threaded his hand through his hair.

The gesture caught her attention and cooled her anger a bit. Which made her even more irritated—this time with herself. She faced forward again.

"I'm going to make it up to her," he said.

She crossed her arms over her chest. "Is that why you picked me up tonight?"

"She asked me to. And yes, that's why. I don't pick up people late at night at the airport on a whim, but I'd do anything for Erma, even if I hadn't made the tragic decision to send her to third."

What a Hayden thing to say, and of course Riley believed him. She doubted he had a mean bone in his body.

After a long pause, he asked, "How was your flight?"

"Long." She hadn't been on a plane since she'd left Mimi's, and she spent the first half hour gripping the arms of her seat when they encountered some turbulence shortly after take-off. Once she realized the plane wasn't going to crash, she'd been able to relax a little. It was hard to fully settle down when her nerves were already stretched thin.

"When was the last time you were in Maple Falls?"

She hesitated. "Nine years ago."

"You haven't visited since you left for New York?"

44

Riley shook her head but didn't say anything else. She didn't want to go there with Hayden of all people.

Fortunately he changed the subject. "Do you like living in a big city?"

"I love New York."

"Seems like I've heard that somewhere before. I lived in a few when I was with different minor league teams." As he drove past the southern suburbs of Little Rock, the lights dimmed, and the interstate became pitch-black except for the red taillights of the few cars on the road with them. "Los Angeles, Dallas, Miami." He chuckled. "I found out real fast that I'm not a city boy. Give me a small town like Maple Falls anytime." He laughed again, and she couldn't help but smile.

"Mind if I turn on the radio?" he asked.

She nodded, and soon country music filtered through the speakers. He left the volume low but loud enough that she could hear the twang.

"Do you like Country?" he asked after a few minutes.

"A little." She'd avoided the music as much as she could, especially during her first few years in New York. Aside from Southern Gospel, it was Mimi's favorite. She leaned back against the seat and closed her eyes. The steady hum of the engine, the lilt of a country ballad, and the cool air blowing through the vents all settled her nerves.

• • •

"Hey," Hayden said, touching her arm. "We're here."

Riley opened her eyes, shocked to see that they were in Mimi's driveway. The 1940s brick ranch house was in front of her, the porch light on. "I fell asleep?"

"Yeah." He smiled. "A few bars into 'She Thinks My Tractor's Sexy.' "

She turned to him, and her breath caught. Mimi had a streetlight at the end of her driveway, and Riley could see Hayden clearly in the light. A thick lock of his blond hair hung over his brow, his mouth forming a half grin. He was beyond handsome, and so darn nice. She needed to get out of this car. "What do I owe you?"

"Nothing." His smile faded. "I'm not an Uber, you know."

"But I want to pay you for gas."

"Forget it."

"I insist."

"This is a favor for Erma, remember?" He opened the door. "I'll bring your bags to the porch. I'm sure she's chomping at the bit to see you."

Riley scrambled out of the car, bothered he wouldn't let her pay him but eager to see Mimi. She hurried to the house and swung open the door. Instantly she was greeted by the smell of arthritis cream, Mimi's favorite vanilla-scented candles, and the sound of *The Golden Girls* blaring from the TV as she entered the living room.

"Riley!" Mimi motioned for her to come to the ancient recliner, her smile big, bright, and the most beautiful thing Riley had ever seen. "Come give me a big hug, sugar!"

Tears welled in Riley's eyes, and not only because she saw the wheelchair next to Mimi—a visual reminder of the pain her stalwart grandmother was suffering. Otherwise, Mimi looked the same. Her silver hair was still cut short in a style Mimi had always called serviceable, and she was wearing her usual evening attire—old sweatpants and a T-shirt that said "I'm a limited edition." In that moment, basking in her favorite person's smile as she saw the love in her blue eyes, she realized how much she missed and loved this woman who had taken her in when her mother abandoned her. Mimi had showered her with the affection Riley hadn't known she craved. She dropped her purse and hurried to her, kneeling on the ground and hugging her thin but still strong body.

"Welcome home, Riley," Mimi said, her voice thick as she hugged her tightly. "Welcome home."

Chapter 3

Hayden yawned as he swept the sidewalk in front of his father's hardware store the next morning. He hadn't made it home until almost midnight, and then it took him at least two hours to fall asleep, mostly because he was thinking about Riley. Why was she still on his mind? It wasn't like he was going to get to know her better while she was taking care of Erma. He was sure she'd want him to keep his distance anyway, especially now that she knew he was to blame for her grandmother's accident.

The smart thing would be to forget about her. He had his job at the hardware store and his new house to focus on. Besides, Riley wouldn't be in Maple Falls very long anyway. Last night she looked like she wanted to jump right back on that plane to New York.

His mind returned to the scene he'd walked in on when he brought Riley's bags inside the house. Neither woman heard him come inside, and he was surprised when he saw Riley crying in Erma's arms. Erma hadn't exactly been dry-eyed, and when she finally noticed Hayden standing there, she motioned for him to leave. He quickly crept out the door. He shouldn't have watched such a private moment, but he had to be sure they were both okay.

He bent over and swept the dirt from the sidewalk into a dustpan as he mused about something else he learned last night. He couldn't believe Riley hadn't returned to Maple Falls in nearly a decade. Even when he was busy with his baseball career, Hayden had made sure to come home regularly to see his family and friends. Maple Falls had always been his keystone, and no one was surprised he decided to stay permanently. He figured he'd just been away when Riley visited over the years, not that she hadn't visited at all. It was obvious from their embrace last night that she and Erma were close, and he was confounded Riley hadn't wanted to return to her hometown even once.

"Mornin', Hayden."

He turned to see Jasper Mathis, a retired carpenter in his eighties and a fixture at Price's Hardware, standing behind him. The older man arrived every morning soon after the store opened, and he was such a staple that visitors who weren't familiar with the store often thought he was an employee. He could be since he knew where every single nail and screw were located, probably better than Hayden did. "Mornin', Jasper. How's it going?"

"Countin' my blessin's and not my problems." He peered at Hayden over his glasses as he took a sip of coffee. "You're lookin' kinda tired, young man."

"I am, a little."

"Long night?"

"You could say that." He opened the front door for Jasper. "Dad's in the back. We got a shipment of paint yesterday and the SKUs are all mixed up."

"I'm sure that's put him in a fine mood."

"Yes, sir." His father had talked to the supplier, who promised them a box of free paint in exchange for keeping his business. Few things ruffled Harrison Julius Price III's feathers, but dealing with shipment problems was one of them.

"I'll see if I can give him a hand." Jasper sighed, but Hayden didn't miss the slight grin on the man's craggy face. Jasper was always happy to help fix a problem.

After emptying the dustpan into the trash bin in front of the store, Hayden went inside and put the broom and dustpan away. They'd opened an hour ago and business was slow, not so unusual for any of the businesses on Maple Falls' short Main Street. He spent the morning straightening up the gardening section, a part of the store that had stayed in constant chaos the past month and a half. It was planting time, and all the gardeners and a few farmers had replenished their supplies. One day Hayden would have his own garden, but that project was on the back burner until he fixed up his house.

Near lunchtime his father and Jasper came from the back of the stock room, arguing about something that had happened twenty years ago, as they typically did. Although nearly three decades separated the men, the Price family was one of the founding families in Maple Falls, as was Jasper's family. The two of them went way back.

"Why don't you take your lunch break?" Dad said, coming up beside Hayden as he wiped off the glass countertop at the front of the store. He sprayed more glass cleaner on a light-blue microfiber cloth and cleaned around the computerized cash register. "It doesn't look like we're going to get an onslaught of customers anytime soon."

Hayden watched for a sign of his father being upset with the slow business, but as usual his dad was upbeat. Family and friends had pointed out that Hayden took after him, in temperament anyway. Definitely not physically. His father was balding, short, and had worn a spare tire around his middle for as long as Hayden could remember. "You sure you don't want to go first? I don't mind waiting an hour or so."

"I guess that'll be all right." Dad adjusted his black suspenders. "I won't be gone long. You up for some lunch at the diner, Jasper? I'm buying."

"Then I'm in."

Hayden smiled as he watched the two men leave, then he looked around the store. It was full of merchandise all carefully organized and tracked. Vastly different from Knots and Tangles, a store he hadn't been inside until yesterday when he asked Erma to join him for lunch. He'd been stunned to see the place filled from top to bottom with yarn and yarn accessories. Was Erma selling yarn or collecting it? He couldn't tell.

The two stores did have one thing in common—they were original Maple Falls businesses, two of the three legacy businesses on the street that were still open. Like those stores, Price's Hardware and Knots and Tangles had struggled with declining business over the last fifteen years. Up until his shoulder healed and he retired from baseball, Hayden hadn't paid much attention to the family business, other than the times he'd visited and worked a few days out of nostalgia. His older brothers, Harrison and Henry, had spent many more hours working for their father than Hayden had. The two of them were part-time employees until they left for college.

Now that Hayden was back in Maple Falls for good, he'd started noticing things. Like how the Sunshine Diner was only open for breakfast and lunch, instead of all day. How Petals and Posies, the floral shop, only operated from Tuesday to Saturday, instead of six days a week like it used to. Erma's operating hours were sporadic at best, and he wondered if she would have to close the shop until her leg healed.

He was most concerned about the hardware store. His father had run it the same way his father had, and other than having updated supplies and a computer instead of a cash register, not much had changed in sixty years. Neither his father nor mother seemed to be concerned, but Hayden was.

The bell over the door jingled, and he turned to see who their first customer of the day was. He lifted a surprised brow. Riley McAllister.

When Riley walked inside the hardware store, she felt like she'd been transported to the past. She usually hadn't needed to buy anything hardware related unless Mimi sent her for something, so she'd only been in the store a few times in her life. Usually her grandmother visited Price's herself and made the purchases, while passing the time talking with Mr. Price, who, like Mimi, never met a stranger and loved to gab. Occasionally Mimi had sent Riley to fetch a part or garden supply, but she never saw Hayden working back then. He'd always been wrapped up in baseball.

He was here now, wearing a navy-blue short-sleeved shirt with the Price's Hardware logo above the shirt pocket, the bottom hem tucked snugly inside a pair of khaki cargo shorts that showed off his sculpted calves. *Focus on his face, not his body.* But then he flashed her a grin that threatened to weaken her knees.

Who was she kidding? Her knees were weak. *Snap out of it.* She should be focusing on the reason she came to see him. Telling herself she needed to apologize for her snippy behavior last night and thank him for picking her up didn't erase the fact that Hayden Price was flat-out gorgeous.

"Hey, Riley." He strolled up to her and slipped his hands in his pockets. "Long time no see."

She tried to smile, but she wasn't in a jovial mood. When she finished sobbing in her grandmother's arms last night, she discovered Hayden had brought the suitcases inside and placed them by the door, then left without her knowing. She hoped he hadn't seen her crying. She rarely cried, and the sudden tears last night had shocked her. Seeing her grandmother laid up, in addition to the stress of flying and having to return to Maple Falls under duress, had cracked something inside her. Now her emotional walls were back up, and she wasn't going to let them crumble again, especially not in front of Hayden.

"How's Erma this morning?" he asked.

"Good." She tried not to notice the concerned kindness in his gray eyes and shifted her gaze to the carousel of batteries behind him. Why couldn't she just say she was sorry, thank him for the ride, and dash out of the store like she'd planned?

"Is she getting around all right? How is she managing those two front porch steps?"

"She goes through the back. There aren't any steps there."

He nodded. "That's good to hear. If y'all need me to build a ramp for the porch, I'd be happy to do it."

"We'll be fine." She faced him, not wanting to linger any longer. "Thank you for the ride last night."

Frowning, he pulled his hands out of his pockets. "You don't have to thank me, Riley. I didn't mind doing it."

Would he have been so eager to pick her up if he hadn't been responsible for Mimi's broken leg? Probably not, although she could tell even from their short interactions that he was far too nice to refuse if her grandmother had asked. She glanced around the hardware store again, her thoughts derailing her purpose. Price's Hardware was as empty as Mimi's yarn shop had been all morning. Mimi had insisted on going in to work today, even though Riley tried to talk her out of it.

"Riley?"

Riley blinked and looked at Hayden again. *Apologize to him already.* "I'm also sorry that I was so short with you last night."

56

His expression relaxed. "No sweat. I could tell you were tired. Long flights can do that to you. It took me a while to get used to jet lag when I was traveling to away games." Shrugging, he gazed at her. "Lately the farthest place I've been is Little Rock."

A shiver went through her. They were just making small talk. But somehow he had moved closer to her without her realizing it, and for a split second she allowed her mind to go back to high school. She suddenly remembered all the times she had noticed him, either sitting at the table across the room from her in art class or walking the halls in school with his fellow jocks and their pretty girlfriends. She remembered all the times she'd wished she had the courage to talk to him. She never saw him with a girlfriend, which only fueled her silly fantasies about the two of them together, and more than once she had pretended she and Hayden were holding hands as he walked her to her next class.

Quickly she gathered her senses again. This wasn't high school. *Thank God.* "Uh, that's all I wanted to say. Bye."

"Riley—"

She ran out of the store before he could say anything else, then hurried down the sidewalk toward Knots and Tangles. When she was a short distance from Price's, she stopped, surprised she had to gasp for air. Her face was heated, and not because the morning sunshine mixed with 85 percent humidity made her feel like she was standing in a swamp instead of on the deserted Main Street.

"That was smooth," she muttered, keeping her head down as she crossed the street.

She opened the door, and the small bell hanging from the glass door announced her arrival. As soon as the door closed behind her, she bumped into a wobbly old shelf filled with alpaca wool. She reached out to steady the shelf, missed, and could only watch as the shelf tipped over and fell against another shelf. To her horror she saw all the shelves fall like dominoes, until the last one hit the opposite wall.

"What in the world is that racket?" Mimi shouted from the back of the store.

"It's just me." Riley cringed and went to set the shelving units upright. Balls and skeins and hanks of yarn littered the floor. The shelves were so old and unstable that she had to steady two of them a second time before she could start picking up the yarn. She scowled. So far the morning was off to a great start.

"Land sakes! What happened?" Bea bustled to the front of the store, her wide hips narrowly missing bumping into other shelves and storage units. Unlike Riley, Bea seemed to know the right path to get through the store unscathed.

"I knocked over some yarn," Riley muttered,

picking up a brown-and-orange commercial skein. She glanced at the label. The production date was from the 1980s, and the colors looked straight out of the seventies.

"*Some* yarn? More like a warehouse full." Bea's heavy gray eyebrows lifted over her small eyes. Bea Farnsworth wasn't conventionally attractive by any stretch, but she was as loyal a friend and as sweet a person as one could find. Riley remembered spending several nights at her house when she was fourteen and Mimi had left to visit her cousin in Missouri. Bea was an excellent cook and taught Riley how to make bourbon balls—minus the bourbon of course. Riley hadn't made them since, but she suddenly had an urge to taste them again.

"It looks like all the inventory is on the floor," Bea added as Riley balanced skeins of ugly yarn on one of the shelves.

"Don't forget all that stuff over there." Riley gestured with a skein of scratchy mauve wool to the other side of the store.

Bea waddled over. "Ah, right. This could have been worse. Let me help you pick up."

Riley held up her hand. "It's my mess. I'll clean it up." She tilted her head toward the back of the store. "What's Mimi doing back there?"

"Trying not to ram into anything with her leg."

"I wish she hadn't insisted on coming in today." Riley had surprisingly gotten a good night's sleep in her old bedroom. With the exception of a new bedspread and sheets, everything in the room was exactly how she'd left it. She had intended to tell Mimi first thing that she was going to clean up her house. Her grandmother had never been the tidiest woman, but Riley could see she had let the housework go.

Her plan flew out the window when the first words from Mimi's mouth were, "After breakfast we're going to Knots and Tangles." Riley had no choice but to comply.

"You know your grandmother," Bea said, dabbing at her forehead with a handkerchief, then sticking it in the pocket of her purple-and-white flowered skirt. "She's gonna do what she wants to do." She glanced back at the entrance to the back room. "I'd better go check on her. We were talking about snacks for tonight's BB meeting."

Riley had forgotten today was Thursday. Every Thursday night, except for holidays and illness, the Bosom Buddies met at Knots and Tangles. She was glad her grandmother hadn't canceled the weekly mainstay on her account.

A slightly less catastrophic crash sounded from the back of the store.

"Mimi?" Riley called out.

"Erma?" Bea said at the same time.

"I'm fine! Just a little mishap."

Bea sighed. "I'm sure it was more than a mishap." She leaned closer to Riley. "We've all been trying to get her to organize the place, but she insists it doesn't need it. She knows where every ball of yarn and every knitting needle is, but the disorganization makes it hard for new customers to browse. Some take one look at the craziness and walk right out."

"Really?" Riley frowned. "That's not good."

"No, it's not." Bea stood back. "Hopefully while you're here you can talk some sense into her."

She thought about her scheme to convince Mimi to sell the store. It was becoming clearer that her grandmother couldn't handle Knots and Tangles and take care of her home, even when she wasn't laid up.

With a smile Bea gave Riley a hug. "It's good to see you, darlin'. I know the rest of the BBs are excited that you've come back."

"I haven't—"

But Bea was already headed to save Mimi from whatever had happened in the back cavern of the shop.

Riley shook her head. She stepped around the yarn scattered on the floor and set her purse on a wooden chest next to the orange laminate countertop, then went back and attacked the mess. She organized the spilled yarn by brand, then by color, and by the time Mimi and Bea made it to the front of the store over an hour later, Riley had filled one of the shelving units.

"That looks nice, sugar." Mimi grinned and rested her forearms on the wheelchair arms. "But how did you manage to knock over five shelves?"

Both Riley and Bea faced her. "It's impossible to move in this store," Bea said.

"It's not impossible," Mimi muttered. "A tad challenging, but not impossible."

As Bea sighed, Riley placed several hanks of cream-colored alpaca wool on another shelf. The crowded shop wasn't the only reason she'd knocked over the shelves. She'd been focused on the way she abruptly ended her conversation with Hayden and hadn't been paying attention. Erma and Bea didn't need to know that tidbit of info.

"I'm not getting into this argument with you again, Erma, so I guess I'll be on my way." Bea picked up her black patent leather purse off the front counter and slung it over her shoulder. Riley was convinced the bag had come straight from the same decade that produced the hideous seventies-style yarn she'd picked up earlier. "Those cheese crackers aren't going to make themselves," she said, turning to Riley. "Maybe we can make some bourbon balls soon. This time we'll add the bourbon." She winked at Riley and then said to Mimi, "I'll see you tonight."

Mimi waved at her, then sat back in her chair, shifting in the seat. "You're welcome to join us, Riley. We're knittin' some knockers tonight."

"You're what?" Riley asked, peeking around the second full shelf.

"Knitted knockers. I'm crocheting mine, but the rest of the girls prefer to knit them. They're for breast cancer patients who have had mastectomies."

"That's a nice gesture," Riley said, picking up the last of the yarn.

"Have you crocheted or knitted lately?"

"No." She carefully placed the last skein of yarn on the shelf, then went to her grandmother. "I've been too busy."

"With your art." Mimi smiled. "Don't worry, picking it back up will be like riding a bike."

"I wasn't good at riding my bike, remember?"

"Oh. That's right. Don't worry, sugar, crocheting doesn't require any athletic ability."

Riley smirked, then sat in the old stuffed chair near the front of the store. The "Man Chair," Mimi called it, since it was available to any poor husband or boyfriend who'd been dragged to the yarn store by his significant other. The chair, upholstered in goldenrod, avocado-green, and burnt-orange flowers, was anything but manly, but it was comfortable, and Riley remembered the snores of more than one male who had fallen asleep in it.

She looked around the store, memories flooding her again. She'd spent a lot of time here, back when the store hadn't been as disorganized and there were more customers, most of them regulars who stopped in once or twice a week to buy yarn and chat with Mimi. Riley had spent her afternoons after school and entire Saturdays working here. When the store had a lull, she worked at the small art center Mimi set up for her in the corner of the back room.

Riley blinked, surprised at the wistful twist her thoughts had taken and the sudden twinge of guilt that appeared as she realized the neglected condition of the store. She shoved it away and addressed what she considered her grandmother's most pressing problem.

"You really have to do something about your inventory, Mimi."

Her grandmother lifted her chin, the loose skin at her neck wobbling a bit. "Don't be bossy."

"I'm not. I'm concerned. I don't want something else to happen to you while you're healing."

"You're acting like this place is a danger zone." She glanced around the shop and frowned. "All right, I may have let things get a little out of control. But I do know where everything is."

"But if it's organized, everyone else will know where things are too."

Nodding, Mimi said, "You're right, of course." Then her face brightened. "What do you plan to do?"

"Me?"

"Darn tootin' you. I can't do anything while I'm laid up. Like I said when I called you, I need your help to run this place. Don't worry, I'll pay you. I know you gave up a lot to come help me."

She met her grandmother's gaze. There was no guile or manipulation in her expression, just an uncharacteristic touch of sadness in her eyes.

"You don't have to pay me," Riley blurted, then mentally kicked herself. Her bank account was worthless, and her grandmother was offering her a job—she was a fool not to accept.

"Nonsense," Mimi said. "I've always paid you when you worked here in the past. I'm not going to change that now."

"All right. I accept." Then she added, "I noticed you don't have regular hours posted on the door anymore."

"That's because I don't have regular hours anymore."

Riley sat up in the chair. "Mimi, how are you supposed to make money if you don't open the shop?"

"Oh, sugar, this store hasn't made money in years."

Riley's brow shot up. "It hasn't?"

Mimi shook her head as she lifted her finger. "There was that one year, I think five or six years ago, that I broke even."

Alarm ran through her. "How are you managing without getting paid?"

"I never said I didn't have any money. Your grandfather left me well taken care of."

Riley saw the touch of sadness in her grandmother's eyes return. It usually appeared anytime she mentioned Poppy, who had passed away thirty years ago. Riley, of course, had never met him, but she'd heard so many stories and seen so many pictures of her grandfather that she felt like she had known him.

"I've also invested well over the years, and I have an excellent financial adviser," Mimi added. "Trust me, sugar, money isn't an issue."

Riley pounced on the chance to put her plan in action. "If you don't need the revenue, then why don't you sell the business? Then if you wanted to travel or—"

"I'm not selling." She crossed her arms over her chest. "Knots and Tangles has been in my family for a long time. I've held out hope it will continue that way."

Another ribbon of guilt wrapped around Riley's conscience, but she ignored it. Mimi knew she had no interest in running the yarn shop, and it wasn't her fault her grandmother was not only being stubborn but also making a bad business decision. Thank God she wasn't broke. *Like me.*

Mimi put her hands on the wheels of her wheelchair and pushed forward, her foot rattling a display of stitch markers that somehow managed to stay upright. "Anyway, I'll put you on a salary." When she mentioned the amount, Riley almost fell out of the chair.

"That's way too much, Mimi."

"Pshaw. I can afford it. I also know you have bills to pay, and while you're here you can't sell your artwork. So now that I'm your boss, I insist on paying you what you're worth."

"Mimi—"

"Insubordination will not be tolerated at Knots and Tangles. You're risking your Employee of the Month status."

Riley laughed. "Other than you, I'm the only employee here."

"And I've won the award every month. It's about time I had some competition." Her eyes grew soft. "I'm so happy you're here, sugar. It fills my soul to have you back in Maple Falls again."

A lump formed in Riley's throat at her grandmother's hopeful tone. She'd have to tell Mimi she was heading back to New York as soon as Mimi's leg healed. But she didn't have to say that now. And while she was here, she might as well get this shop, and her grandmother's home, in better shape.

"I have one condition," Riley said.

"Name it."

"That you let me clean and organize this place."

"Sure thing."

Riley frowned. "You're giving in that easily?"

Mimi shrugged. "Letting you clean the shop won't bother me, because then I won't have to. It will also get the BBs off my back." She pointed at Riley. "But don't you dare touch my house. That's sacred ground."

Riley nodded, smirking. *We'll see.*

Chapter 4

Erma sat in her wheelchair in the back room of her shop, the only room in the entire store that was somewhat tidy. It had to be neat so there was enough space to hold a mismatched set of chairs, a turquoise rag area rug, a scratched but beloved coffee table, and a few TV trays that held snacks and beverages. As the Bosom Buddies entered the room—each carrying her project bag along with a treat to share—her heart warmed. This was what was important. Her friends, good food, creativity, a bit of gossip, and lots of laughter. The icing on the cake was Riley's presence. Her dearest friends were fawning all over her wonderful granddaughter.

"Riley McAllister, you haven't changed a bit," Madge Wilson gushed. She was the youngest of the Bosom Buddies, and her daughter, Harper, was Riley's age. "Still pretty as ever."

Riley's smile was tight as she nodded. "Thank you."

"How long has it been?" Peg Ryan set a bowl of ambrosia salad on the table. "Six years since you've been back home?"

"A little over nine." Riley nibbled on her fingernail, then quickly shoved her hands behind her back.

Erma watched as Riley interacted with the other two Bosom Buddies—Viola Porter and Gwen Brown. Everyone peppered her granddaughter with polite questions, never once hinting that they knew the deeper reasons for Riley's departure from Maple Falls, beyond her wanting to be a famous artist. Erma wasn't sure Riley knew those reasons herself. Her granddaughter not only didn't want anything to do with her mother, but she also didn't want to be anything like her. The BBs were also aware of Tracey's past and the friction between her and Riley. These women were Erma's confidantes, and although they didn't know *everything,* they knew a lot. They also knew when to keep their mouths shut about BB secrets.

Guilt stabbed at Erma, but she shoved it away. She hadn't exactly been forthright with Riley today. The shop hadn't always looked this messy. The BBs helped her tidy it up often enough. Over the past year or so, even before the accident, Erma realized she was losing interest in running the store, which was why she hadn't been open as often as she should. Before she broke her leg, she'd finally started to organize her inventory with the intent to liquidate. She had finally accepted that her granddaughter wouldn't continue the Knots and Tangles tradition, a fact that deeply saddened her.

With Riley here now and working at the shop

again, Erma prayed she would change her mind and see the value of keeping tradition alive. She knew it would take a miracle for that to occur. *Good thing God is in the miracle business.* He'd already provided one miracle—Riley was back. Hopefully soon she would realize that despite the past, Maple Falls could truly be her home.

After all the women filled up their plates with snacks and visited for a while, Erma clapped and wheeled herself as close to the sitting area as she dared, almost knocking her leg into one of the chairs.

"I don't think I'll ever get used to this thing," she muttered, rolling to a stop next to Gwen.

"You'll be on crutches soon enough." Gwen gave her a brilliant smile that was always perfect because her husband was a dentist. His practice was in nearby Malvern, the closest large city to Maple Falls, although calling it large was a stretch.

"Crutches might be worse." Bea chuckled and took a big bite of Peg's salad, then set her plate down and picked up her bag. "Who's ready to knit some knockers?"

Erma glanced at Riley, who was sitting on the opposite side of the room between Bea and Viola. She held a pair of knitting needles and a ball of soft, white pima cotton yarn in her lap. Erma had always preferred crochet, so Bea had taught Riley how to knit.

Erma tried not to frown at the lost look on her granddaughter's face—a look she was all too familiar with. How many times had she seen it during Riley's teenage years? Her heart had ached back then as she wished she could help Riley feel more at ease and make friends. That familiar pain filled her heart now. *At least she's here. That's something.*

"Here, sweet pea, let me give you a refresher." Bea angled her large body toward Riley and began to show her how to use the needles again. As Erma had suspected, Riley picked the knitting back up right away, and soon she was concentrating on the copy of the pattern in front of her on the coffee table.

"How long do you think she'll stay?" Madge whispered, leaning close to Erma as the rest of the women buzzed with conversation and laughter.

Erma shrugged. "I'm not sure."

"Hopefully she doesn't have her mother's wandering genes." Madge, who enjoyed knitting and crocheting, sat back and primly slipped a knot of light-pink yarn on her crochet hook.

Erma held her tongue, a task that always involved a great deal of difficulty. Not only was Madge the youngest in the group, but she was also the newest member, even though she'd been attending Bosom Buddy nights for over two years, at the insistence of Erma herself. More than once Erma had questioned the wisdom of her decision. Overall, Madge Wilson was a good woman, but there were times when her words held a sharp edge, and Erma sometimes thought she was being hurtful on purpose.

She ignored Madge and the urge to put the youngster in her place and focused on crocheting. She'd made so many knockers that by now she could crochet them without looking, which freed her up to visit with her friends, forget about both the pain in her leg and the pain in her behind sitting next to her, and most of all, keep a surreptitious eye on Riley. She hoped her granddaughter could relax enough to enjoy herself tonight. She deserved to have a good time. Erma had a gut feeling that didn't happen much in New York.

Riley was surprised she was able to halfway complete one knocker—and stunned that it didn't look horrible. Nevertheless, she would unravel it later and start again, this time focusing on her tension instead of remembering how to do the stitches, so the project would be as close to perfect as possible. She refused to donate something that wasn't her best work.

She was also surprised at how knitting again helped her forget about her concern for Mimi. More than ever, Riley believed she would have to convince her stubborn grandmother to sell the shop. It had become more of a burden than a joy—anyone could see that. Except for tonight, perhaps. Riley had to admit it was nice to be around a group of people who were enjoying themselves, even if they were decades older than her.

Before she realized it, Bosom Buddy night was over, and Riley helped Mimi's friends pack up their leftover food—because, of course, everyone had made too much. They wouldn't be Southern cooks if they hadn't. Erma bade each of her friends goodbye with a hug and a smile. When the last woman left, Riley turned to her grandmother. She was still smiling, but lines of weariness had appeared on her face. When she moved her wheelchair and winced, Riley hurried over to her.

"Time to go home," she said.

"But we need to tidy things up here first."

Riley scoffed. "Since when have you been eager to tidy up anything?"

Mimi nodded. "True, even though it makes me sound neglectful."

Crouching in front of Mimi's wheelchair and making sure she didn't bump her leg, Riley looked her grandmother straight in the eye and smiled. "You're never neglectful." She patted Mimi's hand, then stood. "But you are stubborn, and I can tell you're hurting. When was the last time you took a pain pill?"

"I hate those things." Mimi averted her gaze and drummed her fingers against her knee.

"Do they help you?"

After a pause, Mimi nodded, rubbing her thumb over her short fingernails.

"Then you need to take them."

"I left them at home." She looked up at Riley. "Did you have a good time tonight?"

Now it was Riley's turn to pause, although she shouldn't have been surprised at the question. Mimi always wanted to know how she was feeling, especially when Riley was a teenager. At the end of every school day, the first thing she would say when Riley walked into Knots and Tangles was, "Did you have a good day today?" Most of the time Riley had nodded, even though it wasn't the truth.

This time when she nodded she was being honest. "I did. I forgot how relaxing knitting can be. Except for those first few stitches."

"Everyone tenses up when they're new." Erma smiled, then winced again and sighed. "I have to admit, I am a little tired."

"That's it. Home we go."

An hour later, after driving Mimi home in her twenty-five-year-old Lincoln Town Car that still had less than 100,000 miles on it, then helping her grandmother get dressed for bed and extracting a promise that she would stay there and sleep, Riley stepped out onto the front porch.

The air wasn't as muggy as last night, and a faint, almost cool breeze ruffled her bangs. She leaned on the banister and looked at Mimi's front yard. The light from the streetlamp at the end of the driveway illuminated the disaster.

The grass needed mowing, weeds had taken over the flower beds, and the Burford holly bushes could use a good pruning. She'd seen the backyard this morning, and it was in even worse shape than the front. Riley had never been a fan of yard work, but after almost a decade of not having a yard, she found herself itching to pull the lawn mower from the shed and attack the overgrown grass.

She sat on the front porch step and propped her elbows on her knees. There was so much work to do—the shop, the house, the yard . . . Everything was unkempt and disorganized. Why hadn't anyone helped take care of these things? Riley knew the answer before she finished the question—stubbornness. Even if someone had offered to help, her grandmother would have turned them down. It was clear that she did need assistance, even before the accident. *Things wouldn't be such a mess if I had stayed here.*

She brushed aside the guilt. It wasn't her fault her Mimi was set in her ways. What was Riley supposed to do, stay in Maple Falls for the rest of her life? She was an artist—at least she was trying to be—and that couldn't happen in a backwater Arkansas town. *Even worse, I could end up like Tracey.*

Scowling, she straightened, batted at the mosquito that landed on her arm, then stood. She'd do what she could to clean up the house and store before she went back to New York. But before she left, she would stand her ground with Mimi. Her grandmother couldn't keep living like this, and she couldn't expect Riley to give up her dreams because she didn't want to change.

And what exactly would I be giving up? Fame, fortune, friends? She didn't have any of that, except she did consider Melody her friend. But just because she hadn't reached her goals yet didn't mean she should hang up her dream, tuck her tail between her legs, and come back to Maple Falls. That was something she would never, ever do.

She went inside and readied for bed. When she laid down and pulled the soft sheet and light blanket over her, she fought to settle her mind. What should she tackle first? The front yard or the back? The store or inside the house? She expected to be up all night trying to come up with a plan, but instead she quickly fell asleep, not realizing she slept until pale sunlight filtered through the gauzy white chiffon curtains covering the bedroom window.

Riley rolled out of bed, ran her fingers through her hair, and threw it up in a messy ponytail.

She quickly dressed in running shorts, a T-shirt, and sneakers, then crept down the hallway and peeked into Mimi's bedroom. Her grandmother was still asleep with her cast propped up on the hill of pillows Riley made for her last night. Soft snores drifted through the room. Riley stepped back, then quietly went outside. The sun was just above the horizon, the sky streaked with shades of blue, lavender, and peach. Birds greeted her with their cheerful chirping. Despite her troubled thoughts from last night, she felt optimistic this morning. A lot of work lay ahead of her, but she would get it done.

Breathing in the fresh, slightly humid air, she sighed. When was the last time she'd gone out for a run? Before leaving for New York, she had enjoyed running and tried to fit one in a few times a week. While art and working at Knots and Tangles were her escapes, she always felt better after a good run. She wasn't a fast runner, and she would rather have a root canal than join a 10K or any kind of marathon, although she had trained herself to run those distances.

When she arrived in New York, she had quickly abandoned running. Art school and the work-study program she was enrolled in had taken up all of her time. After graduating, she was busy trying to make ends meet while working on producing and selling her mixed media creations. She had no time to run, much less ample green space to run through. She'd jogged a few times in Central Park, but it wasn't the same as running in Maple Falls or hitting the trails in nearby Ouachita National Park.

Riley stretched her legs, hearing the snap and creak of her bones and tendons complaining about years of neglect. She jumped up and down a few times, then hit the road, settling on a slow, steady pace. Before long she found herself on the running trail in Maple Falls Park. It was small but had a decent-size pond with a sidewalk surrounding the water where people could run or walk. It was hardly a trail, but it would do.

She was halfway around the pond when she heard someone call her name. She muttered a curse, glad Melody wasn't there to hear her. Naturally, of all the mornings people could run in Maple Falls Park, she had chosen the same time as *him*.

Embarrassment filled her. The last person she wanted to witness her lumbering gait, sweaty face and back, and overall lack of stamina and athleticism was Hayden Price. She didn't want to be a complete witch and ignore him, either, so she peeked over her shoulder and gave him a quick nod of acknowledgment. When she realized he was gaining on her, she picked up her pace. Hopefully he would let her plod along in peace.

No such luck. Letting him know she saw him

was a mistake. He didn't slow down. Instead, he was closing the gap between them. She sped up, and within seconds her heart rate had spiked, she struggled to breathe, and the muscles in her leg burned with every stride. She knew she couldn't keep running at that speed, and she certainly couldn't outrun him. Against her will she slowed, then finally stopped, bending at the waist and placing her hands on her knees. Even her knees were sweaty.

"Hey." Hayden stopped beside her, not sounding the least bit exerted. "Are you okay?"

With effort she lifted her head, still gasping for air. She managed a nod. "F-fine."

His brow furrowed. "You don't look fine. Why don't you sit down for a minute?" He gestured to one of the weathered benches a few paces ahead that seemed to be one weak breeze away from keeling over.

She started to shake her head, hoping he would just leave her alone to catch her breath so she could eventually resume her run. Her breathing wasn't slowing as fast as she wanted it to, and then her legs started to feel like Jell-O in an earthquake, and she knew she had to relent. She made her way over to the bench and plopped down on it, hoping she wouldn't end up with splinters in her butt. *Don't sit next to me, don't sit next to me, don't . . .*

He sat next to her, leaning forward and peering

at her sweat-covered face. "Did you bring any water with you?"

Of course she didn't. She was so unused to exercising, she hadn't even thought about it. "No. I was just going for a quick run."

"Did you run here from Erma's?" he asked. When she nodded, he said, "That's not a quick run."

She eyed him, annoyed. "Where's your water?"

"Uh, at home," he said with a sheepish expression. "I'm just doing five miles this morning, so I didn't think I needed it. Now I wish I'd brought some so I could share it with you."

Riley sat back against the bench, staring at him. Was he even real? The ends of his hair were damp with perspiration, so at least he was human. But how could he be so attractive, so athletic, and so nice? He must have a girlfriend stashed somewhere. Maybe even a fiancée. She glanced at his left hand. No ring, so she knew he wasn't married. He was the type to wear a wedding ring.

She squeezed her eyes shut. The last thing her brain needed was to ponder about Hayden's romantic life. Hadn't she done enough of that in high school?

"Riley?"

Opening her eyes, she finally lifted her gaze. "Yes?"

"Are you sure you're okay?"

Her legs still felt weak, but if she sat here long

enough, she could at least walk back to Mimi's. Running was out of the question, although if she had the strength, she would book it out of here immediately. The next best thing was to encourage him to leave.

"Yes. I'm okay." She tried to hide the fact that she was still slightly breathless. She wasn't sure if it was from the exercise or because Hayden was sitting so close to her. "Don't let me keep you from your run," she said, waving him off.

"You're not. I was almost done." He leaned back against the bench, his shoulder almost touching Riley's. If he noticed, he didn't act like it.

She thought about scooting away, but she was nearly at the edge of the bench and there wasn't any room—unless she wanted to land on the concrete sidewalk. Why were these benches so small?

"Can I ask you something?" Hayden said.

This time when she cast him a quick look, he was staring at the pond in front of them. A group of brown-and-gold-spotted ducks was paddling around the water, and three of them dipped their heads beneath the surface in search of a fish or two for breakfast. She needed to answer his question.

"Um, sure."

"Have I offended you somehow?"

Stunned, she turned to him. That was the last

thing she expected him to ask. "No. Why would you think that?"

"You seem eager to get away from me right now. I got the same impression yesterday when you came into the store." He tapped the rubber heel of his athletic shoe against the walkway. "I guess I just wondered if I'd done something to annoy you when I picked you up from the airport the other night."

She gripped the edge of the bench. Might as well add splinters to her fingers too. "We haven't seen each other in over a decade, Hayden," she said, her tone turning soft. "What could you possibly have done to upset me?"

"I don't know. That's why I'm asking if I've done something wrong."

Riley let out a bitter laugh. "As if that would ever happen."

"Hey, I'm not perfect. Far from it."

He sounded annoyed, so she turned to him. "From what I remember, you were pretty darn close." Oh no, had she really said that out loud?

He smirked. "Interesting. I didn't think you noticed me at all."

"Oh, come on. Everyone knows the great Hayden Price."

"I'm not so great now." Instead of sounding upset, he seemed resigned. "Then again, not everyone can say they blew an entire career on one pitch."

That put things into perspective. While her career had never gotten off the ground, his had launched to the highest peak, only to come crashing down.

"I'm sorry that happened," she said, meaning it.

He shrugged. "Me too. But things happen for a reason, you know? It took me a while to accept that, but now I have." He shifted on the bench again, and now he was facing her, seeming not to care about the precarious sturdiness of the wood. "What about you?"

"What about me?"

"How has life treated you the last ten years? I'm not up on the art world, but I'm sure you've been successful. I remember how good your drawings and paintings were in art class, and that mural you painted on the side of Rusty's Garage for the Too Dang Hot Parade was amazing."

His compliments gave her a boost but not enough to talk about her past. "Is that still going on?"

"Of course. This year it's on August 12. Although it's not much of a parade anymore. Just a reason for everyone to go shopping, get a hot dog and a snow cone, and shoot the breeze."

Riley took that in. The It's Too Dang Hot for a Parade Parade, which had been shortened thirty years ago to the Too Dang Hot Parade, had been one of the few things she looked forward to each year, with the exception of the time she was fifteen and Mimi forced her to join the parade and wear a hat covered with small balls of yarn and a placard advertising Knots and Tangles. That had been embarrassing, not to mention a failure, since everyone who attended the parade already knew about Knots and Tangles anyway.

"I can't believe there isn't a parade anymore."

"Yeah, it's disappointing. But it's also understandable why it disappeared. Lots of people have moved away. The high school band has grown and was invited to do other festivals in larger towns, so they stopped doing the parade. They were always the main draw. Plus, it's too dang hot in August." He grinned. "The name sure was accurate."

"Then why don't they change it to something else? Or have a parade another time during the year?"

"You know how folks are around here. They like tradition. I also think the older ones keep hoping that one day the parade will resume." He looked at her, his expression serious now. "Hope is everything for some people. If you take that away, they don't have anything." He shrugged. "Anyway, you haven't answered my question. What's it like being a big-time New York artist?"

Riley swallowed. She knew about hope. She'd been filled with it when she left Maple Falls. She was going to shake up the art world, and *if* she returned home, it would only be as a success story. She was going to make something of herself and prove to everyone that she wasn't a loser like Tracey. Instead, she found out that while she had been an exceptional artist in a backwater Arkansas town, she had little talent compared to the real artists in New York. How was she supposed to admit *that* to the golden boy?

"I've got to get back to Mimi," she said, jumping up from the bench. "She was asleep when I left, but I'm sure she's up now. I don't want her to be alone for too long."

"Right." Hayden stood. "She's still doing okay, then?"

She couldn't help but smile. He'd asked about Mimi yesterday morning and was still genuinely concerned about her well-being. "She's fine."

"Good." He glanced at the pond again. "I should probably get going too. I'm supposed to open the shop this morning. Dad's going to Little Rock for a yearly tool show." Despite his words, he didn't make a move to leave.

Riley stared at his profile, but instead of focusing on his good looks, she found herself drawn to him for a different reason. *He really is one of the good guys, isn't he?* But she couldn't stand there fawning over him. Well, she easily could . . . She started to back away. "Uh, I guess . . . See you later," she said, the awkward words punctuated with a loud duck quack.

"Yeah." Hayden still didn't move, but he wasn't looking at her either. "Later."

Somehow she found the strength to resume running, and she sprinted away from the park. But once she reached Mimi's street, her legs started to buckle. Thankful Hayden wasn't around to see her fail at running a second time, she slowed to a painful walk. Her body would pay for overdoing it today.

But the ache in her chest had nothing to do with her run and everything to do with Hayden. He had asked her a simple question, and she had bailed on giving him an answer. She'd have to keep her distance from now on. If she didn't, and if he asked about her life in New York again, she might be tempted to tell him the truth—that after almost a decade of pursuing her dream, she was a failure. *Just like Tracey.*

As Hayden lightly jogged back home, he mentally kicked himself. Why had he been so nosy? He should have known better than to pry into Riley's life. She was as closed as a tulip at sunset, and he should have recognized that when she didn't answer his question the first time he asked. But he couldn't help himself. She was still a mystery to him, and he wanted to understand her. Something had been drawing him to her since he first saw her at the airport. Something physical.

He hadn't noticed it at first. She wasn't the kind

of woman he'd been used to dating. High school romance had been out of the question due to his baseball schedule and trying to keep his grades up for college, but he'd managed to have a social life at UCLA. Those girlfriends, if he could call them that, had been stereotypical party girls. He wasn't proud that he'd partaken more than once in certain college social activities, and if he'd continued along that path, he would have put his scholarship in jeopardy.

Thankfully it all quickly grew stale, and he soon nixed his social life to spend the rest of his college days focused on the most important thing in his life—baseball.

Not anymore. His priorities had been forcibly shifted six months ago. It had taken time for him to accept that there was life after baseball, but he fully believed it now. Getting hung up on the past wasn't an option.

Without realizing it, his jogging had picked up speed, and he was at a full run when he reached his house. He was breathing as hard as Riley had been. The thought of Riley triggered his memory of seeing her sweaty, red-faced, and unbelievably sexy. He grinned. The jolt of attraction he'd experienced sitting next to her on that old bench had surprised him. Then again, maybe he had finally grown up.

Hayden caught his breath and put his hands on his hips. Since Riley's arrival he'd been thinking about his teenage years more and more, and it hit him that he'd always thought she was sexy, in a natural and aloof kind of way. Had she always liked to run? Maybe if he'd known that, he would have asked her to join him on a run or two. He'd been running since middle school as part of his off-season training. He shook his head at the dumb thought. She would have told sixteen-year-old him no and sent him on his way. Like she was obviously doing now.

He needed to get a grip. Riley had made it clear that she wasn't interested in him hanging around her, and he needed to respect that. For all he knew, she had a boyfriend back in New York. He wasn't exactly thrilled with the thought. Maybe that's why she was so distant with him, and he couldn't blame her. If she were his girl and some guy was asking her questions, he wouldn't like it one bit. So, no more trying to make friends with her, even though he still wanted to. *And no more prying questions.*

As he entered his parents' house, he wiped the sweat from his face with the hem of his T-shirt. He'd been living at home since returning to Maple Falls, but he had always seen this living situation as temporary. Now that he had purchased a house that he would start fixing up in a week or two, his time in his childhood home would soon be coming to an end. He had to admit he didn't mind staying with his parents. They were easy to get along with, and after years of eating on the road, he could never get enough of home-cooked meals.

When he reached the bottom of the stairs, he saw his mother coming down them, dressed in a light-green short-sleeved blouse, white pants, and white slip-on shoes. She was fiddling with a colorful sheer scarf wrapped loosely around her neck as she walked off the last step and stopped in front of him. "How was your run, honey?"

"Good."

"Where did you go?"

"The park, as usual. I'm going to get a shower," he added quickly before she could ask any more questions and he'd have to mention seeing Riley. He wasn't sure if anyone knew she was back in town.

"All right. There's pancakes and sausage for breakfast in the warming drawer under the oven."

Yes! "Thanks, Mom." His stomach growled as he moved to let her walk past him. "Where's Dad?"

"Finishing up reading the paper on the back porch. He said it's too nice a morning to sit inside. By the way, we won't be back until later tonight. Your father has promised me a fancy dinner at some steakhouse in Chenal. I can't remember the name of it, but he said it had good reviews on the internet."

"Have fun. Let him know the store is in good hands."

His mother smiled and tucked a strand of her shoulder-length blond hair behind her ear, the color courtesy of regular six-week appointments at a salon in Hot Springs. "He knows it is. We'll see you later."

Hayden nodded, then bounded up the stairs, forcing his mind to focus on work and not on Riley. Business usually picked up on Friday and Saturday since people tended to work on their DIY projects more on the weekend than during the week. After a quick shower, he stepped onto the pale-blue bath mat and reached for the matching towel hanging on the hook. He had just wrapped it around his waist when his cell phone buzzed on the double sink vanity. When he saw the caller, he wiped his hands on the towel, then swiped at the foggy screen twice.

"Hey, Erma," he said. "You're on speaker, by the way."

"Good morning, Hayden. How are you?"

"Just fine." He rubbed his shoulder but didn't look at the scar. Occasionally he felt a twinge of pain, but his surgeon had been one of the best in the country, and the healed tendons and muscles rarely ached now. Still, he preferred to ignore the six-inch vertical scar going across the side of his shoulder. He didn't need a visual reminder of the past. "I'm getting ready for work."

"Oh, I won't keep you long then. I have a favor to ask."

"Anything for you, Erma."

"Oh, you really are a peach, aren't you? I promise this will be the last one. Obviously, I won't be able to continue as assistant coach for the church softball team."

Hayden tucked the towel tighter around his hips. "I'm so sorry about that, Erma—"

"No more apologies, understand?"

Her strict tone caught his attention. "Yes, ma'am."

"I hereby officially resign as coach."

"You don't have to resign, though," Hayden said. "I'll hold your place until you're ready to play and coach again."

A pause. "I, uh, I'm not sure when that will be, so it's best I resign. But I do have a replacement in mind."

He wiped his face with the hand towel hanging by one of the sinks. She would probably suggest one of her Bosom Buddies, or BBs, as he'd heard them called. None of them except Erma and Myrtle were on the team, and Myrtle was still on her cruise and wouldn't be back for a while. The BBs were excellent cheerleaders. They'd come to several practices and, of course, the first game. They always brought snacks, too, which was a bonus.

He couldn't imagine who she had in mind.

None of the women, except maybe Madge Wilson, looked like they were in good enough shape to play softball, even in a church league. "Who are you considering?"

"My granddaughter."

Hayden froze, then picked up the phone and took it off speaker. "Are you serious?"

"Of course I am. Is there a reason why Riley can't take my place?"

Other than her not wanting to be around me? "Uh, not off the top of my head, no. Have you run this idea past her?"

Another pause. "I'm sure she'll want to take the position."

Hayden paused. For the first time he heard a note of uncertainty in Erma's voice. "You are?"

"Yes, I am sure, and I have to go. Have a nice day."

"Erma—" She had already hung up.

He set the phone back on the vanity and blew out a breath. He wasn't going to tell Erma no. He said he would do her a favor and he meant it. But he doubted Riley would be interested in the coaching position, and from the way her grandmother hung up on him, he was almost positive Riley had no idea she was being volunteered. He frowned. *So much for keeping my distance.*

Swiping his hand over the foggy mirror, he relaxed, the lines creasing his forehead disappearing in his reflection. Despite Erma's insistence, there was no way Riley was going to agree to be his assistant.

His frown suddenly returned. *Too bad.*

Chapter 5

L ate Saturday afternoon Hayden unlocked the gate to the one and only ball field in Maple Falls. Like most of the town, the field was old and needed some TLC. When he decided to start the church softball team, he spent two entire weekends cleaning up the grounds and creating the infield, killing grass and weeds that had grown over it and building up the pitcher's mound. Fortunately his friend Tanner Castillo helped out when he wasn't working at the Sunshine Diner. Otherwise it would have taken Hayden much longer than two weekends to finish. The end result didn't look great, but it was definitely an improvement and would serve its purpose.

He walked over to one of the dugouts and leaned his huge canvas bag of bats and softballs against the skinny wooden bench, dropping the other bag on the ground. His glove was lying inside the bag on top of the bats, and he picked it up, slipping his hand inside as he'd done thousands of times before. The worn leather fit him like a second skin, which it practically had been for the seven years he'd used it.

As always before practice, he walked to the mound. Common sense told him he shouldn't since there was no reason for him to be there, but he couldn't help himself. The moment the sole of his athletic shoe touched the hard-packed dirt, he was transported to the past, his mind and senses filled with the sights, sounds, and smells of a baseball field during a game. The murmuring of the crowd, the fans wearing their favorite player's jersey, the scents of popcorn and beer hanging in the air. He remembered the feel of the mound beneath his feet, the excitement of staring down a batter and striking him out.

His jaw clenched and he stepped off the mound. There would be no more strikeouts, not from his arm. Now he was forced to experience the game that had meant so much to him a different way— as a spectator, or in this case, a green coach of an even greener softball team. As he stared at the spot where home plate should be, he yearned to pitch again. Sure, he could still throw a few balls overhand, but he'd never reach 70 mph, much less the 100-plus mph fastball he'd pitched in his prime. The memory brought him back to earth.

Hayden jogged back to the dugout and dropped his mitt on the bench, then dragged the other bag to the field, unzipped it, and started placing the bases around the diamond. He'd just finished straightening home plate when he heard a car pull into the gravel parking lot. When he looked over, he saw two cars right behind it—including Erma's.

Surprised, his nerves started to jump. For once the store had been busy yesterday, and he hadn't had time to think about Erma's phone call—until he closed up for the night. The more he'd thought about it then, the surer he was that Riley would tell her grandmother no. But if that was the case, why was she here now? Had Erma actually convinced her to be his assistant? She must have used all her sweet-talking charm to make it happen.

Erma's car stopped a few spaces away from Harper Wilson's red Mercedes. When Harper got out of her car, he wasn't surprised to see her meticulously dressed for a simple softball practice, and knowing her, every item of clothing had a designer label. The first time she showed up at the field, Hayden had been skeptical, especially seeing her perfect manicure, makeup, and brand-new expensive cleats. As it turned out, Harper had played softball when she was younger and was fairly good, not to mention extremely competitive. He chalked that up to her owning her own real estate business. She was his utility infield player, subbing when needed, and was also a backup pitcher.

Olivia Farnsworth, Bea's grandniece, got out of the passenger side of Harper's car. As a librarian, she couldn't be any more different from Harper, both in looks and temperament. Olivia was petite and shy with black hair and olive skin due to her

Hispanic heritage, the opposite of blond-haired, blue-eyed Harper. Olivia possessed a distinct lack of athletic ability but nevertheless put in 100 percent effort, which he appreciated.

The rest of the team started to show up and make their way to the field. Tanner Castillo, who played shortstop, wore his usual Sunshine Diner baseball cap, his long ash-blond ponytail pulled through the snapback of the cap. Hayden and Tanner's friendship had started in elementary school, and although they had gone their separate ways after high school, they picked up right where they left off when Hayden returned to Maple Falls.

The catcher, Jared Young, was the new pastor of their church and only two years older than Hayden. Anita Bedford, a waitress at the Sunshine Diner, where Tanner worked as a cook, played right field. She and Olivia took turns playing right field. The Mathis cousins, Jimmy, Jesse, and Jack, who was known as Jackie—all in their late teens and pretty good players—made up the rest of the infield. Lonnie Finch, a construction worker in his early forties, was a decent pitcher, and bringing up the rear were Junior Dobbs and Eddie Trimble, two men in their fifties who struggled to pick up ground balls due to their love of Southern cooking, not to mention their fondness for enjoying a few beers now and then. They would take Myrtle and Erma's places in the outfield. The team was short on subs, but maybe once the season progressed, more people would be interested in joining.

Hayden smiled as he watched his eclectic team heading toward him. He'd known most of these people all his life, except for Harper, who had attended a private school in Hot Springs, and Jared, who was new to all of them. Hayden was proud of this ragtag group, despite the fact they hadn't gelled on the playing field yet. He was confident they would, eventually.

Once he paired off everyone for warm-ups, he spotted Erma's car again. Riley hadn't gotten out of the vehicle yet, and Erma obviously hadn't accompanied her. Hayden was glad for that. Erma needed rest, and she wouldn't get it here on the ball field since she couldn't stop herself from coaching, even to the point of Hayden having to remind her that he was in charge of the team.

He frowned as Riley remained in the car. Was she all right? Should he go check on her? Then again, he had vowed to keep his distance.

After a few minutes, he couldn't stand it anymore. He yelled to Tanner, who was rolling grounders to Jesse Mathis, "Be back in a minute," then jogged over to Erma's Town Car. Sure enough, Riley was sitting in the driver's seat, hands in her lap, staring straight ahead, the motor still running.

Hayden tapped on the window. She rolled it down and then turned off the engine.

"Hey," he said. What to say next was eluding him. "Uh, did you come to watch the practice?"

She grimaced. "Yes. Sort of." Then she blew out a breath. "Mimi wants me to help you coach."

So, Erma had talked to her. "What did she say, exactly?"

"She wants me to take her place."

"And you don't want to."

Her eyes lifted in his direction. "You don't seem surprised about this."

"She called me yesterday." He put his hands over the top of the door and leaned forward but made sure he didn't get too close to her. "Why didn't you tell her no?"

"Did you tell her no?"

He grimaced and shook his head.

"Exactly." Riley sighed. "I did point out that this was a mistake. I've never played softball before. Then she reminded me that I liked to watch baseball."

Now that was an interesting tidbit of information. "You do?"

"I *used* to," she said quickly. "That doesn't mean I understand how to play the game."

"You're not the only one here who doesn't. I had to teach Olivia the rules at the first practice. At least you're familiar with them."

"Yeah, but that doesn't mean I have a clue

about coaching." She put her hands on the steering wheel but didn't turn on the car. "None of that changed her mind. She said this will be good for me."

He wanted to ask why, then remembered his promise to himself. Riley's business wasn't his business, and he needed to stick to his word, especially since it appeared that she was going to be his assistant whether she liked it or not.

"It's not that hard," he said, hoping to encourage her. "I can teach you about coaching and whatever else you don't know about softball." He surveyed the ball field. Olivia and Harper had stopped practicing and were talking to Anita, who was barely paying attention when Eddie threw her the ball. He needed to get back to the team before this turned into social hour. "Why don't you sit on the bench and watch practice? Then if you still think this is a bad idea, we'll talk to Erma together."

After a moment, she nodded, then got out of the car. As an afterthought, she reached through the window and grabbed the glove lying on the passenger seat. "Mimi's," she said.

He nodded, and they walked back to the field, neither saying anything. He gestured to the dugout. "You can hang out there." She nodded a second time and trudged to the dugout, then sat down on the bench.

Before he gathered the team to start practice,

he glanced at her again. She looked miserable, and that bothered him, probably more than knowing she didn't want to be around him. *But not by much.* There was something else at play here other than her not wanting to coach, and he wondered what it could be.

Riley fidgeted on the bench inside the dugout, wishing she'd been able to stand up to Mimi and tell her she was the worst choice for Hayden's assistant coach. She protested several times when her grandmother brought up the idea yesterday, but Mimi had been insistent.

After Riley returned from her disastrous run sweaty, sore, and still a bit out of breath, she walked into the kitchen to get some much-needed water. She was also just in time to see her grandmother turn off her cell phone.

"Mornin', sugar. Where have you been off to?" Mimi placed the phone in her lap and wheeled to the kitchen table.

Before answering, Riley took a green glass tumbler out of the cabinet and filled it with water, then gulped it down. "Running," she said. If she mentioned seeing Hayden, Mimi would pepper her endlessly with questions.

"Wonderful. Speaking of exercise, I came up with an excellent idea." She folded her hands on the table and grinned.

Riley had turned around to face her grandmother and forced herself not to frown. She was familiar with that smile, and when it appeared it usually meant trouble for her. "You have?"

"Yes. The church softball team needs an assistant coach."

"And you're volunteering? Mimi, that's a terrible idea."

Her smile dimmed. "Excuse me, but *I am* the current assistant coach."

"Oh." Riley filled her glass again and sat at the table, her pulse finally dropping to a normal rhythm. "You can't do that now."

"Correct. Which is why I thought of the perfect replacement." She beamed. "You."

"Oh no," Riley held up her hand. "Not me."

"Why not you?"

An argument ensued, and of course Riley lost. Out of guilt over the condition of her grandmother, the house, and Knots and Tangles, she dropped the subject, hoping Mimi would come to her senses. After working all morning and most of the afternoon at the yarn shop, taking inventory and marveling at how one person could possibly collect so much yarn over the years, she was optimistic that Mimi would see her progress and tell her to stay the rest of the day. However, at three o'clock sharp Mimi ordered Riley to head over to the ball field.

Now that she was here, she felt more uncomfortable than ever—and not because her overworked muscles were still trying to recover from her run. She wasn't surprised that Hayden was taking it all in stride. At least Mimi had the grace to ask him first—or rather, give him advance warning. The fact that she didn't trust her feelings when she was around him was another issue, and now her grandmother was forcing them to work together, under the guise of exercise and fresh air. Riley glanced down at the slight pudge of her stomach, barely camouflaged within her plain, navy-blue T-shirt, and felt the ache in her legs from taking another run this morning. The one thing she couldn't argue with Mimi about was that she needed to exercise more. The fresh air was a bonus.

She stared out in front of her, peering through the chain-link fence surrounding the ball field as the team settled into practice. She had to admit the players were good. Tanner, whom she remembered from high school but never had any classes with, was an excellent shortstop, and the blond woman at second base, whom she did not recognize, was decent too. Even Olivia, who, according to Hayden, still needed to learn how to hold her bat correctly, had a competitive spirit. The petite woman had been Riley's class valedictorian, and she had more guts than Riley did. At least she wasn't hiding in the dugout.

Almost an hour later, Hayden told the players to take a break, and everyone headed toward the dugout and a large upright cooler she'd seen the Mathis boys carry over. Riley jumped up and started filling the paper cups beside it with water and handing them to everyone, glad for something to do. When she handed a cup to the blond woman, Riley realized who she was.

The tall, sophisticated woman looked her over. "Mother said you were back in town." Harper took a sip of water. Even though everyone else was sweating, she was fresh and unbothered. Her muted red lipstick didn't leave a trace of color on the edge of the white paper cup.

Harper Wilson. Riley didn't know her well, but she was all too familiar with her type. Her mother, Madge, was a Bosom Buddy, and there was a strong resemblance between mother and daughter. Harper had a perfect figure, wore perfect clothes, and based on the car she drove, she obviously had money. Tracey always told Riley that women like her were to be avoided.

"They think they're better than us," she'd said after one of the few times she showed up to a parent-teacher conference at Riley's second elementary school in three months. The teacher had been pretty and nice, but Tracey said beautiful women were rotten on the inside. *"She's as phony as the day is long. All them kind of women are. Don't you forget it, Riley Jean."*

Riley never did. Two days later, Tracey pulled her out of that school, and they moved to another apartment in another city with another one of Tracey's endless string of boyfriends.

"Welcome back to Maple Falls."

Harper's kind tone tugged Riley out of her reverie. "Thanks," she mumbled, handing Eddie a drink, which he instantly downed, then held out his cup for more.

"Appreciate it." The large man went to the edge of the bench and sat, a smile on his ruddy face as he joked with Jesse and Jackie. Everyone was enjoying themselves, while she was strung up tighter than a fiddle bow. She poured herself a cup of water and drained it quickly.

"Are you staying with Erma permanently, or will you be looking for a place of your own?"

She turned to Harper again. "Once my grandmother is back on her feet, I'm returning to New York."

"It must be so exciting to live in New York City. I've only been there to see Broadway shows, and of course to shop. They have the most amazing stores, don't they?"

"Uh, I'm usually busy with work."

"You're an artist, right? Mother mentioned that, I think." She laughed and leaned forward. "My mother *loves* to talk. Sometimes I just tune her out. Then again, I suppose everyone stops listening to their mothers from time to time."

Riley's fingers tightened around the cup. Did Harper know anything about Tracey? Did anyone here know the truth about her mother?

"Maybe we can get coffee sometime while you're here." Harper picked up her large red handbag from the bench and fished out a business card. "My personal number is on the back. Give me a call and let me know when is good for you."

As Harper walked over to Hayden, Riley looked at the card. Wilson Real Estate. Harper Wilson, Broker. Riley tucked the card into Mimi's glove. She didn't have any intention of calling or having coffee with Harper. She was here to help her grandmother, not to make friends.

The players had left the dugout and were off in small groups talking and joking with one another. Riley sat on the bench, trying not to notice how close Harper was standing to Hayden. Although Madge was a Bosom Buddy, she had joined the group after Riley left Maple Falls, so all she knew about Harper was that her family was rich, she'd attended private schools, and now, that she owned her own real estate company. Riley had nothing in common with her.

Tracey's words came to mind again. *"They think they're better than us."*

Harper hadn't acted like she thought she was superior to Riley. In fact, she was nice. Friendly. *Or maybe she was just interested in advertising her business.*

She glanced at Harper still talking to Hayden, and she couldn't help but notice what a striking pair they made. Both had blond hair, although Harper's blond-on-blond highlights, while well done, clearly weren't natural. Both were lean, tan, and gorgeous. A surge of envy shot through Riley, and she hated herself for it. What did it matter to her if Harper and Hayden made a good-looking couple? Even their names were obnoxiously cute together. *Yuck.*

A short time later, Hayden sent everyone out on the field again, and when they were all involved with batting practice, he entered the dugout and sat next to Riley. "Thanks for getting everyone a drink," he said, grinning at her. "You're settling in fine as assistant coach."

"Are you thirsty?" she asked, getting up and ignoring his comment about her being his assistant. She also struggled to ignore the electricity she felt when he sat next to her. This coaching thing wasn't going to work. It didn't matter how hard she tried to convince herself that she didn't find him attractive. Her heart and brain weren't listening. He was hot, kind, athletic—the perfect guy. End of story. After today, she'd end the job as assistant coach, no matter what Mimi said.

"I'm fine, Riley." He motioned for her to stay put.

She listened as he began identifying who was on the field. Who played what position, who was their best batter, who still needed lots of improvement, and how Riley would be expected to keep the stats during games.

"Did Mimi do that?" she asked, getting caught up in Hayden's tutoring. She couldn't fathom her grandmother keeping decent records of anything, especially considering the state of her books at the yarn shop. When Riley worked there as a teen, she stayed out of the bookkeeping and finances. Maybe she should have paid more attention.

He shook his head. "Erma was the team cheerleader more than anything," he said. "She appointed herself assistant coach."

"And you couldn't tell her no," Riley said while offering a knowing smile.

"You got it. I didn't mind, though. Team spirit is a key part of the game, and Erma sure did bring the spirit. Olivia was doing stats before, but now she has to play since we're down two members. Hang on a minute." He got up from the bench and walked outside the dugout.

"Anita, put your glove on the ground before the ball comes to you. Right, like that." Then he went back and sat next to Riley again. "I can go over all the duties with you tonight if you want. Maybe we can grab a bite to eat too."

Riley's pulse jumped and her resolve started to weaken. "Oh, um, I don't know about that," she said, staring at her sandals.

"Guess I should have asked if you were free first."

She looked at him this time, the friendly smile gone from his face. She didn't like that her moodiness had erased it. She had to steel her resolve, though, even if she hated herself for doing it.

"I am busy," she explained, telling the truth. "There's so much work to do at the shop and the house."

"Erma's house?" When Riley nodded, he said, "What's wrong with her house?"

"You were there the other night. It's a mess."

"It's a bit untidy—"

"You're being kind." *As usual.* "The yard needs work and the house could really use a few repairs."

"I didn't realize that. Why hasn't she said she needed help?"

"Because she doesn't think she does," Riley explained. "You know my grandmother."

"I certainly do, and you're right, she wouldn't ask for help unless the roof was caving in on her." He rubbed his chin. "I know a good home repair guy I can recommend."

"Really?" Riley hadn't relished the thought of trying to replace the three splintering boards on the front porch or getting the mold off the bricks on the back of the house. "Who?"

Hayden grinned again. "Me."

Tanner ran to the dugout. "We've gone through the batting order, Coach. *Twice.* If you're not

110

too busy, can you tell us what to do next?" Riley didn't miss the smirk on Tanner's face.

"Already?" Hayden shot up from the bench. "Sorry, guess I lost track of time. Uh, bring everyone in. I'll give them the details for the game on Tuesday." He jogged to the infield, and the players gathered around him.

Riley couldn't help watching his every movement. Then she stilled. Hayden had offered to work on Mimi's house. And while she knew it was a bad idea to accept his offer, she wasn't a fool. If he could take care of the outside repairs, she could focus on the inside and on getting Knots and Tangles back in order. Then the image of Harper's business card popped into her mind. While she wasn't interested in becoming friends with her, maybe Riley could enlist her help in convincing Mimi to sell the store. Then, once her grandmother's leg was healed, Riley would be free and clear to go back to New York—that was always her plan. She hadn't imagined having to recruit help, but she'd be an idiot not to.

Feeling a little more relaxed, Riley tidied up the dugout, gathering the used cups and throwing them in the trash barrel near the bleachers, then putting the extra bats in the large canvas bag. Hayden was still talking to the team when she finished getting everything back in order, giving her time to compose what to say to him about working on the house. She had to keep things strictly professional between them. No personal interactions.

Her cheeks heated as several *very* personal interactions with Hayden slid through her mind. *Stop it!* This was why she needed to treat his offer as a business transaction—she couldn't trust herself when she was around him.

When he dismissed the players and everyone except Tanner had gone to their cars, she walked up to Hayden and tapped him on the shoulder.

He turned around. "Hey." Then he shifted his eyes to Tanner and angled his head toward the parking lot.

"I, uh, forgot to tell Eddie something. Be right back."

After Tanner dashed off, Hayden turned to her. "Did you think about my offer?"

"I did. And I accept." *Professional . . . Keep it professional.* "We can meet sometime this week to discuss terms."

His brow lifted. "Terms?"

"For the contract."

His expression switched to confusion. "Contract?"

"I'll call you at work on Monday and we can schedule a time." She began to walk away when he called after her.

"What about the game on Tuesday? You in?"

She paused and shook her head. "I'm sorry, but you'll have to find someone else to help you." With Mimi's glove tucked under her arm, she hurried off to her car, needing to end the conversation with Hayden on that note. She quickly threw open the driver's side door, tossed the glove on the passenger seat as she plopped in, then started the car and sped out of the parking lot.

Only when she had put a decent distance between her and Hayden did she let herself breathe. Having a business relationship with him was something she could handle. It was clear that when she was around Hayden Price, she was weak. She knew from experience that people took advantage of weakness, and that was something she could never allow in her life. Trusting him with anything other than Mimi's house was out of the question.

"What was that all about?"

Hayden watched Riley peel out of the parking lot as Tanner came up beside him. His head was spinning. When he was instructing her about the team and the assistant coaching duties, he saw the spark of excitement in her pretty eyes. She was paying rapt attention, and he doubted she'd even noticed her body angle toward him while he was speaking, her shoulders and torso relaxing. But *he'd* noticed, and it took some strong willpower to focus on what he was saying and not on her—the way her dark-blue T-shirt hugged her soft curves; her long, fair-skinned legs bare beyond the denim shorts; her thick, shiny hair pulled back in a casual ponytail, revealing her fresh face without a speck of makeup. She smelled amazing, like clean laundry and lightly scented soap.

She was so incredibly sexy.

Most importantly, she was opening up to him a tiny bit, and that hit him in the heart. Not to mention how he'd seen her watching him during practice, the desire in her eyes obvious, and that hit him somewhere else. There was something between them. He could feel it . . . and no amount of mental gymnastics was going to dismiss that fact. To him, asking her to join him for a meal was the next logical step.

Then she flipped the script on him, closing up again and talking about contracts and terms, then leaving in a cloud of gravel as she fled once again. *What are you so afraid of, Riley McAllister?*

"Hey," Tanner said, moving to stand in front of him. "Earth to Hayden. What's going on between you two?"

He turned and focused on Tanner, then shrugged. "I don't know what you're talking about."

"You were cozy together in that dugout a little while ago."

Hayden shot Tanner an annoyed look. "There's nothing cozy about me and Riley." *Far from it.*

Tanner laughed. "Right. I haven't seen you that interested in anyone since you moved back here."

Hayden scowled and headed for his bags. He wasn't in the mood for Tanner's ribbing, even though his friend was right. When he reached the dugout, he hefted up the bag Riley had filled with the bats and balls and threw the strap over his shoulder. He liked how she took the initiative to provide water for the players and clean up the dugout even though she hadn't wanted to do the job. He also liked how she respected Erma's wishes, despite her own obvious discomfort. He'd observed her while she was talking to Harper, and she'd been ill at ease with her too.

He was starting to put a few pieces together. For some reason, being back in Maple Falls was difficult for her. Still, she had set all that aside because Erma needed her. Loyalty was important to Hayden, and Riley was obviously loyal to her grandmother.

"Why didn't she practice with us?" Tanner asked, leaning against the dugout entrance. "She brought a glove." After Hayden explained that Riley came at Erma's insistence, Tanner added, "So she's gonna take Erma's place?"

"Apparently not." Which caused a problem for him, since he had an inkling that Erma wouldn't be happy with the news. He had to agree with Riley. It had been a terrible idea. Not because she couldn't do the job. Hayden was sure if Riley wanted to, she would make an excellent assistant coach. But forcing her into it was wrong, and hopefully Erma would realize that. He grimaced and faced Tanner. "I guess you're the assistant, then."

Tanner smirked. "Since you asked me so nicely, I accept. Just don't sit as close to me as you did to Riley, or I'll have to punch you." He started to leave the dugout, then added, "How's the house rehab coming?"

Hayden stilled. Before Riley, his house had been the most important thing on his mind. Now he was trying to remember the last time he'd thought about it. "Still in the planning stages," he said, making a mental note to actually start planning.

"Let me know if you need some help. I'm pretty decent with a hammer and nails."

"I appreciate that," Hayden said, meaning it. "I'll let you know once I get started."

"Cool." Tanner waved at him. "See you at church tomorrow."

"Yeah. See ya."

As Tanner headed to his cherry-red Jeep, Hayden stayed in the dugout, looking at the ball field, the weight of the equipment bags nothing compared to the heaviness on his heart. Even though he was sure—at least he thought he was—that there was a connection between him and Riley, she wasn't open to pursuing it. One-sided interest was new to him, and he had to admit it pricked at his ego.

Shaking his head, he walked out of the dugout and stalked to his Subaru. Maybe he was imagining things. It wasn't as if he didn't have plenty of other things to keep him occupied, and he just added fixing up Erma's house to the list.

By the time he'd put the bags in the trunk of his Subaru and started the engine, he realized Riley was right. Contracts were always a good idea, even though it bugged him a little since she and Erma were his friends. Correction—Erma was. He didn't know what he and Riley were.

What he did know was that he needed to focus on the reality of his own life—working his job, rehabbing his house, and coaching the church softball team. He'd wasted enough emotional and mental energy on Riley McAllister.

Chapter 6

The bells of the Amazing Grace Church rang out clear on Sunday morning as Riley and her grandmother arrived for service. Riley maneuvered the car into the handicapped spot in the parking lot, then pulled Mimi's wheelchair out of the trunk. When she unfolded the chair and pushed it to the passenger side of the car, Mimi frowned.

"Next Sunday I'm using crutches," she said as Riley helped her slide into the chair. "I hate this thing."

"We'll see what the doctor says on Wednesday."

"I don't care what he says." Mimi adjusted the strand of pearls at her neck. She always wore them to church and for any other special occasion. "This chair can go in a dumpster fire when I'm done."

"It's a rental, Mimi."

"Oh. Scratch that."

Riley couldn't help but smile as she pushed her grandmother into the foyer. Immediately the BBs rushed their wounded friend, and Riley was surrounded by flowered dresses, lilac and geranium perfume, and the squawk of ladies talking. Bea took over pushing Mimi, and the ladies made their way into the sanctuary, leaving

Riley behind. Or rather, forgotten. Which was fine. *I'm used to it.*

She pushed away the bitter thought. Mimi had never forgotten about her, and it wasn't fair to think that. She was surrounded by her friends, and Riley was grateful for them. She had taken the BBs for granted growing up, but she knew they all watched out for one another. Riley had always watched out for herself, except when Mimi did, and for the most part she preferred it that way. But since returning to Maple Falls, she wondered what it would be like to have a group of friends as devoted as the BBs. Not that it would ever actually happen, but she still wondered.

She walked into the sanctuary, planning to sit with Mimi and the rest of her group when she heard someone say her name. She turned to see Anita Bedford motioning for Riley to sit next to her. Riley hesitated. She barely remembered Anita from school. Although she preferred to sit with Mimi or by herself, she didn't want to turn Anita down and risk hurting her feelings, especially when she had such a sweet, expectant expression.

"I'm sorry I didn't get a chance to talk to you at practice yesterday," Anita said, her smile growing bigger as Riley approached. "Welcome back."

Riley nodded, unsure if Anita was talking about Maple Falls or church. Probably the former since Riley hadn't been a regular church attender when she was a teenager. The first year she lived with Mimi she was forced to go to church, but instead of finding the peace and community interaction all the other churchgoers seemed to experience, she felt resentment. It was harder to pretend to be invisible among such close-knit people. Her opinion about church had never been favorable anyway, since Tracey never took her and had been quick to point out how judgmental church folks were. When Riley was there, all she'd ever felt was judgment, even though people rarely spoke to her beyond small talk.

Finally Mimi stopped forcing her to go when Riley started arguing with her every Sunday morning—as long as she agreed to attend during the holidays, which she had. Now she couldn't remember the last time she'd stepped foot inside a church. Probably the last Sunday she'd spent in Maple Falls. The only reason she'd agreed to go today was because her grandmother needed a ride.

Anita nodded toward Mimi. "She looks good today. A lot better than she did after the accident. It's hard to keep her down, isn't it?"

Riley nodded. Harper and Olivia entered the pew on the opposite side and sat next to Anita.

"I just hope I'm that spry when I'm her age," Anita said.

Harper leaned over to greet Riley. "Good morning."

"Morning." Now seeing the three of them, Riley felt underdressed in her black three-quarter-sleeved shirt and frayed jeans with her usual sandals. It was one thing for her grandmother and her friends to wear dresses and pearls to church, but quite another to see women her own age almost equally dressed up. Harper was the most sophisticated of the three with her pale-peach sleeveless dress, orange high-heeled espadrilles, and dangling turquoise earrings. Olivia was more tailored, wearing a light, white cardigan over a red blouse and navy-blue pencil skirt, while Anita was the most casual in a flowing lavender maxi dress.

A man with a guitar stepped on the stage and started playing, and Riley realized it was Jesse Mathis, the oldest of the three Mathis cousins who were at softball practice yesterday. He began to sing, and the rest of the congregation stood and sang with him. Riley had never heard the song before, and despite the words displayed on the screen, she didn't try to sing along.

Instead, she observed her surroundings and soon saw Hayden standing in his pew, his parents beside him, all three singing. She tried to pull her gaze from him, but she couldn't stop herself from checking him out. Crisp white collared shirt rolled up to the elbows, fitted blue jeans, and she caught a glimpse of his slip-on tan suede shoes. She'd never really been interested in portraiture, but an exception could be made if Hayden was the model.

She jerked her focus and thoughts back to the front of the church, where a large wooden cross was framed by frosted glass windows. She was surprised God hadn't struck her down for having such thoughts in a house of worship.

For the next hour she forced herself to pay attention to the service, and she had to admit that Jared was pretty good at delivering a sermon. From what she could remember of the former pastor, Jared was much more interesting and exuberant than his predecessor, who had been a mainstay at the church for almost thirty years.

When the service was over, she said a quick goodbye to Anita, Harper, and Olivia before they could say anything to her. This was her MO—arrive as late as possible and leave as soon as the service was over. That way she hopefully wouldn't get stuck talking to anyone. She headed outside to wait for Mimi, certain one of the BBs would bring her out of the building. She walked to the car and leaned against it, then saw Hayden exit the church with Tanner.

He turned and their eyes met. She steeled herself, expecting him to walk over and strike up a conversation, either about repairing Mimi's house or, God forbid, trying to convince her to be the assistant coach. When she arrived home last evening, she had stood firm with her grandmother and told her that she not only wasn't going to be the coach but also wasn't going to attend any of the games. If Mimi wanted to go to one, she'd have to rely on one of the BBs to take her. Her grandmother had seemed taken aback, but to Riley's shock, she didn't try to change her mind.

Hayden was surprising her right now. Instead of walking over to her, he gave her a curt nod, then turned his back and launched into conversation with Tanner. As other people poured out of the church, he began engaging them in conversation too.

Riley frowned. He was acting like he barely knew her, when just yesterday he was sitting so close to her she could see the scar on his right knee, one she had wondered about last night when she couldn't stop thinking about him as she tried to sleep.

Wasn't this what she wanted, though, for him to leave her alone? And not just him, but everyone else too? As she stood alone by Mimi's car, longing washed over her. For Hayden and for something else she couldn't put her finger on. Everyone here seemed relaxed and happy. Two things she was not.

The noon sun was beating down, and she wiped perspiration off her forehead as she waited for her grandmother and questioned her decision to wear jeans on such a hot day. She hadn't brought anything else other than shorts. She didn't even own a skirt.

"Riley! Yoo-hoo!"

She looked up to see Bea pushing Mimi toward her, Peg strolling alongside. Mimi was grinning as they approached her. "We're going to The Orange Bluebird for lunch," Erma said.

"Is that new?" Riley asked. The Sunshine Diner had always been closed on Sundays, and since it was the only restaurant in Maple Falls, The Orange Bluebird must be in another town.

"Heavens, no." Mimi's fingers touched her pearls. "It's been around for years in Rockfield. It used to be called Gas and Guzzle because it was part of a gas station. Then it was sold to The Orange Bluebird owners and they changed the name."

Riley couldn't decide which name was worse.

"They have a delicious all-you-can-eat brunch." Bea was practically licking her chops.

"Peg said she would bring me home," Mimi interjected, gesturing to her friend.

That was unexpected. "You don't want me to take you?"

"You've been running nonstop since you got here. I figured you'd like some time for yourself, so go on home and take it easy. I'll be back this afternoon. Come on, girls!" She waved forward Bea and Peg. "I want to get there before they run out of buckwheat pancakes."

Riley stood by the Town Car as her grandmother and friends climbed into Peg's gold minivan. It was a bit comical watching the two women figure out how to get Mimi in the back seat, then wrestle her wheelchair into the trunk. Finally Junior Dobbs sauntered over and helped them out. After several profuse exclamations of gratitude from the women and a tip of Junior's baseball hat, he and her grandmother and friends exited the parking lot.

When she scanned the lot, she saw that everyone else had left, including Hayden. Now she really was alone. There was nothing to do except go back to the house.

When she pulled in the driveway, she parked and went inside, ignoring the stacks of magazines, catalogs, unfolded laundry, and layers of dust on the furniture. She slipped out of her sandals and placed them neatly near the front door, then walked into the kitchen, intending to fix a glass of iced tea. Instead, she paused at the table, listening. She heard the hum of Mimi's ancient refrigerator, felt the cool, smooth, outdated vinyl flooring beneath her feet, saw the row of dust-covered small ceramic roosters sitting on the ledge of the kitchen window. Like everything else in the house, nothing had changed in this room since she left. But instead of lamenting that her grandmother was stuck in the past, she found the familiarity of the kitchen comforting.

Although not the silence. It was too quiet, especially when she was used to hearing the TV blaring or Mimi chatting on the phone with one of her friends. Quiet canceled out comfort, and she slapped together a ham and cheese sandwich, poured herself a glass of tea, and went outside.

The sun was hidden behind the clouds, but the heat and humidity lingered in the air. She wandered through the tall grass in the backyard, stopping in front of an old tire swing. She used to play on it when she was little and visited Mimi. She'd even swung on it a few times after she moved in as a teen. She sat on the raggedy tire and pushed her toes in the dirt, swinging back and forth as she ate her sandwich.

How many times as a child had she sat on this swing while her mother and grandmother were in the house, having a talk that usually ended in an argument with Tracey storming out and dragging Riley with her? She had no idea, but she clearly remembered wishing she could live here instead of with Tracey. Mimi's house was always nice, always comfortable, and always filled with food and love. Mimi read her bedtime stories and fixed her cookies and milk, but only if Riley had eaten her vegetables at supper. She would let Riley take bubble baths and play dress-up, and she always told funny tales about her life with Poppy. Tracey had never done any of those things. Living with

Mimi would solve all her problems. Riley had been sure of that.

Then she moved in with her grandmother, and while her life had been different and better, it hadn't been the paradise she'd imagined. She hadn't felt any more connected to Maple Falls than she had to all the transient cities she'd lived in with Tracey. *Whose fault was that?*

She popped up from the tire, shoving the past out of her mind. She should have gone with Mimi to The Orange Bluebird. At least there she would be distracted by the food and company. Here her only companions were memories she didn't want to relive.

As usual when she was out of sorts, she thought about her art. She went back inside and put her partially eaten sandwich and glass of water on the kitchen table, then climbed upstairs to her bedroom. She searched the small dresser in the corner of the room, and in the bottom drawer she found a small stack of cheap sketch pads, exactly where she'd kept them when she lived there, along with a pack of charcoal pencils.

Riley took one of the pads and one of the pencils and went back to the backyard, this time sitting in a white plastic chair on the pitted and peeling deck. She put her feet up on the short deck railing and began to sketch the elm tree in front of her. She was halfway through with it when she looked at it and frowned. The sketch was uninspired and two dimensional. She glanced at the tree again, disappointed that her drawing hadn't done it justice. Working in mixed media for most of a decade had eroded her drawing skills. She turned the page over to a fresh white sheet.

Closing her eyes, she let her creativity take over, as she often did when she felt blocked or off her game. She allowed the pencil in her hand to take the lead, giving control to the art instead of forcing it. After a few minutes of sketching, she opened her eyes, eager to see what was on the page.

She groaned. An outline of Hayden's face stared back at her.

Riley started to turn the page again, then paused. She studied the light pencil strokes, thinking of how she could flesh out the image. Maybe she could get him out of her mind by getting him on the page. At this point she was willing to try anything.

She continued drawing, sketching out his facial structure, which of course was perfect. Then she started on his hair, making sure to add the way the ends touched the collar of his shirt at church this morning, and the one cowlick at the crown that she'd noticed the first time she saw him in high school. Soon she was engrossed, focusing on her craft as much as she was the subject of it.

The sound of a car door slamming brought her

out of her zone. She folded over the sketchbook and set it on the rusty white wrought iron table next to her chair, then went inside, put on her shoes, and opened the door to help Peg with Mimi.

When she stepped on the front porch, she was stunned to see Olivia, Anita, and Harper coming up the steps, holding bags of takeout.

"You left before we could invite you to lunch," Anita said, smiling as she stopped in front of Riley.

"So we decided to bring a late lunch to you." Harper held up a plastic bag from a restaurant Riley had never heard of. "We planned to get here earlier, but Mother asked me to run an errand." She rolled her eyes. "Sometimes she refuses to take no for an answer."

"I hope you like Mediterranean food," Olivia said. "The spanakopita is amazing."

"So is the hummus." Anita chuckled. "I hope you aren't planning to kiss anyone this afternoon, though. They put tons of garlic in it."

Hayden's face appeared in her mind, and Riley's cheeks flushed. Then again, she had been drawing him for twenty minutes, so thinking of him didn't necessarily mean she was thinking about kissing him. *Liar.*

She scratched at her forearm. "You didn't have to do this," she said as Harper opened the front door.

"I don't know about y'all, but I'm starving." Harper walked inside like she owned the place.

"We better eat before it gets cold." Olivia smiled at Riley. "It's nice that you came back to be with Erma. She's a firecracker, but everyone needs help sometimes." She followed Harper inside.

"Is it okay that we did this?" Anita asked, her eyes darting to the table and back to Riley. "We saw Erma leaving with Peg and Bea, and then you left by yourself . . . Well, we didn't want you to eat lunch alone."

A lump formed in Riley's throat. She couldn't remember the last time someone had been this hospitable to her. Melody, of course, but she and Melody were roommates and good friends. She barely knew these women.

"Yes," she said, her voice sounding thick. "It's okay."

"Good, because Harper ordered enough to feed six people."

Riley motioned for Anita to go inside, and then followed. Harper and Olivia were in the kitchen, talking as they unpacked the bags. The spicy scent of the Mediterranean food wafted through the house. Riley's stomach growled.

"Did we interrupt your lunch?" Olivia gestured to the sandwich on the kitchen table.

She paused, then shook her head. The food they brought was way better than ham and cheese any day. "Sorry the house is such a mess."

Harper raised her flawless eyebrows. "I thought it was a little neater than it was the last time we were here."

"It is," Anita added.

Riley was surprised to hear that they had been here before. "When was that?"

"Three months ago, I think." Olivia opened a plastic container of hummus and set it in the middle of the table. "Erma and Harper's mom, along with their other friends, were playing bunco, and they invited us to join in."

"That was a fun night," Anita said wistfully. "I wish my mother had a group of friends like that."

"She has the Junior League," Harper said, rolling her eyes.

"Don't remind me."

Feeling at loose ends, Riley went to the cupboard and pulled out plates and glasses, then opened one of the drawers and gathered silverware. It wasn't long before all four of them were seated at the table, filling their plates with pita triangles, hummus, tabbouleh, rolled grape leaves, spanakopita, and chicken skewers.

The three other women continued chatting, but Riley felt a bit uneasy. She added two grape leaves and a spoonful of tabbouleh to her plate. Ten minutes ago she was lonely and completely alone. Now she wasn't sure what to do about having company. *I'm such a mess.*

"Girls, I don't know what to do." Erma picked at the stack of blueberry buckwheat pancakes in front of her. She loved these pancakes, and The Orange Bluebird's brunch in general, but her appetite had disappeared. A shame because the restaurant didn't allow doggie bags.

"About what?" Bea had no problem polishing off her stack and was working on a second, along with three strips of crispy bacon and a tall glass of milk.

"Hayden and Riley."

Peg's and Bea's forks clattered onto their plates.

"What?" Peg said, her hand going to the tacky red bead choker around her neck. Erma loved Peg dearly, but the woman had horrendous taste in jewelry. "There's something going on between Hayden and Riley?"

"I had no idea." Bea grinned. "But how wonderful. He's such a nice young man, and if anyone deserves a nice young man, it's your Riley."

"True." Bea's words made Erma feel a little better, and she ate a couple bites of her pancakes, then took a sip of her French roast coffee. "Unfortunately I don't think she believes that, and that's why I don't know what to do." She filled Bea and Peg in on her spur-of-the-moment plan to get Riley and Hayden together. It had formulated the day she asked Hayden to pick Riley up at the airport, and then grew when she came up with the idea for Riley to take her place as assistant coach. What better way for them to be in each other's company at least two days a week? That backfired when Riley resisted going to practice and then came home so unsettled and told Erma in no uncertain terms that she didn't want anything to do with coaching or softball. Now Erma was wondering if she'd made a mistake.

"Maybe you should mind your own business," Bea said before biting into a strip of bacon.

"Riley *is* my business, Bea." Erma didn't try to hide the edge in her tone.

"Of course she is." Bea's expression turned contrite. "I just meant that if Hayden and Riley are meant to be, let them come together on their own."

"From what I can tell, that's not going to happen." Erma set down her fork. "I have to admit I'm surprised there wasn't a spark."

"Why? Did you expect there to be one?" Peg asked.

Erma scoffed. "He's smart, comes from a good family, has impeccable Southern manners, and you'd have to be blind or dead not to notice how handsome he is."

"Why, Erma Jean, I think you have a crush on the young'un." Bea giggled and winked at Peg.

"Very funny." Erma leaned back in her wheelchair, now wondering if she should have brought this topic up at all. She knew she couldn't reveal the real reason she hoped for Riley and Hayden to click romantically. She was ashamed even to think about it because she was being singularly selfish. *But I want Riley home.*

Falling in love with Hayden would ensure that. His dad had mentioned a few days before Erma's accident that Hayden bought a fixer-upper on the edge of town, which meant he was staying in Maple Falls. She remembered being a little jealous. At least Harry had one son home. Besides, what man wouldn't think Riley was a catch? And who wouldn't want Hayden Price as a grandson-in-law?

"I'm surprised someone hasn't snatched up Hayden since he got back." Peg cut into her eggs with the side of her fork. A huge cobalt-blue and emerald-green ring adorned her finger. It would have been pretty except it was in the shape of a beetle. "There are several single young women in our town."

"Maybe he's not interested in dating anyone," Bea added. "Did you ask him about it, Erma?"

"Of course not. I'm not that nosy."

Bea and Peg smirked. "Right," they said in unison.

"Not about romance, and not when it comes to my granddaughter." She sighed, realizing she was contradicting herself. "You two are no help. You know that?"

"I'm going to get some fruit," Peg said, pushing back from the table. "Do you two need anything?"

Erma shook her head, but Bea said, "Another piece or two of that bacon, please. Wait, make it three."

When Peg left, Bea turned to Erma, her expression serious. "All right, Erma, what are you really up to?"

Surprised, Erma frowned. "I just told you. I want Riley and Hayden to get together."

"I've never known you to be a matchmaker."

"There's a first time for everything." Erma lifted her chin. "Besides, we all agree that Hayden's a keeper."

"He is, but I suspect that's not the only reason you want him and Riley together." Bea leaned forward. "You can't force her to stay, hon."

Drat. Leave it to Bea to figure it out. If Myrtle had been here, she would have known Erma's real motives too. *The perils of having best friends.*

"I know that," Erma snapped. Then she reached for Bea's hand. "I'm sorry." Tears welled in her eyes. Bother, she didn't want to break down here in a crowded restaurant. As it was, half of Maple Falls seemed to have the same idea she and her friends did, and the last thing she wanted to get around town was that she'd been seen crying at the brunch buffet. "I miss her so much. I don't know if I can bear it if she leaves again."

"Oh, honey." Bea squeezed her hand. "I know you're worried. But we're here for you. Just like we have been all these years. We BBs don't let each other go through hard times alone."

Erma nodded, swallowing her tears. She released Bea's hand. "Thank you. I just wish it didn't have to be this way. I always prayed things would be different."

"Keep up that faith, Erma. Just don't try to force anything, especially something as important as a romantic relationship. If the good Lord wants Riley and Hayden to be together, he'll make it happen. He doesn't need your help."

That was for sure. Erma adjusted the napkin in her lap as Peg rejoined them, then handed a small plate of bacon to Bea. The woman did enjoy her pork products. Erma sat back and watched her friends discuss Jared's sermon. A feeling of calm came over her. She would enjoy Riley's company as long as her granddaughter was here, and she wouldn't ruin their time together by trying to press her into doing something she didn't want to do—and that included taking over Knots and Tangles and coaching the church softball team. She'd already given silent agreement to Riley last night, and when she returned home she would call Hayden and let him off the hook too.

A pain creased her heart. She'd lived on hope

for too long. Her dream of handing over Knots and Tangles to Riley needed to die. Just because her granddaughter, who had always possessed gumption, had been working in the store to get it organized and cleaned up, didn't mean she was interested in running the business. In fact, she'd made it clear she didn't want to. Earlier in the week, Riley had even mentioned that maybe Erma and Myrtle could move in together. Erma pretended to chew on the idea, but it was preposterous. She adored Myrtle, but being roommates would certainly fray their relationship. They were too independent to share a residence.

There was also another thing Erma needed to face. Knots and Tangles wasn't much of a business anymore, and not just because she hadn't been giving it her full attention over the past few years. All the businesses on Main Street were in various states of decline, including Price's Hardware and the Sunshine Diner. Why would she want to saddle Riley with a losing proposition? That wasn't fair, and it wasn't respectful of what Riley really wanted to do— be an artist. She was an excellent one with a true gift. Erma had to accept that her granddaughter's home was in New York.

Somehow she would have to deal with the loneliness that had been encroaching over the past several years, although she hadn't admitted it to anyone. If the Bosom Buddies thought for a minute that Erma was lonely, they'd never leave her alone. She wasn't lonely for friends; she was blessed with the best. The empty hole in her heart could only be filled by family, and her only family was Riley. That was too much of a burden to put on her grandchild, who had already been burdened with so much in her life.

"Do you want some fresh pancakes?" Bea asked, breaking into Erma's thoughts. "Those have grown cold by now."

Erma nodded. She hated to waste food, but she couldn't choke down cold buckwheat pancakes. "Just two," she said. She would eat those at least. If she went home from the buffet hungry, Riley might think something was wrong.

At least she had settled a few things in her mind. She'd butt out of Riley's life, both professional and romantic. That was the right thing to do. She'd failed so many times with Tracey and partly blamed herself for her daughter's mess of a life. She couldn't bear it if she messed up Riley's.

"What's it like being a famous artist?" Olivia asked, scooping a small bite of hummus with a pita triangle.

"Glamorous, I'm sure." Anita sighed.

"Erma is really proud of you." Harper smiled and looked at Riley. "She said one day she would like to display your artwork in the yarn shop."

"She did?" Riley wondered why Mimi hadn't mentioned it to her before. She also wondered why she hadn't offered to send Mimi some pieces.

"I was always amazed that you could draw and paint so well," Anita said before taking a sip of iced tea. "I can barely draw a stick figure."

Olivia nodded. "Same here. What do you paint now?"

"I don't paint anymore." Riley explained about her mixed media projects, and she was pleased to see the girls were interested and had a lot of questions. As long as the topic stayed on art or New York life, Riley was fine. More than fine, actually. Not only was she enjoying the food, but she was also enjoying the conversation. Still, she kept up her guard in case the subject shifted to something more personal.

To her surprise, it never did. She saved a plate of food for Erma to heat up later and told the women she didn't need help cleaning up the kitchen. Then she walked them to the door, Olivia and Anita saying goodbye and heading for Harper's Mercedes.

Harper lingered on the front porch and turned to Riley. "I was serious about getting together for coffee," she said. Before Riley could answer, she added, "I know what it's like."

"What do you mean?" Riley asked, confused.

Harper tucked a strand of blond hair behind her ear, revealing a single twinkling diamond stud in her ear. "Coming back home and trying to find your place again. I left for college right after graduation, and then I worked in Dallas for four years. When I decided I wanted to have my own business, I came back here." She frowned slightly. "I've always been kind of an outsider here since I didn't go to school with everyone else. It took me a while to ease back into friendships."

Riley wasn't sure what to say. She couldn't admit to Harper that there were no friendships to ease back into. Of course Harper wouldn't know that.

"So be sure to call me. Or maybe I'll call you." She made her way down the steps. "I know where you live, after all." She grinned and waved as she walked to her car.

Riley watched them leave, and the lump in her throat reappeared. It had never occurred to her that anyone in Maple Falls would understand what she was going through. Not back then and definitely not now. But Harper did, to a certain extent.

Would Hayden?

She shook her head and went back inside. It didn't matter if Hayden understood her or not. While she was changing her mind about possibly taking Harper up on her coffee offer, she stood firm about not getting any closer to Hayden.

Chapter 7

To Hayden's surprise, Monday morning was almost as busy as Saturday had been. Several customers had purchased paint, including one woman who had taken more than an hour trying to decide on the perfect shade of white for her kitchen. Hayden always thought white was a bad color for a kitchen, especially if the family had kids. He intended to paint his own kitchen a light golden yellow, once he got that far into the project. But white and gray and wood tones were in right now, and when she finally decided that Ice White was the perfect shade, he told her she had made an excellent choice, when in reality he was just glad she'd made a decision at all.

"I'll be back to pick out hardware for the cabinets," she said as he rang her up.

"Great. Is there any particular kind you're looking for?"

"I haven't decided. I'm considering bright silver or matte silver. I have to think about it a little longer."

"We'll be here when you're ready. I'll take this out to your car for you."

"Thank you so much. I'm so glad I stopped in here." She pushed her long black hair over her shoulder. "I had gone to the big building store in Malvern, but they didn't have the right shade of white. You have no idea how many shades of white there are out there."

He nodded and smiled. *I sure do now.*

After he put the paint in her car and went back inside the store, he helped another customer find grass seed for his lawn, then described the difference between a Phillips and a flathead screwdriver to a young man he thought should have known the distinction already. Hayden had learned all the types of screwdrivers and hammers they had in the store by the time he was eight, but he had to remember that not every kid was interested in hardware. By the time lunch rolled around, he realized he hadn't taken a morning break.

"This takes me back," Dad said as the last customer left and the store was empty for the first time since they opened that morning. "I remember when we were this busy most of the time."

Hayden smiled, glad to see his father happy. Even though Dad usually rolled with the punches, Hayden suspected he was concerned about the downslide in business for the past several years. Or maybe he wasn't as concerned as Hayden thought he should be.

When the phone rang, Hayden said, "I'll get it. You go grab lunch."

Dad nodded and went to the back of the store as Hayden picked up the portable phone off the counter. "Price's Hardware, where we have the best price in town. This is Hayden, how may I help you?"

"Hi, Hayden. It's Riley."

He gripped the phone, instinctively turning around and putting his back to the door. "Hi, Riley," he said, making sure to keep his tone businesslike, as if she were just another customer. The drumming in his heart wasn't exactly cooperating. "How may I help you?"

"I said I would call you today." She paused. "About helping me with Mimi's house."

"Oh, right." He sounded like he had forgotten, but that couldn't be further from the truth. It had taken everything he had to keep a cool distance and not approach her at church yesterday. He wasn't used to struggling this much. Calming his emotions had always come easy to him. As a pitcher, he couldn't allow himself to feel excitement or pressure or anxiety, and especially not during a big game or when the score was on the line. Being on autopilot and leaning on his training was key.

But how did he go on autopilot when it came to Riley? Somehow he would have to figure it out because Erma needed help, and fixing up her property was something he wanted to do for her.

"Could you stop by tonight?" Riley asked. "I

can show you what needs work, and we can draw up the contract."

"Is your lawyer going to be there?" He meant for it to come out sounding like a joke, but his tone was too sharp. *Great.* So much for keeping cool.

A pause. "I'm capable of writing a simple agreement."

She sounded a little touchy, and he couldn't blame her after his lawyer dig. He tempered his tone. "I'll be there after six."

"Thank you." She hung up.

He stared at the phone, cleared his screen, and put it in his pocket. Whatever. He'd finish Erma's projects, and then he and Riley wouldn't have to cross paths again. He was even questioning what he saw in her in the first place. Good. He needed to hang on to that attitude if he was going to work with her.

Hayden went back to the office, expecting his father to be at his desk eating the lunch Mom packed for him this morning, since Jasper hadn't shown up today. But his father wasn't there, and Hayden saw the note he'd left.

Gone to the diner for lunch. Call if you want me to bring you anything back.

He sat on the swivel chair and thought about what he wanted to eat. It was better than thinking about Riley. As he tried to decide between a chef salad and chicken tenders, he straightened a stack of tool catalogs on his father's desk, then saw a piece of paper with familiar letterhead at the top. *Henry Price, Esq.* His brother's law practice. Why was his brother sending a formal letter to their father?

Hayden picked up the letter and read it, his stomach churning by the time he finished. Despite the fancy header, the contents weren't about legal business. Instead, it was about his father selling the store.

Reeling from what he'd just read, he set the letter back on the desk and covered it with a catalog. His father had found a buyer and asked Henry to look over the contract since Dad wasn't using a real estate broker and was selling the property on his own. Henry had scrutinized everything and said it was a fair offer. But his brother's last words had driven the sharp point home. *"Don't hesitate to accept."*

Hayden stood and yanked his cell out of the pocket of his cargo shorts and tapped his brother's number. The phone rang a few times before Henry answered.

"Hey, Hayden," he said. "How's it goin'?"

"Dad is selling the store?"

Silence.

"Yes. How did you find out?"

Hayden explained. He didn't care if Henry chastised him for reading information not meant

147

for him. Right now he had to get down to the bottom of why their father was giving up on the family business.

But Henry didn't say anything about Hayden reading the private correspondence. "So, I take it he hasn't said anything to you yet."

"Not a word. Does Mom know?"

"Yes."

Hayden thrust his hand through his hair and started to pace. "Why didn't they tell me?"

"I'm sure they have their reasons."

"I bet Harrison knows."

Henry sighed. "Yes, he does. Hayden, this has been in the works for a while."

"How long?"

"At least two years."

"Two years?"

"Hayden, don't get upset." Henry's voice carried its usual calm tone. His brother, like Dad, rarely got upset about anything. That made him a great lawyer but irritating to talk to sometimes. "Mom and Dad didn't want to bother you with it. You had just gotten drafted by the Tigers when they started talking about selling, and then your accident happened—"

"I've been living with them for six months. I've worked here every minute the store has been open since I got back. It's not like I don't see them every day."

"You'll have to discuss it with them. I'm sorry

you had to find out this way, but I can't get involved in something that's between you and them. Look, I've got a client coming in a few minutes, so I have to let you go. I'll give you a call back later."

"But—" The phone went dead on the other end.

Hayden shoved the phone back into his pocket and scowled. Henry was a busy attorney, and deep down he knew his brother was right. But that didn't stop the betrayal from winding through him right now. His whole family had been planning on selling the family business, and no one thought to mention it to him, using his now nonexistent career and then his injury as an excuse. Didn't they think he had an opinion? Did they bother to consider that he would?

When he heard the bell above the front door jingle, he gathered himself, shoving his feelings inside like he'd always done when he was in pain or hurt. The years of keeping his emotions wrapped tight were failing him. He took a few deep breaths to calm his mind. Finally he was collected enough to greet the three customers who had walked in, and to do so with a friendly smile—just as his father taught him the first day he started working in the store.

When Dad came back from lunch, they were still busy with customers. Hayden skipped lunch, which was fine since he didn't have an appetite. He also didn't have a chance to talk to his father, and by the time they closed for the day—an hour later than normal—he needed to head over to Erma's.

"Today was a good day." Dad pulled out the cash drawer and started for the back. "I'll lock up, son, so you won't be late. Lord knows Erma is a fussbudget when it comes to punctuality."

Before Hayden could say anything, his father was halfway to the back of the store. Probably a good thing, since this wasn't going to be a quick conversation.

"See you later," he managed to say.

"Bye, son."

Usually after closing, Hayden left the store through the back, where he parked his car in the small lot behind the store. Today he walked out the front door, needing the longer walk to gather himself again. The sun was low, and they hadn't gotten a break from the hot, swampy air. He passed Petals and Posies and saw it was already closed. Then he noticed the peeling paint on the front facade, a contrast to the bright and cheerful floral display in the picture window.

He paused, noticing a bit of dry rot on the bottom left corner of the doorframe on the building. Turning, he took a good look at Main Street. The yarn store, the bakery, the diner at the end . . . Each of their facades were worn and in various states of disrepair. Then there were the empty buildings in between the decades-old businesses. For Sale and For Rent signs were posted on the glass. One, only half attached to the inside window, had been there so long the bright yellow paper with black lettering had faded to white and gray.

Why would anyone choose to shop in Maple Falls when there were bigger stores in surrounding cities? For the first time he saw hometown businesses with a critical eye and realized that the town's mainstays were literally dying away. Could he blame his father for wanting to sell?

An unexpected wave of sadness hit him. What would happen to these historic buildings once they were sold? Would any of the legacy businesses survive? He didn't know if the prospective buyer of Price's Hardware would even keep the business the same.

A more chilling thought entered his mind. What would happen to Maple Falls if there were no businesses? No parades? Nothing to draw people here to spend their money and enjoy what used to be a quaint, and yes, a little bit quirky, town. Would Maple Falls end up like so many other small Southern cities and become a ghost town?

Could he allow that to happen? Did he even have the right or the means to stop it?

Riley pulled back one of the pleated sheer panels that covered the front window in Mimi's living room and peeked at the driveway. Hayden still hadn't arrived. She frowned, kicking herself for being so snippy to him earlier. Then again, he had been a bit snippy himself by mentioning her having a lawyer. Was he making fun of her business sense? Or was he expressing frustration with her insisting on a contract for a few common repair jobs? She suspected it was the latter. *Can't blame him for that.*

After calling she had worked the rest of the day at Knots and Tangles. She'd had to force herself to focus on organizing the back room so she didn't think about seeing Hayden later or worry that she had driven him away.

She'd decided to move all the shelves, the table, and boxes of yarn away from the walls so she could clean behind them. Once everything was in the middle of the room, she saw that the space needed a paint job and added that to her ever-growing punch list. Between the shop and Mimi's house, there was no way she could finish even half of what she wanted to do without help.

When she arrived in Maple Falls last week, her sole goal had been to take care of Mimi until she got back on her feet. Now that goal had changed, and she wanted her grandmother to have the house and business she deserved, instead of settling for what Riley considered subpar. The thought that it might not happen all because she'd gotten into a snit over a trivial comment bothered her. She didn't like that she had become so touchy lately. It wasn't Hayden's fault she liked him. Well, it was a little, but he couldn't help being himself. She was the one who had a problem, and she needed to get a grip on it.

She looked out the window again. There was nothing she could do except hope she hadn't driven him away

"Don't fret, sugar. He'll be here soon." Mimi tapped the end of her ballpoint pen against her temple, then said, "Aha! That's it." She filled out the final squares of the newspaper crossword. "Viola! Done. That was a toughie."

Riley turned to her. "You must be the last person who gets a physical copy of the newspaper."

Mimi took off her reading glasses and gave Riley a stern look. "I'm sure I'm not, or there wouldn't be any newspapers available. Also, doing a crossword puzzle on a computer isn't the same." She set the paper on the table next to her recliner, then started to use her free leg to push the footrest down.

Riley hurried over to help before Mimi hurt herself. If she ever made any extra money, she was buying Mimi an electric recliner, one with a remote and massage capability. Her grandmother would fuss, but Riley knew in the end she would like it. Though that would be a long way off. The idea of extra money was a pipe dream.

"I'm fine, Riley. Look, I can even scoot into the wheelchair myself." Mimi positioned herself in the chair, then grinned with satisfaction. "See? No problem."

"Until you fall off the recliner. Why won't you ask for help?"

Mimi's expression grew serious. "I'm not used to it," she said in a low voice.

Riley almost nodded. She had difficulty asking for help, too, a trait she must have inherited from Erma. While it could be annoying to others, she was proud of being independent, and she was glad to have that in common with her grandmother. Funny how the characteristic had skipped a generation when it came to Tracey.

"There he is," Mimi announced, perking up.

"How do you know?" Riley glanced at the front door.

"I heard the car door slam."

Riley hadn't heard it, but Mimi's hearing was impeccable. Her pulse started to thrum, and she was relieved he hadn't changed his mind about helping.

"Are you going to tell me why you and Hayden are meeting tonight?" Mimi asked, wheeling closer to her.

"Eventually." Riley smoothed her hair, which was pulled back in a bun at the nape of her neck.

Mimi touched her hand. "Don't worry. You're pretty as a posy."

"I'm not thinking about how I look—" A knock sounded at the door.

"Be right there!" Mimi hollered, then shoved Riley toward the door.

Off balance from the unexpected shove, Riley steadied herself before opening the door.

"Hi, Hayden," she said, keeping her tone as neutral as possible.

"Hey." He wasn't paying attention to her. His gaze scanned the yard as he added, "Sorry I'm late." Then he turned to her. "Ready to talk?"

"Yes." She started to frown. Now he was examining the front of the house, his normally bright expression twisted in a studious grimace. Wow, she didn't think the house was that bad.

"Come on inside, Hayden," Mimi called out behind her. "I've got fresh sweet tea, extra sweet, of course, and lemon cookies in the kitchen."

Hayden nodded, and before Riley could fully open the door, he walked inside, passing right by her as if she were Mimi's butler. He leaned down and kissed her grandmother on the cheek. "How are you today, Erma?"

Riley watched as Hayden gave Mimi his undivided attention while she listed her complaints, the chief one concerning her wheelchair.

"I don't need this contraption anymore," she griped, sneering at the armrest.

"Is that what the doctor said?"

"Doctors don't know everything." Mimi sniffed, lifting her chin. "If he tells me when I see him Wednesday that I have to keep using this, he's getting an earful."

Hayden's brow lifted. "Glad I'm not that doctor."

While he was still listening to Mimi and nodding as she continued her tirade on the medical profession, Riley noticed he was tapping his foot, as if he were impatient. *As if he wants to get this over with.* For some reason that irritated her, and she could feel herself getting prickly again. If he didn't want to help anymore, he should have canceled the meeting.

She marched to the kitchen and started pouring tea into two crystal-cut tumblers Mimi had insisted they use, along with a matching pitcher that her grandmother only brought out for special occasions. Riley also noticed when she got home from the shop that the living room and kitchen had been tidied up. Was she trying to impress him? Were the green glasses they normally used not good enough?

Riley leaned against the kitchen counter and let out a deep breath. She was starting to sound like Tracey again, and she hated it. Never had she gotten the impression from Hayden or the Prices that they were stuck up or thought they were any better than anyone else. Why had that crossed her mind now?

"Erma seems to be feeling better."

Riley turned to see Hayden standing behind

her, his expression impassive. She nodded, taking a moment to steady her nerves before handing him a glass of tea. "She's in a hurry to get well. I don't want her to rush her recovery."

"Good idea." He glanced at the tumbler in his hand. "Nice glasses." He walked over to the table and sat down, then started drumming his fingers against the vinyl flowered tablecloth Mimi must have dug out from the depths of her linen closet.

"Is this a bad time?" Riley crossed her arms over her chest. *Be pleasant.* "We can reschedule if you're too busy." Her tone had successfully tempered.

His fingers stilled, hovering over one of the large red poppies printed on the tablecloth. Then his shoulders slumped. "Sorry. Tonight's fine. I just have a lot on my mind." He picked up a lemon cookie and set it on a small white dessert plate but didn't take a bite. Instead, he lifted his gaze and met hers, a determined look in his eyes. "Ready to get Erma's house shipshape?"

His words steered her back to the topic at hand, and she sat across from him at the four-person table and picked up a small notepad she'd found in her bedroom. Correction—her *former* bedroom. This wasn't her home anymore, and she needed to remember that.

Before she could say anything, he started talking. "I checked around the house before I knocked. You're right, this place needs some work." He started listing everything that needed to be done—making several front porch repairs; power washing the siding; and stripping, sanding, and staining the back deck, along with some smaller jobs.

Most of those she had already thought of. "That's not too bad," she said, trying to convince herself.

"Oh, there's more. Let's talk about the roof." He sat back in his chair.

"What about the roof?"

"It needs replacing."

"That sounds expensive." She wrote it down on her list.

"It is. Very expensive." He folded his hands and placed them on the table. "What's your budget?"

Riley paused, her enthusiasm sinking. "Slim."

Hayden frowned. "How slim?"

"Shoestring slim." When she told him how much she had to spend, he shook his head.

"That will cover the deck. Maybe." His expression turned troubled. "I didn't realize Erma was having financial difficulties."

"She's not." Riley looked down at the table, staring at the seventies-style flowers covering the cloth. She'd have to tell him the truth if she was going to get anything done with the house. "I wanted to surprise Mimi and cover the expenses myself." Technically Mimi would be paying for the repairs, since Riley was using the money she was earning at Knots and Tangles, but Hayden didn't have to know that.

He didn't say anything for a long moment. "I think I can make your money stretch a little more. I'll give you the deepest discount I can on anything we need from Dad's store, so that will help. Of course the labor will be free, and that will save you quite a bit right there."

"I can't let you do that—"

"I'm doing this for Erma."

She blinked. A dogged look shone in his eyes that she hadn't seen before, along with something else. Hardness. Gone was the charming glint that had seemed to be a permanent fixture in his gorgeous eyes.

"Right," she said tightly. "This isn't about me."

Hayden sighed. "I didn't mean it that way, Riley." He leaned back again, this time keeping his gaze on her. Finally he asked, "What do you think about Maple Falls?"

Talk about a loaded question. She had a lot of thoughts about Maple Falls, almost all of them negative. "Why are you asking?"

"Have you noticed anything off about Main Street since you've been back?"

She shook her head. "I tend to stick with Knots and Tangles."

"Oh." He rubbed his eyebrow with his index finger. "I was hoping to get your perspective

159

on something, just to make sure I'm not losing my mind."

His words intrigued her. "What do you mean?"

She listened as he described the downhill slide of the business district and the worn-out appearance of buildings that were almost a hundred years old.

"I don't think I ever took the time to pay attention to downtown before," he said, rubbing the back of his neck. "I've mainly been focused on helping Dad and nudging him toward updating the store. He's not too open about that."

Riley could relate. "Have you seen Knots and Tangles recently?"

"I was in there the day before I picked you up from the airport. It's a little—"

"It's a *big* mess. You know it. I know it. I think the whole town knows it."

"I wouldn't count on that." He took a sip of tea. When he set down the glass, he said, "I'm not sure there are many people left who shop locally."

She thought about that for a moment, then realized he was right. Other than the Bosom Buddies—who, in addition to coming to the shop on Thursday nights, individually stopped by at different times during the week—she hadn't had more than two customers, and neither stayed very long or purchased anything.

"I've been working on the inside of Mimi's

store," she said. "I want it to be organized and functioning more by the time I go back to New York."

He lifted his gaze to hers, and she thought she saw a faint grimace. "Does it matter what the store looks like inside if there aren't any customers?"

He was right, of course. Even if the shop was pristine on the inside, the outside still showed neglect. "Would refurbishing the outside help?"

"It can't hurt. Knots and Tangles isn't the only one that needs some TLC. Every building on that street does." He sighed again, then waved his hand. "Sorry. I didn't mean to hijack the conversation. We're here to talk about Erma's house, not the decline of Maple Falls. Are you ready to draw up that agreement now?"

"What agreement?" The kitchen door swung open as Mimi rolled into the room.

Riley jumped, then spun around in her seat. Mimi had excellent hearing, but she wouldn't have been able to discern their conversation unless she had been nearby. "Don't tell me you were eavesdropping."

"Of course not," she said, sounding offended. "I needed a drink of water, and I just *happened* to hear you talk about an agreement."

"You just happened." Hayden smirked, but the twinkle reappeared in his eyes. "Did you *happen* to hear anything else?"

Mimi rolled over to the table. "As a matter of fact, I did. You two shouldn't talk so loudly."

"Maybe you shouldn't park yourself right outside the door," Riley pointed out.

"Never mind about that." Mimi moved her gaze from Riley to Hayden. "I don't like secrets. Tell me what's going on, or I'll take my lemon cookies and give them to someone who deserves them."

"Ouch." Hayden put his hand over his heart. "You got me right here with that, Erma."

Riley looked at him, and he turned to her. Her toes curled at the teasing yet genuine smile on his face. She'd never been more attracted to him than in that moment. Something shifted inside her. This wasn't just physical attraction or appreciation of Hayden's kind nature. He might be helping her out because he felt guilty over Mimi's broken leg, but she could see that he cared about her grandmother. That meant more to her than anything. Hayden's heart far surpassed his handsome exterior.

"Well?" Mimi said. "Spill."

Riley pulled her gaze away from Hayden. "I want to fix up your house," she said, knowing it was pointless to skip around the truth when her grandmother was in a demanding mood.

"We want to fix it up," Hayden added.

"Bless your hearts." Mimi's eyes turned soft. Then she raised her chin. "My house is fine."

"Your roof is fixin' to spring a leak any day."

Hayden pointed to the ceiling. "About right there."

Mimi blanched. "It is? I had no idea. I guess I'll call a roofer in the morning."

"I can recommend a couple people," Hayden said. "You should get more than one estimate. We also sell roofing materials at the store. I can get you a good deal once you decide on a roofer."

"All right," Mimi said. "Sounds good. What else have you two been planning to do?"

Riley watched as her meeting with Hayden suddenly turned into a powwow between him and her grandmother, with neither acknowledging her as they talked about not only the jobs that needed to be done but also the budget and the timeline. She waited for them to include her in the conversation, but after a few minutes she felt invisible. Normally she would have been okay with that, but suddenly it rankled.

"Hey," she said, interrupting. "This was my idea. Remember?"

"And it's a good one." Mimi patted Riley's hand, then turned back to Hayden. "Now, what were you saying about stain colors?"

Riley's gaze darted between her grandmother and Hayden, her fists clenching under the table, her face growing hot. For some bizarre reason she wasn't thinking about house repairs or business rehab. Instead, painful memories flooded her—feeling like an outsider at every school she'd attended, which had been too many to count until she was in high school. Never fitting in with the New York art crowd or various social events she'd attended with Melody. Although she enjoyed lunch the other day with Anita, Harper, and Olivia, she still didn't feel like a part of their group. She'd sat in silence as they talked about people she didn't know or had barely known. And now, even in her grandmother's kitchen, she was feeling shut out of her own plan.

Worse, she was familiar with the bitter knot forming in her stomach and the hot ache suffocating her head. She'd experienced those sensations over and over growing up. Loneliness. Abandonment. *They don't care what I think. They don't care about* me.

Suddenly she jerked back from the table and jumped up from her chair. Without looking back, she ran out the kitchen door and into the backyard, heaving in gulps of warm evening air until she reached the tire swing.

Hadn't she put all this in the past? All the pain and isolation she'd felt for years . . . Why was it back now? Over a discussion of home improvement, of all things.

Why now? Why here? Just . . . Why?

"Oh dear," Erma whispered. "I was afraid of this."

Hayden's gaze had been pinned to the back

door of the kitchen since Riley ran out. Her reaction was so sudden and intense, he was worried about her. Turning to Erma, he saw her eyes glazed with tears. Uh-oh. That wasn't good.

"Did I do something wrong?"

She shook her head. "No, sweetie." Then she sighed. "She'll be okay."

Hayden wasn't so sure. She wasn't just a little upset. She was distraught. Her fleeing the kitchen out of the blue like that confirmed that something was seriously wrong. All he wanted to do was go outside and put his arms around her, which was a terrible idea. But that fact didn't change his feelings. It only convinced him not to act on them.

Erma rubbed her temple, her fingertip brushing the short silver hair above her ear. Then a faint smile appeared on her wizened face.

"Leave it up to her to want to do something sweet for me," she said, her bottom lip trembling. "She spent all day working in the shop and insisted that I take it easy. She would handle any customers that came in. We only had two. Hardly a rush."

Hayden nodded. Her words convinced him that something had to be done about the state of downtown Maple Falls, but right now he couldn't focus on anything but Riley. He glanced at the back door again.

"You want to go check on her, don't you?"

He thought about lying, but Erma would see right through it. He nodded. "Just to see if she's all right."

She smiled. "I think that's a good idea."

Hayden shot up from the chair and dashed out the door. Riley was standing by an old tire swing that was probably as busted up as everything else seemed to be in this town. Her back was to him, and he slowed his steps, not wanting to surprise her. Her arms were wrapped around her body, her shoulders hunched. He took another step forward, and to his surprise, she turned around and straightened her shoulders, her expression as unapproachable as always.

"Did you and Mimi figure everything out?"

The sun had dipped below the horizon, dimming the light to dusk, but he could clearly see her guarded expression. It was as if she had transformed from the vulnerable woman who ran out of the house to someone who was completely in control. He was starting to understand that it was just a mask, that underneath the veneer of calm was a turbulent storm.

"Are you okay?" he asked, knowing full well she wasn't.

"I'm fine." She took a step back and bumped into the swing. As he suspected, the tire was sagging in the middle and part of the treads were hanging off. She steadied the swing but didn't look at him again. "After Mimi and I discuss the budget, I can write up the agreement—"

"Would you shut up about the agreement?" He moved closer to her. "I don't care about some dumb contract between you and me. I trust your word. I'd like to think you trust me . . . but I can see that's not the case."

She glanced up at him. "It's . . . it's . . ."

"It's what, Riley?" He softened his tone. "You're hurting. I can see that. I just don't understand why."

She turned away. "You don't know me, Hayden," she whispered.

That was the opening he'd been hoping for, despite everything. He moved closer until his chest was nearly pressed against her back.

"I want to, Riley. I've wanted to get close to you since I saw you at the airport. I don't know why, and I don't think it matters anyway." He swallowed. "What does matter is you. And if you want me to go away, I will. Just say the word, and I won't bother you again."

Riley shivered but couldn't bring herself to face Hayden. She couldn't believe what he was telling her, even though she'd heard him say the words. *He wants to get close to me.* How could that be possible? He'd always been in a different league. She'd always been the outsider and still was. He didn't know her past or her family. And if he found out—

"Riley?"

She closed her eyes at the low, smooth sound of his voice close to her ear. When he put his hands on her shoulders, she couldn't pull away. Something broke inside her, and she leaned against him. This fantasy would end soon enough, but right now she desperately needed Hayden's touch.

He wrapped his arms around her and drew her against him. She marveled at how the back of her head nestled perfectly against his broad shoulder, how safe and secure she felt at this moment. When his hands moved down to her waist, then clasped around her, his palms covering the band of her jeans as he embraced her tighter, it was as if he'd given her something she hadn't known until this moment she was starving for. Closeness. Connection.

"Riley," he whispered in her ear.

Hearing her name broke the spell, and she pulled away from him, her heart hammering. Embarrassed, she couldn't meet his gaze. She'd had a moment of weakness, and she couldn't allow it to happen again. Steeling herself for his anger, she said, "You should go."

A pause. "Not until you look at me, Riley."

Slowly she turned around, keeping her distance. Instead of censure, she saw acceptance.

"Thank you," he said, his smile gentle.

Stunned, she blurted, "For what?"

"For giving me your trust, even for a moment."
His smile widened. "I intend to earn the rest."

Unable to help herself, she asked, "Why? Why
would you bother with me?"

His smile dimmed, but the sweetness in his
eyes hit her very core. "Because I want to. The
last thing you are to me, Riley McAllister, is a
bother. I aim to show you that truth too." He took
a few steps backward. "I'll call you tomorrow."

"What?" she asked, fighting to keep her feet in
place so she didn't make a fool of herself running
after him. "Why would you do that?"

"So we can figure out a schedule for the repairs.
Operation Erma must go on." He grinned, then
turned around and walked away.

Was he actually whistling? What nerve. If he
thought things had changed between them, he
was wrong.

She was lying to herself and she knew it. When
she remembered how good his well-muscled
arms felt around her, the feel of his heartbeat
against her back . . . she couldn't stop herself
from smiling.

Chapter 8

The cell phone on Riley's nightstand buzzed, jerking her out of a dream. A wonderful dream about her and Hayden and . . . Well, she would savor that dream for a long time to come, but right now she had to answer the phone before she threw it against the wall. She picked it up and looked at the screen. Melody. Sitting up in bed, she answered the call.

"Hi," she said, her tangled hair falling in a curtain around her face.

"You're up?" Melody sounded surprised. "I figured you'd still be asleep. I was going to leave you a message."

"What time is it?" She squinted at the old clock radio on her nightstand. Seven a.m. She should have been up an hour ago. "I'm putting you on speaker," she said as she scrambled out of bed, then switched over the audio. "I'm running late."

"For what? Why haven't you called me? I've been worried about you and Mimi."

"I'm sorry." Riley threw off her T-shirt and sleep shorts and hurried to her suitcase. She was down to her last outfit and would have to do laundry today at some point. "I've been making Mimi breakfast every morning."

"Wait. You? Cooking?" Melody chuckled. "I never thought I'd see that happen."

"Yeah, well, every once in a while, I go crazy and do something domestic."

"Anytime you want to do that around here, you have my blessing. What else is going on in small-town America?"

Riley filled her in on her plans for Knots and Tangles and fixing up Mimi's home. "There's so much work to do around here." She slipped on a sports bra, a scoop-neck short-sleeved shirt, and then jean shorts. "I had no idea."

"Wait, hold up. You're working at the yarn shop?"

Riley finger-combed her hair into a ponytail, realizing she had a lot to explain to Melody. She decided to leave Hayden out of the updates. If her friend knew about him, or worse yet, how Riley felt about him, she would never hear the end of it.

"Yes, but just until Mimi can work full-time again."

"How is she doing?"

Riley slid her sandals onto her feet. "Ready to get back to normal. We see the doctor tomorrow and find out when she can use crutches."

"That sounds promising. So, you're coming back soon, then?"

She paused, her second foot halfway into its sandal. "Um, I might be here longer than I planned," she said hesitantly. "Will that be a problem?"

"Actually, that's what I wanted to talk to you about. I was going to tell you not to worry about the rent next month. Charlie is still here, and he said he would cover it."

Riley sank on the bed with relief. "Thank God."

"I thought you'd be happy to hear that."

"I totally am. Tell him thanks for me."

"I will. I've gotta go, but give me a call soon and tell me more about everything going on. I miss you."

"I miss you too. And I promise, I'll call you when we have more time to talk." She ended the call and inhaled. Not having to worry about the rent while she was taking care of things here lessened the load on her shoulders. When she went back home, she was giving Charlie a huge hug.

Home. She glanced around her teenage bedroom, which had never looked like a typical teenager's room. She hadn't put posters on the walls or kept any kitschy or personal items scattered around. She'd learned long ago that personalizing a space was a waste of time and money, and she hadn't decorated any of the four New York apartments she'd lived in. This bedroom had been hers longer than anything else.

Riley pressed her fingers against her forehead. What was she doing traveling down memory lane again? Hadn't last night been enough torture? Her emotions had overwhelmed her, and look what happened. *Hayden happened.* That thought led to her remembering the best parts of the dream she just had. Those were some images she didn't mind revisiting . . .

She jumped out of bed and batted at her cheeks. *Focus on something else.* Anything was preferable to being stuck on this confusing merry-go-round of emotions she was riding. She hated every minute of it. *Well, not every minute . . .*

She opened her mouth to utter a curse, but out of habit she checked herself. "Dagnabbit," she muttered. The ridiculous word yanked her out of her mental rut. The best way to stop the ride was to be busy, and she had plenty to do. She headed downstairs to prepare her grandmother's breakfast.

When she walked into the kitchen, Mimi was already at the table, sipping her coffee, a small plate with two pieces of toast sitting next to the newspaper she was reading. She glanced up, peering at Riley over her purple reading glasses. Mimi seemed to have different colored glasses for each day.

"Good morning, sleepyhead."

"I'm sorry I overslept." Riley hurried to the pantry. "I'll have your oatmeal ready in a few minutes."

Mimi scoffed. "I'm tired of that slop."

"Really? I thought you loved oatmeal."

"My cardiologist does. I'm not a fan." She gestured to her toast, which Riley now noticed was slathered with butter. "This and my coffee are good enough. Why don't you get your breakfast and join me?"

"I thought I'd pick up something on the way to the yarn shop."

Her grandmother pointed to the seat across from her. "The shop can wait."

Detecting the seriousness in Mimi's tone, Riley nodded, and a few minutes later she was pouring milk over a bowl of cornflakes as her grandmother pushed her newspaper aside. "I want to talk about last night."

Riley stared at her cereal. "I'm sorry I acted so childish."

"Not that," Mimi said. "Although, for the record, you weren't being childish. You have the right to get upset sometimes, sugar. You don't always have to be so strong."

Riley met her compassionate gaze. "There's getting upset, and then there's acting like an idiot."

"You didn't act like an . . ." Mimi shook her head. "Let's agree that's water under the bridge. What I really wanted to talk about was your plans for *my* house."

"Oh." Riley dug into the cereal, glad for the

change in topic. "What did you and Hayden decide?" she asked before taking a bite of the flakes.

"Nothing, really, other than taking care of the roof. Everything else around here is fine."

"Did Hayden say that?"

"Well, no—"

"Because it's not true." Riley set down her spoon, not caring that her breakfast would be soggy in a few seconds. She couldn't believe how deeply her grandmother was digging in her heels. "Let me do this for you, Mimi. I want to make your house as beautiful as it used to be when—" She almost said when she lived there, but she caught herself.

"I know you do." Mimi's voice grew soft. "But I'm concerned you might also be doing this out of obligation or guilt."

"I'm not," Riley said quickly.

"Are you sure about that?" She set her glasses on the table. "You don't have to feel bad for pursuing your dreams in New York. I encouraged you to do exactly that, remember?"

Riley nodded. Her grandmother had always been her biggest cheerleader, and even though she'd cried all the way from Maple Falls until Riley walked through security at the airport, she never once made Riley feel bad for leaving. *"Happy tears,"* she'd said before giving Riley a tight, final hug. *"They're happy tears, sugar.*

I want you to take New York by storm. Just like I would. If I wasn't terrified of planes, that is." That had made Riley laugh and given her the freedom to leave.

"I do remember, Mimi."

"I realize I've probably put a burden on you all these years, asking you to come back here for visits. That was selfish of me."

Now that did bring up some guilt. "Mimi, you're never selfish."

"Oh, I am. It was no skin off my nose to come visit you in the big city. Who knew flying could be so much fun? And I enjoyed my visits, actually. Wouldn't want to live there, but I can see why it appeals to you." She bent back the corner of the newspaper. "But there's something else I've put on your shoulders, and I should have realized before now that it was wrong."

Riley stilled. She'd never heard her grandmother speak like this, and she was starting to worry, although that was nothing new when it came to Mimi. "Mimi, what's wrong?"

"Nothing's wrong, honey. It's just that I was never able to give up on one of my dreams . . . until now."

It had never occurred to Riley that Mimi had her own unfulfilled dreams. Riley always thought she was perfectly settled and happy with her life in Maple Falls, especially the last two decades or so. If she wasn't, then she wouldn't be so insistent on keeping the store open, since it tied her to the town. Then again, when had Riley stepped out of her own self-absorbed world and paid attention to her grandmother's life? *Talk about being selfish.*

"What dream?"

"The one where you're running Knots and Tangles." Mimi sighed. "I've made it pretty clear that I want to keep the business in the family. But I've been doing a lot of thinking the past few days. I think maybe this broken leg happened for a higher reason, not just because I was being reckless. I'd prayed that when you came back, you would want to stay." When Riley started to speak, she held up her hand. "But I was wrong to think that way. This isn't your home. I can see that now."

"It used to be." Riley's voice sounded thick. "This was the only real home I ever knew, Mimi. I'm so grateful to you for that."

Tears slipped down Mimi's wrinkled cheeks. "Bother," she said, picking up a paper napkin and dabbing the corners of her eyes. "I told myself I wasn't going to cry."

"It's okay to be upset, remember? A wise woman told me that once. About ten minutes ago."

Mimi chuckled. "I am wise, that's true. But I mean it, Riley. I won't pressure you anymore about coming back here or about the shop. I want you to live your life without feeling saddled with a dream that isn't yours. The time has come for me to sell my yarn store."

Riley sat back, absorbing her grandmother's words. She couldn't believe how fast the tables had turned. She never expected her grandmother to willfully give up Knots and Tangles.

Somehow Riley didn't feel the satisfaction she'd anticipated. Getting Mimi to let go of her shop was the biggest challenge on her to-do list, and she had been gearing up for a battle. It never entered her mind that her grandmother would surrender so easily.

"And since I know you so well, Riley Jean, I don't want you to worry about me or the store," Mimi continued. "I'll take care of getting it cleaned up and put on the market. I'll get Harper to help me when the time comes. That being said, I want you to stay away from the shop for the rest of your visit."

Shock coursed through Riley. "Why?"

"You need a vacation. I know for a fact you've been spending too much time holed up in that apartment."

"I've been working, Mimi." Riley felt a bit defensive. "The apartment is also my studio."

"Which proves my point. You're always either at work or working. That's no way to live. This is beautiful country here. You can go hiking or go jogging again. I remember you used to like that insanity."

Riley hadn't gone on a jog since last week, and her muscles only just stopped hurting two days ago. "I'm more suited for brisk walking now," she mumbled.

"Exercise is exercise." Mimi sipped her coffee. "You know, you could also work on your art, just for fun. I remember when you used to do that, and I haven't seen you drawing or painting since you arrived."

Riley decided not to tell her about the sketch of Hayden she'd worked on a little more last night before bed. She considered taking Mimi's suggestions, then changed her mind. The last thing she needed to do was rest right now, even though her grandmother was right, and she did need a vacation. Riley couldn't remember the last time she'd taken more than a couple days off from her work. And while hiking and jogging and creating sounded appealing, she couldn't block out her thoughts.

"I appreciate your vacation offer," she said. "But I'd like to finish what I started in the shop. I don't like leaving things half done."

Mimi frowned. "Well, I know it will be done right if you do it. Okay, but promise me you'll take time for yourself while you're here."

"I will. In between working on the shop and the house."

"You are so stubborn." Her grandmother slapped her hands on the armrests of her wheelchair. "I have no idea where you get that from. Fine. Do what you want, as long as it's what you want, and not what you *think* you should do." Mimi frowned. "I'm not sure that made sense."

But it made perfect sense to Riley. And while her cornflakes were now little limp blobs floating in milk, for the first time since she returned, she didn't feel completely at sea. "I love you, Mimi."

"I love you, too, sugar." She put her glasses back on and started reading the paper again, as if they hadn't just finished one of the most important conversations they'd ever had. But that was her grandmother. She didn't dwell on things for long.

Riley stood and picked up her bowl. As she walked to the sink to dump out the soggy cornflakes and fix something else, "Boot Scootin' Boogie" rang out from Mimi's cell phone. When her grandmother didn't answer it after several seconds, Riley frowned and turned. She was still perusing her newspaper, but Riley caught her glance at the phone before focusing back on the paper.

"Aren't you going to get that?"

"No." Mimi continued reading. "It's just a solicitor."

The phone stopped singing, and Riley reached for the bag of bread in a basket near the toaster. "Boot Scootin' Boogie" started up again, and once more her grandmother ignored it.

"Same number?" Riley asked, slipping two pieces of bread into the toaster slots and pressing down the lever.

"Yes," she replied, her tone tight.

Riley watched her and saw the strain at the corners of her mouth as she sipped her coffee. "You could put your number on the do-not-call list if they're bothering you."

Mimi didn't say anything as she glanced at the phone, then turned it over so the screen lay flat on the table. As soon as the ringing stopped, she picked up the phone and dropped it on her lap.

"Time to get dressed for work," she said.

"I think you should stay home today."

But Mimi was already wheeling out of the kitchen faster than Riley had seen her move before. She frowned. That was weird, even for Mimi.

The toast popped up, and Riley blinked. She turned to the toaster and started preparing the bread, adding a small pat of butter to each slice. After she finished eating, she would tell her grandmother what she tried to before she hurried out of the kitchen—that she shouldn't go to work today, considering tomorrow would be a long day since they had to go to Hot Springs to see her doctor. Riley didn't like the idea of closing the store, but then she remembered that Mimi hadn't had normal business hours in a long time.

One day wasn't going to make any difference.

A short time later, Riley arrived at Knots and Tangles, having convinced Mimi to stay home and rest up for tomorrow's trip to the doctor. She parked in the lot behind the store, then unlocked the back door and walked through the store to the front door. Ready for another workday, she flipped the Closed sign to Open.

But instead of starting straight to work, she stepped outside on the sidewalk, remembering what Hayden had said about the decline of the buildings. Now that she was paying attention, she could see he was right. She took in the old architecture, seeing it with an artist's eye for the first time. It would be a huge undertaking, not to mention expensive, to restore some of these buildings. She doubted the town or the businesses had that kind of money. A less ambitious plan would be to freshen up the storefronts, including Mimi's. But what did that matter if she was going to sell the shop anyway?

Riley frowned. Now that her grandmother had accepted that Riley wouldn't take over the shop and had agreed to sell the store, what would she do? Travel with Myrtle, maybe. The Bosom Buddies would have to find another place to hold their gatherings too. Riley wondered where they would end up. At someone's house? Or the church?

She walked to the curb and stepped onto the

street, which had been empty since she walked out of the store. In the middle of the road, she turned and studied Mimi's storefront. What would happen to this place once her grandmother sold it? Would it continue to be a yarn store or become something else? The idea of Knots and Tangles turning into a different business, or worse, shuttering altogether like so many other stores on this street, bothered her. How ridiculous. She didn't have an emotional attachment to anything here. But she couldn't deny her unease.

She glanced over her shoulder at Price's Hardware. They were open too. A sandwich board stood out in front of the big picture window, announcing a sale on garden tools. At least Hayden didn't have to worry about anything happening to the hardware store. They seemed to have decent business, and even she knew how much his father enjoyed working there from the few times she'd gone into the store. There was no way Mr. Price would sell his business. *You thought the same thing about Mimi.*

"Excuse me, are you open yet?"

Riley turned to see a pretty blond woman, whom she guessed to be in her midforties, standing on the sidewalk, her smile bright and cheerful.

"Yes, we are," Riley said, opening the door for her. "Come on in. Excuse the mess. We're doing a bit of reorganizing."

184

The woman surveyed the store. "There's so much yarn here! Oh, I'm in heaven!" She started to walk around, checking out the bins of yarn, stopping to pick up a skein. She turned it around in her hand, scrutinizing the label. "You have some vintage products," she said. She turned to Riley, who was brushing a bit of stray dust off the Man Chair near the front windows. "I'd like to introduce myself. My name is Lorri, and I own a yarn shop too. Mine is in Malvern."

"Nice to meet you. I'm Riley." She walked over and shook Lorri's hand. "This is actually my grandmother's store."

"It's really neat." Lorri's eyes sparkled. "I love visiting yarn stores when I'm out and about. It's nice to see what other places carry. I always find something different that I don't have in my store."

It was nice to see a new customer who was passionate about yarn the way Mimi and the Bosom Buddies were.

Not wanting to keep Lorri from shopping, she said, "If you have any questions about anything here, let me know. I'm still learning the inventory, but I'll help if I can."

"Wonderful. I'm off to browse!"

Riley walked to the checkout counter to organize the paperwork her grandmother had shoved on the shelves, while Lorri took her time going through the store. Over the past few days of working here, Riley had found some interesting yarn and set it aside for herself. Not to knit or crochet with, but to take back to New York to incorporate into future art pieces.

Her thoughts went back to Mimi selling the store. Her grandmother had told her not to feel guilty, and Riley tried not to. Mimi not having the energy or interest to keep running it was more than enough reason for her to sell. But as Riley glanced at Lorri a time or two while she shopped, taking the time to touch the yarn, look at the labels, and compare colors, she missed the days when she used to do the same thing while she worked here, searching for just the right color and texture to experiment with. That had been the fun part of being in Knots and Tangles, the part that spoke to her creative soul, and she was just now realizing it.

When Lorri was finished shopping, she brought several hanks of beautiful vintage yarn to the counter, yarn Riley didn't know they had. The woman must have dug through a lot of piles to find those. What other treasures were hiding in this store?

As Riley rang up her purchases, Lorri said, "Let me give you my card. If you're ever near Malvern, come see me at my shop." The card she placed on the counter was white with a pink state of Arkansas and the shop's logo printed over it. "I also dye my own yarn," she continued. "If you're interested in seeing some of it, you can visit the shop's website too. The URL is on the back."

"I'll definitely do that." Riley placed the yarn in a plain paper bag with handles. "Is dyeing yarn difficult?"

"Not at all. I love it. I'm a knitter at heart, but when I started dyeing the yarn, it brought out another part of my creative side." She handed Riley a credit card. "I'll be happy to show you my setup sometime if you'd like."

Riley almost accepted the offer, excited to see another yarn store and for the briefest moment thinking it might give her ideas for Mimi's shop. *But the shop won't be here much longer.*

"I'm just here visiting," she said, her heart sinking a bit. "But thank you for the offer." She returned Lorri's credit card, put the receipt in the bag, and handed it to her. "And thanks for stopping by."

"You're welcome. I'm sure I'll be back." She grinned. "Have a great day!"

Despite her mixed emotions, Riley couldn't help but smile as Lorri swept out of the store. The woman was like a breath of fresh air, and her enthusiasm was almost contagious.

She looked around, seeing empty white walls above the shelving units. Her imagination suddenly took flight. She didn't want Knots and Tangles to close or become another business. To keep that from happening, she would have to showcase the store's potential. It wouldn't be too hard to decorate the place in addition to organizing it. If she had time, she could also make a custom piece using yarns from the shop—and she knew exactly where she could hang it.

For now, there was nothing she could do about the outside of the building. She didn't have the time or money to fix it up. But she could renovate the inside and make it a beautiful, creative space. Inspired, she grabbed one of the papers from the stack of discarded paperwork she had just sorted. She flipped it over to the blank side and started to sketch.

"Something on your mind, Hayden?"

Hayden looked up from his lunch of taco salad with extra sour cream. He'd barely touched it since Anita brought it over to him. He met his father's inquisitive gaze. Did he have anything on his mind? His mind was filled to the brim, mostly with confusing thoughts making him feel off-kilter, the norm lately rather than the exception. How could he explain the way he was seesawing between savoring the memory of Riley in his arms and the painful betrayal of Dad selling the store? Even if he wanted to talk about either, he wouldn't bring them up in a public place like the crowded diner. He might as well advertise them in the local paper instead.

He had to tell his father something, so he

shrugged and dove into the taco salad with a brief, "Not really."

"Hmm."

Hayden glanced at him, knowing what that utterance meant. Unsurprisingly, his father wasn't buying what Hayden was selling, since his ability to hide his emotions was quickly eroding. He decided to change the topic.

"What do you think about sprucing up the front of the store?"

His father lifted one eyebrow, now more gray than blond. "What made you think about that?"

"I was just taking a look at the businesses on this street and realized it might be a good idea to fix things up before the Too Dang Hot Parade."

"Didn't I tell you? The event is canceled this year."

Hayden gripped his fork. "No. You didn't."

"Yeah, we had a chamber of commerce meeting two weeks ago and decided there wasn't enough interest to continue the parade."

"What about the money it brings to Main Street?"

"The parade hasn't been the moneymaker it used to be for a few years now. Last year we didn't come close to breaking even. We realized the event has run its course. How's the taco salad?" Dad took a bite of his all-American burger.

Forget the taco salad. How could his father

be so blasé about Maple Falls' only tradition? "I can't believe there won't be a parade," he mumbled.

"Nothing lasts forever, son. Things change, whether we want them to or not."

Hayden knew that better than anyone. He'd never imagined his hometown would slowly die while everyone watched from the stands, doing nothing about it.

"Not everything has to change, Dad. Some things are worth saving."

At that moment Jasper walked into the diner, and Dad motioned for him to come over and join them. Soon the old man and Hayden's father were engrossed in conversation, as usual, while Hayden picked at the lukewarm taco meat. This couldn't be happening. First, Dad was selling the hardware store, and now the town had ended a decades-long parade and town event. True, the parade had first started as a joke, but eventually it became a beloved tradition that everyone anticipated. Hayden hated that he'd missed so many of them since the parade happened during baseball season, and he'd been excited about being at his first Too Dang Hot Parade, minus the parade, in over a decade. Now he didn't even have that.

He pushed his salad away. "I've got to get back to the store," he said, sliding out of the blue vinyl booth. He couldn't sit here and pretend to enjoy his food while his life was being turned upside down. He pulled out his wallet and put several bills on the table. "Lunch is on me."

"But you didn't finish your salad," Dad said.

"I'm not hungry." Before his father could say anything else, he rushed out of the diner and headed back to the hardware store. An empty, helpless feeling washed over him. His baseball career was over, but he had been ready for a fresh start in Maple Falls, fixing up his house, working at the hardware store, and laying down some roots, God willing.

Frustration overtook him, and he clenched his jaw. His college coach once said Hayden must have ice in his veins because he was so cool under pressure. What a joke. He felt anything but cool right now. As it was, he was itching to punch out a window in one of the abandoned buildings. No one would care about the damage anyway.

Everything was changing too fast, and that made his head spin. When the doctors told him he'd never pitch again, he tried to prove them wrong and ended up setting back his recovery in the process and ensuring that he'd never play competitive ball again. That had been hard to accept, but knowing he had a place to come home to and a job waiting for him had given him hope. Now even those weren't what he thought they would be.

As he reached the store, he spotted Riley at

the end of the street, coming out of Petals and Posies. Instantly he slowed, watching as she held a bouquet of flowers, then brought them to her nose. He'd sold so many packets of flower seeds over the years that even from this distance he could name the flowers in the bouquet—red roses, pink and orange gerbera daisies, and at least two purple carnations. Riley was so beautiful in the sunlight, and when he saw her smile, it was as if an electric shock ran through him.

He watched her for a few seconds, mesmerized by her amazing smile. Instantly he relived the bliss he'd felt holding her last night when she had accepted a little bit of comfort. Unable to stop himself, he walked toward her.

"Riley," he called out, unnerved by the cracking sound in his voice. Great, he sounded like a preteen whose voice hadn't completely changed. Or an upset man who needed to be around the one person he inexplicably knew could calm him down.

When she turned toward him, he half expected her to run off like she usually did, but instead she waited. As he neared, he could see the concern on her face. That made everything worse. The Ice Man was losing his cool, and he couldn't do anything about it.

"What's wrong, Hayden?" she asked, moving the flowers away from her face.

He wanted to tell her that things were fine. That

nothing bothered him, that what was happening around him wasn't rocking him to his core. But they would both know he was lying.

"Everything, Riley," he said. "Everything's wrong."

Chapter 9

R iley tucked the flowers into the vase sitting on the counter.

After she'd taken a break from sketching earlier, she went back to organizing and cleaning out the bins and paperwork under the counter. When she saw the vase at the very back of a shelf next to a tin of rusty buttons, she rinsed it out in the sink in the bathroom, then decided to give Petals and Posies a little business. A small bouquet of flowers wouldn't have a huge impact on the shop, but it would be something. Sophie, the woman who owned Petals and Posies, had been happy about the sale.

She hadn't expected to encounter Hayden, and from the anxious way he'd called out her name, she knew something was wrong. The pained expression on his face confirmed it, and she didn't think twice about inviting him into the store.

Now he was sitting on the old but still comfy lime-green velour sofa in the back room. She'd had to clear a spot for them to sit. As soon as he parked himself on the cushions, he raked his hand through his thick hair, then stared at the coffee table covered in boxes of knitting needles that hadn't been unpacked yet.

For once, Riley hoped they didn't have any

customers. She sat next to him but didn't say anything. Not because she wasn't curious or concerned, but because she sensed he wasn't ready to talk yet. When he was, she would be here to listen.

After a few minutes, he lifted his head and blew out a breath. "I'm supposed to be at work right now. We were so slow this morning that Dad decided to close shop for lunch. He's probably still at the diner jawing with Jasper, not worried about a thing."

"Should he be worried about something?"

"Yes, he should." Hayden held his hands in front of him. "He should be as mad as I am that things have gotten so bad around here." He dropped his hands to his knees. "But he's not. He's moved on."

Riley was confused, but she listened as Hayden continued to talk, expressing his anger over the cancellation of the Too Dang Hot Parade. That news surprised her too. She never imagined the town would cancel such a long-standing tradition.

He continued lamenting the fact that no one seemed to care what happened to Maple Falls. "Dad's selling the store," he explained, surprising Riley even more. "My whole family knew about it except for me. I guess I was supposed to find out when the sold sign was slapped on the front door."

"Hayden, I'm sorry." She wasn't sure what else

to say. She agreed it wasn't right for his family to keep him in the dark like that, but it wasn't her place to say so.

He leaned back against the lime-green upholstery and continued staring straight ahead. "Ever since I can remember, I've had my whole life planned. From the time I picked up a baseball bat in T-ball until the end of my career, I knew what I wanted—to be a pro ball player. And I would do anything to reach that goal."

"And you did." Which was more than she could say about her own career. He had actually achieved his goal, while hers was still out of reach.

"For one game. One friggin' game. But there was always another constant in my life. This town. I traveled so much and lived in so many places, but I could always come back home. Sure, I would notice changes here and there when I visited. But I didn't realize how different things were until I moved back here. My career was over . . . The thing I loved more than anything was gone." His voice broke. "But at least I had my hometown. Now I'm not sure of anything anymore." Then he shook his head. "Wow. I never told anyone that before. Not even my parents. I didn't want anyone to know I didn't always have everything together. Even after my shoulder injury, I kept up the ruse. I had a reputation to protect."

Without thinking, Riley angled her body toward him so she could look at him directly. She knew what he was talking about. Hadn't she done the same thing? Not only when she lived here, but also right now? Pretending that she wasn't bothered about being a loner or not having a normal childhood? Afraid of repeating the past?

"I get that," she said softly, then drew in a breath. This was what she'd wanted to avoid—revealing anything personal to him. But he was so distraught and so honest with her that she couldn't stop herself.

"I never felt that way about Maple Falls, or any place, for that matter. My mom and I moved around a lot before I came to live with Mimi. Motels, trailer parks, a cheap apartment or two. I can't remember them all. I missed a whole year of school when I was eight because we didn't have a permanent home. Mom dropped me off at Mimi's when I was thirteen, and I haven't seen her since."

"Riley, I'm so sorry." Pain entered his eyes. "I had no idea you had it so rough. I knew you lived with Erma back then, but I didn't know anything else about your family."

She averted her gaze. "No one did at school. At least I kept hoping they wouldn't find out."

"As far as I know, they didn't. I never heard anyone talk about your mom . . . or you."

That sounded so pathetic, even though it had

been necessary. "That was the goal. If I kept my distance, no one could ask too many questions I didn't want to answer."

"Which was why you kept to yourself." He paused, shifting on the couch to face her. "Is that the reason you're so distant now?"

Maybe she should have kept her mouth shut. But there was something inside her that wanted to continue talking. Just admitting that she'd been afraid of the school kids finding out about Tracey gave her some relief.

"Yes. It's hard to keep secrets in a small town, and I'm sure there are people here who know about my mother. The Bosom Buddies all know, of course, and they did a good job of knocking the gossips down a peg whenever they could. But there were people who did talk about us behind my back. I didn't want to dig up the past again." She swallowed the lump in her throat. "I shouldn't have said anything. You're the one upset, and here I am talking about myself."

His mouth lifted in a half smile. "Hey, I'm glad you shared that with me. It can be hard to show people the real you, the one who struggles and hurts. I haven't been able to. Until now." He leaned closer to her. "I don't have to pretend with you, Riley. I know I can trust you."

"How can you be so sure?"

"Because I feel it here." He took her hand and put it over his heart. "What do you feel?"

She felt his muscled chest beneath his Price's Hardware work shirt. She also felt the hammering beat of his heart against her palm, spiking her own pulse. "I feel . . . you."

He leaned forward, his eyes turning smoky gray. A smile played on his lips as he lightly kissed her. When she responded, he drew her close and extended the kiss.

More than once during her teen crush on Hayden she had imagined kissing him, and even more recently she'd thought about it a few times, knowing it would never happen. But fantasy and reality had collided, and she was in heaven.

When he drew away, lightly nipping her bottom lip one more time before they separated, she could barely breathe.

He was grinning at her. "I gotta say, I feel a whole lot better now."

The distant sound of the bell ringing above the front door of the store brought her back to earth. *Now* she had a customer? How was she even supposed to stand up after experiencing a kiss like that?

"I should see who that is," she said, breathless.

"I better get back to work too." He moved his face closer to hers. "Thanks," he whispered.

"For what?" she managed to say.

"Listening. Talking. And . . . the other stuff." He winked and got up from the couch. "I'll show myself out," he said, then left through the back door.

She leaned back against the sofa, her fingers pressed to her lips as she tried to regain her senses. *Customer. There is a customer up front. Right. I should go see what they want.*

Finally her brain engaged, and when it did, she felt another shock. Against her better judgment, she had revealed too much to Hayden. On the other hand, that reveal led to a kiss that reached into her soul and left her wanting more. It also left her wondering where she and Hayden went from here.

Somehow Hayden had managed to make it through the rest of the workday without losing his mind. Quite a feat since all he wanted to do was go back to Knots and Tangles, grab Riley in his arms, and kiss her senseless. Not only had he felt like he'd unloaded a burden he'd been carrying with him for longer than he could remember, but her response to his kiss sent his senses skyrocketing.

Beyond the kiss, though, something important had happened. Riley had opened up to him, and more pieces were falling into place. He'd had no clue she lived such a difficult life before moving in with Erma, and he suspected she was still holding back a lot about how bad her childhood really was. Her confession also made him realize how ridiculous he'd been for thinking her distant attitude had anything to do with him. If he'd experienced the same kind of neglect and then felt the need to hide it from everyone, he wouldn't have been in any hurry to come back to Maple Falls either.

With all that on his mind, how was he supposed to focus on hammers and nails?

Finally closing time came, and he drove over to the ball field for Tuesday's practice, Riley still on his mind. At least his frustration over his family and the changes in his hometown had settled, or he'd be jumping out of his skin, not a good look for a softball coach, even for a church league team.

When he reached the field, he shifted his focus to softball and coaching the players. After what happened with Riley today, he was glad she hadn't ended up being his assistant. It was hard enough not to think about her when she wasn't here.

Then just as the team started warming up, he noticed Erma's car pull into the lot. His heart rate jumped. Had Riley changed her mind? He was thrilled to see her exit the car, despite thinking a few minutes ago that she would be too much of a distraction. Then he saw her go to the passenger side of the vehicle and help Erma out of the car. He laughed. He should have known Erma wouldn't stay away from the ball field for long.

He gave Riley and Erma a wave, then ran the practice as efficiently as possible, which wasn't difficult with this team. Once he got the players started on batting and fielding practice, he turned to see Riley sitting in a lawn chair next to Erma, who was positioned as close to the fence as was safe.

"Lift that bat higher, Tanner!" Erma shouted. "You look like a girl out there."

Hayden smirked as Tanner shot her an annoyed look. Riley ducked her face behind her hand, then removed it when Tanner slammed the next pitch over the fence. He turned and started jogging backward, giving Erma a sarcastic salute, then made his way around the bases.

"That's how you motivate a young man, sugar." Erma sat back in her seat, seemingly proud of herself. "Most men, really. Appeal to their egos."

"Tanner doesn't need much motivation, and he has plenty of ego." Hayden crouched next to Erma's chair, but not before he checked over his shoulder at Riley. She had gotten up and was organizing the dugout again, probably more to get away from Erma's method of coaching than anything else. She was moving the nearly empty ball bag to the other end of the bench from where Hayden had dropped it when he arrived, and out of the way of the entrance, so no one would have to walk around it or trip over it. Then she sat on the bench, and he saw what seemed to be a sketchbook next to her. She picked it up, pulled a pencil out of her crossbody bag, flipped the book open, and started to draw.

"She's okay, Hayden."

He glanced up at Erma, who was smiling. "I know," he said, believing it. The conversation they'd had this afternoon had shifted things between them. *Not to mention the kiss.* But he knew he still had to tread lightly with her.

"She came home from the shop in a good mood today." Erma faced the field again. "I asked her if something had happened."

Hayden stilled. Surely Riley wouldn't tell her grandmother about their kiss. Then again, the two of them were close. "Uh, what did she say?" he asked as Lonnie pitched a perfect strike to Jared, who had yet to miss a ball behind the plate.

"That it was an ordinary day."

Ouch. Maybe he had read Riley wrong again. Then their kiss came back to mind, particularly how she had responded to him. He definitely hadn't read that wrong.

"Hayden," Erma said, drawing him out of his thoughts. A good thing considering the path they were on. "I meant to tell you last night that I'm sorry for asking you to take on Riley as your assistant."

"It's okay—"

"No, it wasn't, especially for Riley. But it was

also wrong for me to put you in an awkward position. Occasionally I have to admit that not all my ideas are good ones."

This was a side of Erma he hadn't seen before. "Don't worry about it."

"Thank you," she said, her voice barely audible. Then she turned to Hayden. "Riley has something up her sleeve, though. She's had her head in that sketchbook since she got home from the shop. She even had it next to her while we ate supper. I encouraged her this morning to spend time on her art while she was visiting, but I didn't think she would do it right away. I haven't seen her this excited in a long time." She elevated one eyebrow. "Are you sure there aren't any other secrets you're keeping from me?"

"Uh . . ." Hayden peeked at Riley again. She happened to look up at the same moment and meet his gaze. He expected her to ignore him, or worse, give him that blank expression that bothered him so much. Instead, she smiled, then went back to her sketch.

He grinned and got to his feet while Erma told Jared to get lower in his stance behind the plate, preventing Hayden from answering her question. He glimpsed the dugout again. *We've officially turned a corner, Riley McAllister.*

He couldn't wait to see where they went from here.

• • •

As the softball practice continued, Riley kept sketching in her book. The ideas were flowing now, and although she only needed a rough drawing of her plans, she had become engrossed in filling in the details. Other than doodling around with her sketch of Hayden, she hadn't done much drawing since she'd moved to New York. She was never one to map out her art, because she preferred to discover each creation organically. This was different. While her drawing was a far cry from artistic, it suited the purpose and filled a dry spot in her soul. Soon she would explain her plan to Mimi, but right now she was enjoying the creative process.

She lifted her head occasionally to watch the practice. Or more accurately, to watch Hayden as he ran the practice. She leaned one elbow on her knee and rested her chin in her hand as she watched him correct Lonnie's pitching form on the mound. Although the team played in a slow-pitch softball league, Hayden was just as comfortable pitching underhanded as he had been pitching a baseball. *And just as fine. What a gorgeous man.* She sighed.

"Something wrong, Riley?" Mimi leaned forward, studying the field as if she were still Hayden's assistant coach.

She straightened. "No. Nothing. I'm good." She glanced at her sketch again before closing the book. She'd done more drawing today than she had in years, and it was time for a break.

She set her sketchbook on the bench and left the dugout to stand by Mimi. The warm wind had kicked up, a soft breeze fluttering the leaves of the elms and oaks around the field. She scanned the chain-link fence surrounding the ball field, noting numerous patches of rust. Then she took in the metal bleachers that were also dotted with orange spots of rust. The last time she was here she'd been so uncomfortable and out of sorts that she hadn't noticed. Now she was seeing every decrepit detail. The splintered and warped wooden roofs above the two dugouts, the lack of a scoreboard, the rusted signs—their faded lettering impossible to decipher—stuck on the fence behind the outfielders.

Hayden was right. Maple Falls was dying away. The things that made a town vibrant—strong businesses, safe open spaces where families could spend time together, activities that attracted both young and old—were disappearing. She shouldn't care. This town represented nothing but disappointment to her, except for being home to Mimi and the Bosom Buddies. Still, for some reason, the declining state of the town over the past ten years saddened her. Where would Maple Falls be in another decade?

Where will I be? The question popped into her mind out of the blue. What did she have to show for her past ten years in New York? An empty bank account, extra pounds she didn't need, and a few sales at the flea market. Maybe she had more in common with Maple Falls than she wanted to admit.

"Olivia!" Erma hollered as the woman approached the plate, hefting the bat as if it weighed fifty pounds instead of less than sixteen ounces. "Sugar, keep your eye on the ball this time."

"Yes, ma'am!" Olivia touched the brim of her light-gray baseball cap, her chin-length, straight black hair tucked behind both ears. She held the bat at such an awkward angle that Hayden held up Lonnie's pitch and jogged over to her. He repositioned the bat, gave her a few instructions Riley couldn't hear, then scooted away from the plate. Lonnie released a pitch, and Olivia connected with it, hitting a weak grounder to Jimmy at third base.

Riley smiled as Jimmy took his time fielding the ball without making it obvious. He threw Olivia out seconds before she reached first base, but she looked pleased. Riley was happy for her. Funny how a simple game could bring joy to so many people, players and spectators alike. Her grandmother was certainly enjoying herself. Then again, anytime Mimi had a chance to be bossy, she was in her element.

"It's good to see you smile, sweetie." Erma

reached out and took Riley's hand. "Real good."

"It feels good," she whispered, too low for Mimi to hear. But it didn't matter. The dread she'd felt over the past few days was dissolving, giving her space to breathe, to think clearly, and to relax, at least a little. She had Hayden to thank for that, in part.

When practice was over, Riley passed out cups of water like she had on Saturday, this time hanging around the players instead of escaping into the dugout. Anita motioned for her to join her, Harper, Olivia, and Kingston, a tall, blond man who hadn't been at the previous practice. Mimi had told her his name when he caught a ball in the outfield earlier. She paused, then walked over.

"Do you know my brother Kingston?" Anita gestured to the man, who was probably the only one on the field who could hold a candle to Hayden in the looks department. Still, Hayden edged him out, in Riley's opinion.

Kingston held out his hand. "I don't think we've met."

As Riley shook his hand, Anita said, "King is five years older than us, so that's probably why." Anita grinned. "He was in medical school when we graduated."

"Gotcha." Riley smiled. "Are you on the team too?"

"When I can be. I have pediatrician practices in Malvern and Arkadelphia, and I'm on call a lot at the hospital. But when I can make the practices and games, I try to. Hayden's done a good thing here, putting this team together."

"I agree." Olivia beamed. "It's been a lot of fun learning how to play. I feel like a kid again."

"My legs are getting a workout, that's for sure." Harper did a hamstring stretch.

Riley didn't quite believe her. Harper's trim, fit figure didn't happen naturally. She should know. She'd let her own figure go to pot.

"We were just thinking about grabbing some ice cream," Kingston said, looking at Riley. "There's a place right outside town that serves the best in the area."

"You should come with us," Anita added.

Riley paused, surprised she was considering their offer. But what if they started asking questions? Just because she'd trusted Hayden with a small piece of her past didn't mean she was ready to share it with anyone else.

"Maybe another time. I'm Mimi's ride home."

"I'm sure Junior wouldn't mind dropping her off," Kingston said. "Doesn't he live right around the corner from her?"

Riley had forgotten about that. Why hadn't Mimi asked him for a ride instead of practically begging Riley to take her to the ballpark tonight? Then again, her grandmother's decisions didn't make sense to her half the time, especially recently.

"So, are you coming with us, then?" Kingston flashed her another grin, his straight white teeth gleaming. He looked more like a model than a doctor, although she could see him as one of those too.

"Where y'all going?" Hayden joined them and stood next to Riley. Very close to her, she noticed, and between her and Kingston.

"Swirlies." Anita tucked her glove under her arm. "It opened a few weeks ago. Their hot fudge sundaes are to die for."

"Do they have sorbet?" Harper asked. "I'm lactose intolerant."

As Anita listed the different flavors of sorbet available at Swirlies, Hayden turned to Riley. "Are you going?" he whispered.

She paused. Once again, she was tempted. A part of her wanted to join the group, to eat two huge scoops of cookie dough ice cream and enjoy the company. Then, as it always did, reality slammed into her. What was the point of making friends when she wasn't sticking around?

And what about Hayden? She trusted him more than she had anyone else other than Mimi. Even Melody didn't know about Tracey. Had telling him been a mistake? She felt better after their talk—and kiss. But she hadn't given any thought to the future. Would she end up getting hurt when she had to leave?

"Riley?"

She met Hayden's expectant gaze and knew the answer. *Yes, I will. I always do.* Turning from him, she looked at the rest of the group. "Thanks, but I need to get Mimi home."

"Rain check, then," Kingston said.

She barely nodded, then hurried to Mimi, who was in a lively debate with the three Mathis cousins about the best old-school rap group. Riley frowned. When did Mimi ever listen to rap music?

"Oh, there you are, sugar." Mimi gestured to the three sweaty young men. "Tell them I'm right."

"Uh, you're right?"

"Of course I am." She gave the boys a queenly wave of her hand as they chuckled and shook their heads.

"Ready to go?" Riley asked, moving behind her grandmother and starting to push her along. The sooner she got out of here the better.

"I guess so." She inhaled a breath of air as a breeze flowed around them. "It feels wonderful out here. Thanks for coming with me, Riley. It's good to get out of the house."

Riley nodded, feeling a little guilty for dragging her away from everyone. But if she didn't leave now, she might change her mind about going to Swirlies.

"I'm glad you had a good time."

"I really wish I could play again," Mimi said as they slowly made their way toward the car.

The rest of the players were also heading for the lot, talking and laughing on the way there. Riley fought the impulse to search for Hayden, but she kept her focus on pushing Mimi. Her shoulders tensed. So much for being able to relax.

They were halfway to the parking lot when she heard him call her name. She cringed, knowing she was being a jerk again, and ignored him.

"Sugar, don't you hear Hayden calling you?"

Now she had no choice but to turn around. She stopped Mimi's wheelchair and turned halfway to look at him. He was jogging toward them, her sketchbook in his hand. How could she have forgotten her sketchbook? She started to mumble a curse, then stopped herself. Funny how her language had cleaned up since she'd gotten here. But right now her mind was filled with less than ladylike words.

"I'll be right back." She turned, forcing herself not to dash toward him, dread pooling in her stomach. *Please don't open that book.*

As he neared, he said, "You forgot this—" He tripped, and the sketchbook flew out of his hand and landed on the ground.

A wind stronger than any of the previous ones kicked up and blew open the cover of the sketchbook. Several pages flipped as she scrambled to get the book.

But Hayden picked it up first. He glanced down at the picture on the open page.

Chapter 10

S tunned, Hayden stared at his image on the white page in the sketchbook. It made him remember Riley's skill as an artist. She had captured him well, even the cowlick on the side of his head. Then realization dawned. *She drew a picture of me.*

He looked up to see her standing a few feet away, wisps of her brown hair blowing around her beautiful face. Without a word he closed the sketchbook and handed it to her.

She took it and hugged it to her chest. "Thank you," she said, icicles hanging from her words.

And with that she was distant again. He marveled at how she could turn from warm to frigid in a split second. But he wasn't irritated. He understood why, but that didn't mean he wanted her to leave. When she started to walk away, he jumped in front of her.

"Don't," he said, keeping his voice low. A few members of the team were still in the parking lot, but he didn't want to risk getting their attention.

Her eyes turned cold. "Mimi's waiting on me."

He saw Erma talking animatedly with Junior. "She's occupied right now." He looked at Riley again, this time at a loss for words. What was he supposed to say to her? *Don't leave? Don't be an ice queen? Let me hold you again?* Obviously, she had been thinking about him and, from the accuracy of her sketch, watching him. He didn't mind that one bit. What he did mind was that she was running away from him again when she didn't have to.

"I really need to—"

"Wait. Just . . . Wait right here." He ran over to Erma and Junior. "Hey, man, would you mind taking Erma home?" he asked Junior, who was so easygoing that Hayden was sure he would say yes. He also hoped Erma understood that he wanted to spend time alone with Riley.

"Sure thing, Hay." Junior tilted up his sweat-stained ball cap. "Anythin' for Miss Erma here."

"Why, Junior, you charmer." Erma lifted her brow at Hayden and gave him a small nod before turning to her willing chauffeur.

Thank God Erma was so sharp.

"I'd be glad to catch a ride with you," she continued. "You can finish telling me about that fish you caught last week. Twenty pounds, you said?"

"At least." Junior started to push Erma toward his light-green pickup truck. "Might have been twenty-two."

"My goodness!"

Hayden blew out a breath, relieved that Erma was taken care of and that Junior had someone to talk about his fish with. Then he turned around, glad to see that Riley hadn't moved. She didn't look so happy, though, and now he wondered if he hadn't made things worse by taking care of Erma without asking Riley first. But he wasn't going to let her get away so easily this time. He rushed to her, skidding to a stop on the grass. "Junior's—"

"Taking her home. I can see that." She scowled. "Why did you do that, Hayden?"

"Because I didn't want you to leave." There. The truth was out. "I think we have some things to talk about."

"Like what?"

"Us, for starters."

"There is no *us*." She moved her index finger back and forth between them.

He took a step back but kept his gaze steady. "I think there is."

"You're wrong." She hugged the sketchbook to her again.

She was stubborn, he would give her that. Then again, she was Erma's granddaughter. He also suspected that some of that stubbornness had been honed during her childhood. Reminding himself of that helped him keep his patience. He glanced at her sketchbook.

"Nice picture, by the way," he said. "Interesting choice of subject matter."

Her cheeks turned bright red and she averted her gaze. "I was practicing."

"Uh-huh." He scratched the corner of his forehead, then went for broke. "You can't honestly tell me that you didn't feel anything when we kissed."

"N-no. I-I didn't."

"Wow, you're a terrible liar." He grinned. "I like that about you."

"Hayden, don't."

"Don't what?" He took another step forward, and she moved back. "Don't worry, Riley," he said, softening his tone. "I'm not going to kiss you again. Even though I want to."

"You do?"

"Of course I do. But I can see you don't want me to."

A pause. "I never said that."

"Now, those words I believe."

She moved away from him again, holding the sketchbook as if it were a life preserver. "We shouldn't have kissed," she said.

That hit him hard. He understood she was protecting herself, and now he understood a little about why she felt like she had to. But to act like there weren't feelings between them . . . What was he supposed to do with that? *Slow down.* That's what he needed to do, for both their sakes. He'd never been one to jump into a relationship, and he'd never even been in a serious one. There was a learning curve to this, he was discovering.

"You're right," he said, following her lead and

moving away from her. "We haven't known each other that long. But we can change that."

She pressed her lips together and then pushed the stray strands of hair away from her face as she stared at the empty ball field. "No, we can't."

"Riley, please look at me."

She couldn't keep from facing Hayden, not when she heard the pleading in his voice. The sun was setting behind him, casting a soft amber glow around his incredible body. She wasn't being fair or honest with him, and he deserved better. She was stuck, like a pig in a mud wallow, as Bea might say.

She could walk away from Hayden right now, get into Mimi's car, and drive off. She could tell him she didn't need his help to fix up Mimi's house. Now that she didn't have to worry about the rent this month, she had extra money to hire someone else. It wouldn't be ideal, but it would solve a problem. She could make sure she never crossed paths with Hayden again before returning home to New York. That would make everything less complicated—and less painful.

But she remained in place. Every cell in her brain was telling her to flee, but with each pounding heartbeat, she grew further from leaving. She couldn't pull her gaze from his questioning one. Couldn't stop wishing things were different and wanting to launch herself into his steady arms. She couldn't reveal her heart either. She dropped her chin, the metal spiral coil binding the notebook digging into her arm.

They stood there at an impasse. Finally Hayden spoke. "Remember I told you I would earn your trust? I can't do that if you won't even let me try."

Riley lifted her chin, feeling it quiver. "You could have any woman you want, Hayden. Why are you bothering with me? I'm no one special."

He shook his head. "That's where you're wrong."

"Fine. Mimi thinks I'm special." She felt the bile rise in her throat. "She has to, being my grandmother and all."

"Ah, Riley." He moved closer to her, and before she could stop him, he brushed back the hair from her face and slipped it behind her ear. "First of all, you're putting me on way too high a pedestal. How many people do you think stuck around when my career was over? Sure, they were there for me at first, when there was still hope that I might come back. But eventually we all had to accept that wasn't happening and move on. The first one to go was the woman I was dating at the time."

Envy suddenly wound through Riley. "I'm not interested in a play-by-play of your romances, Hayden."

"Good, because you're not getting one. Besides, there weren't that many. I don't even know what happened to that woman, actually. I'm sure she found another baseball player to latch on to. Hopefully things worked out for her."

"You're not bitter she left you?"

He shook his head. "No. I think we had gone on a total of three dates. She wasn't interested in nursing a broken player back to health, and that was fine by me. I didn't need to be distracted." He took another step closer. "But know this, Riley. I'm distracted right now. *Very* distracted, in the best way."

As his words sank in, a pleasant shiver ran down her spine. *He even says all the right things.* How could she not put him on a pedestal?

"I can't claim to understand everything you've gone through or the pain you've felt. We've both been broken, in different ways. But I can tell you this—you can put the pieces back together. I want to help you do that."

"Why—"

Hayden pressed his finger over her mouth. "Just listen, please. I like you, Riley. You might have thought you were invisible back in high school, or at least you did everything you could to make yourself be. But I remember you. I noticed you, and I was interested in you back then."

Her eyes grew wide. "You were?" Her words were muffled against his finger.

He chuckled and dropped his hand. "Yep. But my focus was on other things. Still is. I haven't

221

talked to my father yet about selling the store, but I'm going to. And I've been thinking a lot about making some changes in this town. Good ones, of course. I'm hoping people will see them that way. That's going to take some time, I know, but I can at least try. I also have my new house to fix up, Erma's repairs, the softball team—"

"And I'm getting in the way of all that."

"No." He paused, his gaze intensifying. "Even with all this going on, the number one thing I'm thinking about is you."

Suddenly she couldn't breathe. This was too much all at once, and the strength of the emotions running through her were almost more than she could bear. She didn't know what to do.

Then she latched on to the conviction she'd seen in his eyes as he talked about improving Maple Falls. She thought about the drawing she had worked on earlier in the day of Mimi's shop. "Speaking of improvements," she said, keeping her tone light, as if he hadn't just made her heart sing. She opened the sketchbook and showed him what she had been working on all day.

He scanned the drawing. "Is this Knots and Tangles?"

"I'm hoping it will be. I've figured out a way to redesign the whole store."

"Wow. You sure have."

She found herself on solid ground now that they were talking about something practical. "I think instead of having the Bosom Buddies hold their group in the back of the shop, they should sit here." She pointed to a large seating area she had created in the middle of the store. "I want to paint all the wooden shelves pure white, which will be a great contrast to the colorful yarn."

"I know all about white paint," he mumbled with a half smile. "Just let me know when you need it."

"I have to see if Mimi is on board first. She hasn't been taking advantage of those huge picture windows in the front of the store. Seeing people inside, even if it's just Mimi's friends knitting and crocheting and having a great time, will draw customers in."

"That's a great idea." He checked the drawing again, then looked at her. "We're on the same wavelength with improving things around here, I see."

"Yes, but also keeping within the character of Maple Falls. This place has Southern charm." She had to give credit where it was due. "I don't think it should lose that."

"I agree." Hayden took the sketchbook from her and studied it. The sun was almost gone from the sky, but there was still enough light to see.

The tension in Riley's back started to ease. She could handle talking about buildings and home improvements. What she couldn't handle were the feelings he was bringing out in her a few moments ago. She also couldn't admit the truth—that she had been thinking about him all the time too.

Suddenly he started turning the pages of the sketchbook. Before she could grab it away from him, he came to her drawing of him. "And what about this?"

Her cheeks started to burn again. "Give me that back." She tried to take the sketchbook from him, but he held it above her head out of her reach. "I was just fooling around!"

"Just fooling around, huh? You just happened to be drawing a picture of me, even though you could have drawn anyone else? Erma, or one of the Bosom Buddies?"

"Stop being a jerk." She couldn't keep from giggling as she reached for it. He was only a few inches taller than her, but his arms were much longer, and the book was well out of her grasp.

He held it above his head. "I will, on one condition."

Her guard came up again. She didn't like conditions. But the teasing glint in Hayden's eyes tempered her automatic reaction. "What?"

"Have dinner with me tomorrow night. Not a date—I'll make that clear. Just two friends getting together to discuss their ideas for Maple Falls. How does that sound?"

She paused. That actually appealed to her. As they were looking at the sketchbook earlier, she'd gotten excited again, like she had in the shop when the idea first struck her. Besides, agreeing to dinner seemed like the only way she was going to get her sketchbook back. Unless she tackled him to the ground and took it, which wasn't going to happen. He was too big, too strong—and she was too weak to resist the thoughts that instantly traveled to an intimate place she couldn't risk dwelling on, not with him standing a few inches from her and her resolve wilting.

"Fine," she said, trying to sound casual. "What time?"

"I'll pick you up at five thirty tomorrow night. There's a steak joint a block down from the ice cream shop. They have decent sirloins and a gigantic food bar." He frowned. "Don't tell me you're a vegetarian."

"Definitely not."

"That's a relief." He handed her the sketchbook. "I'll see you tomorrow, then." He grinned at her, then turned and jogged back to the dugout to collect the softball equipment.

She clutched the sketchbook and walked to Mimi's car, got inside, and drove home in a daze. As usual, Mimi was sitting in the recliner watching TV and working on a crochet project when Riley walked inside. Riley paused, ready for Mimi to ask what took her so long to get home.

"You're blocking the TV." Mimi raised her crochet hook and waved Riley away, then slipped a loop of yarn over the hook. "I'm just about to find out who the killer is."

"Sorry." Riley nodded, relieved that her grandmother hadn't asked any questions. She went upstairs and sat on the edge of the bed, finally allowing herself to think about what Hayden had said. That he had noticed her in high school blew her mind. That he thought she was special blew it even further. Remembering his words and the honesty in his eyes warmed her to her toes. She grabbed a pillow and squealed into it, feeling like a teenager again. Except she had never felt like this in her teens—or ever.

Her clothes were still in her suitcase. She'd refused to unpack, not wanting anything about her time here to feel permanent. Did she have anything suitable to wear to a steakhouse? She would have to make do since there wasn't any time to shop.

Riley ground her thoughts to a halt. This wasn't a date, so it didn't matter what she wore. And that's how it should be. Like Hayden said, they were two friends discussing ideas. Nothing more.

But for the first time in her life, she wished she owned a skirt.

The next morning, Riley was working at Knots and Tangles, trying to focus on boxing up some old yarn Mimi had agreed to donate to an online knitting group. She was also trying to keep her thoughts off her upcoming supper with Hayden.

Her grandmother's doctor had called earlier and canceled Mimi's appointment but rescheduled it for tomorrow. Mimi wasn't happy with that, of course, but after pouting for a little while, she called Bea and they made plans to spend the day together.

Riley glanced at the clock on the wall above the counter for the tenth time. Barely eleven thirty. She had been sure it was past lunchtime. The day was crawling, and she could hardly keep the mix of nervousness and excitement at bay.

She heard the bell above the front door and turned around. Harper walked inside, dressed in a sharp royal-blue pencil skirt and white blouse, her thick blond hair tousled strategically over her shoulders.

"Hello!" she said, grinning brightly. "I brought some goodies for you."

Riley froze in front of the box. "What?"

Harper set a large white shopping bag with two handles on the counter. "When you said you weren't free for dinner tonight when I called you earlier, I put two and two together." She placed her hands on her slender hips. "You and Hayden are going out, aren't you?"

"Uh . . ." Riley felt the sting of embarrassment fill her cheeks. "Not *out* exactly—"

"I knew it. When you two were hanging out after practice yesterday, I suspected something was up."

Knowing she had to nip this in the bud, Riley said, "It's not a date. Seriously. I have some plans for Knots and Tangles, and I wanted to run them by him. He . . ." She wondered if she should say anything about him wanting to improve the town, then decided against it. "That's it. We just agreed to have supper at the same time. We both have to eat, you know."

"Right." Harper eyed Riley's clothes, the usual plain T-shirt and jean shorts. "You're not wearing that, are you?"

"No," she replied, feeling somewhat defensive. "I'm going to change into jeans."

Harper sighed. "I was afraid of that. Friendly dinner or not, it won't hurt for you to dress up a little. I brought some things that might work for you."

Now Riley felt humiliated. Was her appearance that bad? Her clothes weren't fancy, but they were comfortable—way better than what she'd had when she was with Tracey. More than once she had been pulled out of class by a kind teacher or the school nurse and given a new pair of jeans that didn't have holes in them or a jacket that actually fit. The clothes themselves were old, but they were new to Riley, and they were clean, something her clothes rarely were.

"Hey." Harper's tone grew serious. "I didn't hurt your feelings, did I?"

Riley picked up a full box of yarn. "Of course not." But she couldn't meet Harper's eyes.

"Oh, I'm pretty sure I did." She hurried over to Riley and put her arm around her shoulders. "I can be so thoughtless sometimes," she said, sincerity filling her tone. "Usually I try to catch myself, but . . . I just wanted to do something nice for you, that's all. Mother said you had dropped everything to come help Erma, and I figured you wouldn't have had time to pack much. But if I've offended you, I'm really sorry."

Riley could see Harper was being genuine. She could also see that she was upset. Riley set down the box. "It's okay." She paused. "You're right, my wardrobe could use a little help. I didn't pack very much when I left New York. I was in too much of a hurry."

"Well, if it's okay, I brought a few things I thought might fit you." Harper gave her a sheepish grin. "But you don't have to look at them if you don't want to."

Now Riley was curious, and she also didn't want to make Harper feel any worse. "I'd like to."

Harper brightened. "Oh good!" Her heels clicked on the worn tile floor as she walked to the other side of the counter and started pulling clothing out of the bag. "You have such beautiful fair skin, I thought these would be pretty on you."

She handed Riley a pale-pink scoop-neck blouse with a thin band of lace edging on the hem, along with a flared skirt that was a shade darker.

Once again, she was glad the store was empty. She examined the outfit. She couldn't remember the last time she'd worn anything pink. "You didn't buy these, did you?"

"Not yet. I have a friend who owns a boutique. She let me bring the clothes here. If you don't like any of them, I'll take them back. You can purchase whatever you want to keep." Harper pulled out three more outfits, each one just as nice as the pink one, and fancier than what Riley usually wore, but still more casual than Harper's style. She had to admit Harper had done a good job picking out the clothes. She checked the sizes. Harper had nailed those too. Riley wasn't sure if that was a good thing or not.

Then she spied the price tags and stilled. She couldn't afford a single one of these items, much less an entire outfit. When Harper started pulling out matching jewelry, Riley's stomach churned.

The front bell jingled, and Bea walked in, then held the door for Mimi as she rolled into the store.

"Hello, Harper," Mimi said. "How's the house-selling business going?"

"A little slow right now, but it will pick up." She handed Riley a long, green beaded necklace meant to go with the second outfit.

"What's all this? Bea walked over to the counter where the clothes and jewelry were spread out. "Such pretty clothes. Are these yours, Harper?"

Riley continued to study the outfits as Harper explained to Mimi and Bea what was going on, telling them she and Riley had plans tonight, instead of revealing that Riley was having supper with Hayden. Riley would have to thank her for that stroke of genius later. She didn't like the idea of fibbing to Mimi, but she also didn't want her grandmother to get the wrong idea.

She touched the pink shirt again, loving the soft feel of the silky fabric. The other outfits were brighter and more playful, but she was drawn to the pink clothing for some reason.

"Try them on, sugar."

"I don't know . . . ," she said to Mimi, who had rolled closer to the counter.

"You can change in the bathroom, then model for us. We'll help you decide which one you want."

Riley leaned over the counter. "I can't afford these," she whispered.

Mimi smiled. "Don't you worry about that, honey."

After a pause, Riley relented. She took the clothes to the back and hung them on the hook on the back of the door. She selected the red-and-white pantsuit first, ignoring the price before she put on the clothes so she wouldn't feel any more guilty than she already did. Harper even brought shoes, and they fit too. The woman had a good eye—that was for sure.

Riley stood back to see her whole body in the mirror above the sink. The clothes not only felt good but were flattering. Better yet, she felt . . . pretty. When was the last time she'd felt that way, or even cared enough to think about it? She scrutinized her face in the mirror and smiled.

Erma held back tears as she watched her granddaughter model the beautiful clothes Harper had brought. *Bless that child.* How she managed to figure out Riley's sizes, Erma didn't know, but every single ensemble was a perfect fit. At first Riley seemed uncomfortable showing off the clothing, but Harper's and Bea's enthusiasm helped her relax. Erma would have joined in, but she was content to be quiet and observe for once.

Of course she didn't believe Harper's poppy-cock about a girls' night. These weren't outfits for dinner with a girlfriend. They were more suited for something special. *Like supper with Hayden Price.* Erma wasn't 100 percent sure that was what was going on, and she wasn't going to pry—she'd promised to stay out of Riley's personal business. But she had seen the gleam in Hayden's eyes when he asked Junior to take her home last night, and she'd also noticed Riley watching him while he was coaching.

Erma didn't miss much, especially when she was paying attention.

Riley came out in the last outfit, a lovely pale-pink blouse and skirt that hugged her curves in all the right places. Erma had noticed that her granddaughter had finally put a little meat on her bones, and she was lovely. The color was perfect for her skin tone, and the delicate gold necklace added the perfect final touch.

"That's the outfit," Bea said, clasping her hands together and smiling.

"That's the outfit," Harper added, giving her a thumbs-up.

"That's the outfit." Erma nodded and rolled closer to Riley. "You've never looked more stunning, sugar." When Riley smiled, Erma's heart melted.

"I'm not used to wearing heels," Riley said, shifting back and forth on her feet.

"They're wedges, and they're barely an inch and a half." Harper went over to her. "You'll be surprised how comfortable they are to walk in."

"More comfortable than those stilts you're wearing," Bea said to Harper. "I don't know how you don't fall over in those."

"Practice, Bea, practice." She turned to Riley. "Now, about your hair—"

"Riley, don't you think you should get back in your own clothes?" Erma asked. Not only was Riley's hair fine as it was, but a new hairstyle would also be a bridge too far for her granddaughter's comfort. But Harper didn't know that. "In case we have customers."

"Yes, I should." She turned and hustled to the back room.

Erma had been disappointed this morning when her appointment was canceled, but spending the morning with Bea and window-shopping antique stores had put her in a better mood. Besides, she was finally getting pretty good at maneuvering her chair.

Erma spun in her wheelchair and faced Harper. "That was very sweet of you, Harper," she said, meaning every word. She took the young woman's hand and squeezed it. "Just let me know how I need to pay."

"I'll take care of it, and you can pay me back," Harper said, packing the rest of the clothes back in the bag. "That will be the easiest."

"I can reimburse you in yarn, then." Mimi winked.

Harper laughed. "No, thank you. Crafting is Mother's thing, not mine." She smiled at Erma and Bea. "She does look pretty, doesn't she?"

Erma nodded. "She certainly does." She was positive Hayden would think so too.

When Riley came out of the bathroom, Erma and Bea were already in the back room discussing the work Riley had done in the shop so far. She left the outfit on its hangers in the bathroom so it wouldn't wrinkle.

"I'm going to say goodbye to Harper," she told the ladies. "I'm sure she has to get back to work."

Mimi nodded, giving Riley a wink, then turned back to Bea.

Riley walked up to the front of the store. Harper was sitting in the Man Chair, scrolling through her phone, the bag on the floor next to her.

Riley pulled over the stool she'd used to reach the top of the shelves and sat near Harper. "I can't believe you got my sizes right."

"Fashion is my passion. Besides, you have such a cute figure. You need to show it off more."

Cute wasn't the word Riley would use, especially next to the lithe Harper. Still, that didn't change the fact that the new clothes had made her feel good and attractive. That wasn't the goal, of course, especially since tonight wasn't a date. It was a meeting between two friends to discuss a common interest. She wished she didn't have to keep reminding herself of that.

"What time is Hayden picking you up?" Harper asked, slipping her phone into her purse.

"Five thirty." Her nerves spiked again, and to distract herself, she continued talking. "He's taking me to some steakhouse a little ways past Maple Falls."

Harper chuckled. "Sounds like you're getting some of your Southern accent back."

Riley frowned. "I am?"

"A touch. You don't have a New York accent for sure, but you don't sound Southern either." She leaned forward. "Once you start callin' me sugah dumplin', then I know you're here to stay," she drawled.

Riley didn't bother to correct her. She couldn't keep telling everyone she would be leaving soon. They would find out when she was gone.

Harper got up from the chair and grabbed the bag of clothes. "Have a great time with Hayden," she said, hitching her purse strap over her shoulder. "He's a good guy."

"You're not interested in him?" She hadn't meant to ask the question out loud. It just popped out. She couldn't imagine anyone not being attracted to Hayden.

"Oh, he's cute. Can't deny that. But he's not my type." She smirked. "He's definitely yours, though." She walked over to the door and opened it, letting in warm, humid air. "We girls will expect a full report later on," she said.

"Girls?"

But Harper was already out the door.

Riley stood there, stunned by what had just happened. She figured Harper meant herself, Anita, and Olivia. But a full report of what, Riley wasn't sure. She wasn't used to having girlfriends to report to. She was also finding she didn't mind it so much.

She thought about the pink outfit again and Harper's thoughtfulness. This was the nicest thing any woman had ever done for her, with the exception of Mimi or one of the BBs.

Riley smiled, blinking back something she wasn't used to—happy tears.

Chapter 11

Hayden slicked back his hair, the ends still damp from the quick shower he took before he went to pick up Riley from Knots and Tangles. He could have just changed his work shirt in the back room of the hardware store, then got in his car and picked her up behind the store instead of rushing home first, but that didn't feel right for some reason. Even though he spent the day reminding himself that dinner tonight wasn't a date, his nerves sure made it feel like one.

At 5:30 p.m. sharp he opened the door to the yarn shop. The bell above him dinged as he walked inside. When he didn't see her right away, he paused in the middle of the shop, noticing how much room there was now since Riley had arrived and put her organizing skills to work. He wasn't sure what to do. Should he wait for her at the counter? Holler that he was here? Text her? He was pulling out his phone from the pocket of his jeans when she walked through the doorway that led to the back of the store.

He froze, phone in hand, unable to take his eyes off her. She was wearing a light-pink top that dipped a little low, but not too low to be indecent, and a flowing skirt that skimmed the tops of her knees. Her hair was pulled back in a loose ponytail with a few strands framing her face. At the base of her neck was a simple gold necklace. Her cheeks were rosy, as if she were blushing. She was so beautiful he could hardly breathe.

"Hi," she said, looking at him but keeping her distance.

He swallowed. "Hey." Great, he sounded like a bullfrog. He cleared his throat. "Uh, ready to go?"

Riley nodded. "Let me get my purse." She went behind the counter and picked up her crossbody bag, hanging it over her shoulder.

"I parked in the back," he said, walking over to her.

She nodded and walked around the counter. Then she suddenly tripped and started to fall forward.

Hayden curved his arm around her waist, steadying her, seeing that she'd tripped over the corner of an old area rug that was curling at the edges. He noticed she had on a pair of white strappy shoes with cork-colored heels. When he faced her, he realized they were nearly nose to nose.

"New shoes." She sounded like she'd swallowed a squeaky dog toy. "I'm not used to them."

The words hardly registered. Besides their kiss

the other day, he'd never been this close to Riley before, not that he hadn't wanted to be. He should let go of her, but his arm remained firmly in place. He could feel the softness of her shirt and the curves underneath, see the light sprinkling of freckles across her nose that were only visible this close up. Kissing her again would be so easy, so pleasurable—*so wrong.*

He dropped his arm and stepped away. "Can't help you with that," he said, letting out a chuckle about her new shoes and hoping he didn't sound stupid. "I prefer cleats myself."

"They wouldn't exactly go with the outfit."

That made him laugh—and broke the awkwardness of him holding on to her longer than was polite. Before he could say anything, she started walking away.

"I don't want to be late for our reservation," she said.

The steakhouse didn't take reservations, but he didn't correct her. He followed her out the door, trying to keep his gaze straight ahead and not on her. He wanted to blame the clothing for his intense attraction, but who was he kidding? She could wear a muumuu and he'd find her just as desirable.

When he saw that she was almost to the passenger door, he hurried and opened it for her. He couldn't decipher the look she gave him before getting in the car, and he figured he was really pushing things now. But he'd open the door for any woman. Those manners were ingrained in him since his youth.

As he drove to the restaurant, he searched for something to say. This was supposed to be supper with a friend, and conversation should have been easy. Instead, he turned on the radio and they listened to country music on the way to the steakhouse. When he pulled into the parking lot and turned off the engine, she started to open the door.

"Wait," he said, instinctively touching her arm to stop her. When she glanced down at his hand on her arm, he pulled it back. "My mother would never forgive me if I didn't open the door for you."

Her lips curved into a half smile. "Southern manners?"

"You know it." Relieved, he smiled back, then dashed out of the car and opened her door, holding out his hand. When she slipped her hand into his palm, he tried to imagine he was helping one of the BBs out of a car, something he had done a time or two. It didn't work, of course, and he realized how nice Riley's hand fit in his the same moment she let go.

After they walked into the restaurant and were taken to a table, Hayden insisting on pulling out her chair for her, they sat down and read over the menus. More silence, and that had diminished his good feelings from moments ago when she had smiled at him.

Maybe he'd made a mistake by asking her to dinner. They probably should have met at Erma's, which would have been neutral territory, sort of. The waitress showed up and they ordered their food, then handed the menus to her before she took off. When he saw Riley fidgeting with the corner of her red cloth napkin, he was sure tonight was going to be uneasy at best, and possibly a disaster. Since his track record with her wasn't great, he steeled himself for a long, uncomfortable evening.

Although she tried, Riley couldn't stop feeling uncomfortable. It had started when she first saw Hayden staring at her when she came from the back of the shop. All the confidence she'd had in the bathroom evaporated when he kept gaping at her, not saying a word. That was what made her nervous—Hayden was rarely silent. She couldn't tell what he was thinking. Did he think her new outfit was ugly or that she'd overdressed? She couldn't read his expression, and when he didn't say a word about her clothing, she figured she'd made a mistake wearing it. She should have stuck with her original jeans and T-shirt plan, although she noticed that Hayden not only looked nice but smelled amazing. She probably smelled like old yarn and cardboard boxes.

243

She had to admit that she was disappointed. Hayden was straightforward, and she liked that about him. If he liked her outfit, he would have said something.

Then there was the moment she tripped over the rug. She'd meant to get rid of that old thing already, but it kept slipping her mind. And while she might have caught her toe on the corner while wearing the sandals, it only made things worse that she had new shoes on—shoes Hayden didn't seem to notice, either, until she pointed them out.

The waitress came by with glasses of water, and as she set them on the table, Riley tried to relax. She quickly picked up the glass and took a big gulp, only to spill half of it on her shirt. She was mortified. She couldn't even do a friendly supper right. She put the glass down and picked up her cloth napkin, dabbing it at her neckline. Then she saw Hayden was staring at her again, only to clear his throat and take a sip of his own water. Of course he didn't spill a drop.

She sat back in her chair. This was ridiculous. She refused to spend another minute ill at ease. This was Hayden, and they were here to discuss their ideas for Maple Falls, and they couldn't do that if they weren't speaking to each other.

"Let's talk about Maple Falls," she said, getting to the point. She never thought she'd ever say those words out loud.

He shifted his gaze for a split second, then

looked at her again. "Okay, well, my first plan is to convince my parents to sell me the store."

Her brow lifted. "You want to buy it?"

"Yes. I can't accept that it won't be our family business anymore. The only way to make sure that happens is if I own it outright."

It didn't escape Riley that they had very different opinions on the value of family businesses. "What about your house? Isn't it going to be expensive to fix up?"

He shook his head. "Not if I do the work myself. I crunched some numbers, and although it will take more time than if I contract out some of the work, if I do as much as I can, I'll save a good chunk of money, and I'll put that toward the hardware store. Money isn't the issue. Talking to my folks will be."

"Why?" She took another sip of her water, this time making sure she didn't spill it. "You have a good relationship with your family." Something she was a bit envious of.

"I'm still irritated that they didn't tell me about the sale." He frowned. "I understand their reasons, at least the ones Henry told me. But they left me out of a family decision and didn't give me a chance to put in my two cents."

Riley was acquainted with that feeling, at least in other parts of her life. To be fair, Mimi had always tried to include her in Knots and Tangles, only to meet resistance.

The waitress brought their order—a rib eye, baked potato, and vegetable medley for Hayden, and a filet, mashed potatoes, and salad for Riley. The filet was a bit on the pricey side, but she was paying for her part of the supper, and thanks to Mimi's generosity, she could afford to splurge a little.

After they started eating, they continued to talk. Riley suggested telling his parents what his plans were for the hardware store, and they brainstormed ideas to get more customers into the shop. Then they switched to discussing Knots and Tangles, and Riley explained her plans concerning the shop and Mimi's house in more detail. She pulled out the budget with the estimates she'd worked on and gave it to Hayden, who perused it before tucking it into his pocket.

"Would you two like to look at the dessert menu?" the waitress asked as she cleared their empty plates.

Riley started to shake her head, but Hayden said, "Do you still have hot fudge sundaes?" When she nodded, he told the waitress, "One sundae, two spoons."

After the waitress left, he looked at Riley, "Just in case you want a bite or two."

She was nearly full after the wonderful meal but wasn't sure she could resist a sundae. "Maybe one bite," she conceded.

As they waited on dessert, Hayden brought

up his ideas for revitalizing Maple Falls. "Eventually I want to get the Too Dang Hot Parade back on track, but I know that's going to take time. Until then I want to visit with the Main Street business owners and talk about sprucing up their storefronts. I thought we could also get the school kids involved to clean up the park and ball field. I'm going to contact the vocational school in Hot Springs, too, and ask about commissioning some new benches for the park."

"Wow, that all sounds great." So great that for a moment she wished she would be here to see it all come to fruition. But she couldn't let his enthusiasm sway her into staying in Maple Falls longer than she had to.

The sundae arrived and was large enough to serve two people. Hayden moved it to the center of the table and dug his spoon into the mound of vanilla ice cream, which was melting under a puddle of thick hot fudge.

When he took a bite, he smirked. "Delicious. Bet you can't stop at one bite."

She took it as a challenge and lifted her brow at him, then scooped up a huge bite of the sundae. When she tried to fit it in her mouth, she had to laugh as whipped cream landed on her nose.

"Here," he said, reaching over and wiping it off with his napkin before settling back in his chair. "That counts as two bites, by the way."

"Oh no it doesn't." She grinned. "You never specified the size of the one bite."

He lifted another spoonful. "Good point." Then he waved the spoon a little closer to her. "Sure you don't want another bite?"

For the first time in her life, she didn't glance around to see if anyone was watching her. Somehow Hayden inspired her to let go of her self-consciousness, even if it took a while to get there. She shook her head, then snatched the cherry that was sliding off the top of the sundae. "I'm done."

"Hey, what if I wanted that cherry?"

"You did?" Her guard immediately went up again. "I'm sorry. I should have asked—"

"Riley, I'm teasing. I don't even like cherries."

She turned her head slightly and gave him a sidelong glance. "Is that true, or are you just being nice?"

He set down the spoon and put up his hands. "You caught me. I love any kind of cherries."

"You're a terrible liar too." She grinned and crossed her hands on the table as he finished off the dessert. She was tempted to grab another bite but held her ground. He didn't need help polishing off the ice cream anyway. The waitress dropped off the check as he was scraping the last bit of hot fudge from the bottom of the dish.

When Riley reached for her bag, Hayden shook his head. "It's on me tonight."

"I'm paying my share."

He looked at her. "I suppose it's useless to argue with you."

"Correct." Again, she couldn't stop herself from smiling.

"All right. But I still get to open the car door for you, right?"

Her smile widened and she sighed dramatically. "If you insist."

They paid the bill and made their way to the car, Riley letting Hayden open the door. As they went back to downtown Maple Falls, they continued talking about their future plans, Riley leaving out her determination to leave as soon as she could, and Hayden never bringing up the subject.

It was dark by the time he pulled into the parking space next to Erma's car in the lot behind Knots and Tangles. She could see a few fireflies hovering around the two small bushes that edged the parking lot. She hadn't been able to figure out if they were planted there as a beautification project that was never finished, or if they simply weren't pulled out when the lot was poured. They had always seemed out of place to her.

Hayden left the car running as he turned to her. "I had a great time tonight. Thanks for helping me talk through my ideas and how to approach my parents. I feel more confident about that now."

"You're welcome." The silver light from the single lamppost in the parking lot shone inside the car, lighting up his face. Her hand went to her necklace and she fiddled with the gold chain, her nerves spiking again. For a supper that had been friendly, the electric tension between them right now definitely wasn't. She wouldn't have to move much to kiss him. Just a few inches and she could experience another wave of bliss like their last kiss. More than anything she wanted to do just that.

"Riley—"

"I've gotta go." She opened the car door, forgetting that she had agreed to let him do it. "Mimi has an early doctor's appointment." Which was true, but it wasn't that early. She scrambled out of the seat. "Thanks. Bye." She slammed the door and fumbled in her purse for her keys. She didn't glance back as she got in the car and fled from Hayden—again.

Although this time she had to do everything in her power not to go back to him.

On Thursday morning, Hayden was ready to talk to his parents. That, however, was not what was on his mind after he'd gone for a quick run before breakfast. Riley was, particularly the way she ran off last night. He'd been serious about having a good time with her, especially when she relaxed while they were discussing business. Then she'd turned playful during dessert, and that was when he'd been a goner. Although she sped out of his car like a jackrabbit, he'd been sure she wanted to kiss him again, maybe as much as he wanted to kiss her.

Strangely enough, he was glad she hadn't. That would have complicated things, and he'd rather be around Riley as friends than kissing her and destroying their fragile friendship. The best thing he could do right now was get her off his mind and focus on his meeting with his parents.

After returning from his run, he quickly showered and dressed, then went downstairs and into the kitchen where his mother was finishing breakfast. When they were all seated at the table and had started eating, he told them he wanted to talk.

"About what, dear?" Mom sipped her white coffee that was mostly milk and sugar with a splash of actual coffee.

"The store."

Both parents gaped at him. "You want to talk about the hardware store?" his dad asked.

"Yes." Hayden leaned forward. "I know you're selling the business."

His parents exchanged a glance, then his father spoke. "How did you find out?"

Hayden told them, apologizing for reading personal mail. "I called Henry and he confirmed it, but he didn't give me any details."

"I'm sorry, Hayden." Mom grimaced. "We were going to tell you—"

251

"—when the time was right," Dad said.

"You've been so busy with baseball and then rehabbing your shoulder."

Hayden moved his hands under the table as he tried not to clench them into fists. His parents had never been deceptive about anything before. He needed to hear them out.

"I understand," he said evenly. "But I've been back more than six months."

"We didn't have a deal in place until recently." Dad tapped the handle of his coffee cup. "I thought—"

"We thought," Mom interjected. "It was a joint decision."

"We thought we would tell you after the sale." Dad turned to Hayden. "I'm surprised you're upset about this."

"Why wouldn't I be upset?"

"We weren't keeping it a secret from you," Mom insisted.

That was debatable but not the point. "I don't care that you didn't tell me. I'm upset about the sale. I can't believe you don't want to run the store anymore."

His shoulders drooped. "I'm tired, son. I've been tired for a while. It's hard having a business nowadays. Not just in a small town, but in lots of places. Although small-town businesses have been hit the worst. People are shopping in bigger cities, bigger stores."

"Those strip malls." Mom sniffed. "They and online shopping have been the death of small businesses."

"I'm tired of fighting, son. Maybe if I was younger I'd be able to handle it better." Dad sighed, then took Mom's hand. "We have things we want to do. Travel. Go see the grandkids together. We always have to take separate trips because someone has to mind the store."

Hayden sat back in his chair. "I didn't realize how difficult it was for you."

"Oh, you know your father," Mom said. "Never wants anyone to think he's anything but a ray of sunshine."

Dad frowned and tugged on his salt-and-pepper mustache. "That's not true. Not totally anyway."

"Honey, it's a done deal. Your father is signing the papers tomorrow afternoon."

Hayden stilled. He'd hoped for more time than that, but beggars couldn't be choosers, especially in a situation like this. "I want to buy the store."

"What?" his parents exclaimed.

"I have a good chunk of money saved from playing ball. Enough to make a decent offer, I'm sure." He didn't think it was necessary to explain financial details further than that.

"It's not about the money," Dad said. "You don't understand what you're getting into."

"Then tell me. Explain everything I need to know about running a hardware store. I can't imagine there's anything else you didn't teach me about the place when I was growing up."

"There's a few things. That's still not the point. Hayden, it's not just hard. Running a failing business is defeating."

Hayden thought for a moment. "Maybe it doesn't have to fail. What is the buyer planning to do with the property?"

"I'm not sure. Henry is handling the sale, and I've never met the guy, but he's bought up two other buildings on the street too."

That didn't sound good at all. Mass purchases of buildings or land usually meant new development. Hearing that made him more determined than ever to go through with his plans for Maple Falls. He'd just have to get through to his parents first. "That doesn't bother you?"

"It does, but what can I do about it?" Dad frowned, his expression somber. "I don't want to saddle you with this, Hayden. I'm sure you have other things you'd rather do with your future."

"Other than finish rehabbing that house I bought two months ago, I can't think of anything more important than this." Riley instantly came to mind, but he had to keep his focus on Price's Hardware right now. He had to get his point across to his parents.

"You've had a lot of changes in your life in a short time." Compassion filled his mother's eyes. "It's been less than a year since . . ."

"Since the injury that ended my career. You can say that, Mom. We can talk about it too."

Dad shook his head. "I don't see how you accepted it so easily." His gaze was direct. "I'm not sure I believe you have."

Anger flared inside Hayden, but he tamped it down, reminding himself that his parents didn't know the whole story. Maybe it was time they did. "Two years before I signed with Detroit, I started seeing a counselor."

Mom drew in a breath. "You did? Why?"

"I was having trouble keeping my emotions in check." It wasn't easy to admit this, and he hadn't said anything because he didn't want his parents to worry. But he could see the alarm on their faces. "I'm in a good place now, ironically. Better than I have been in a long time. But I was frustrated back then. I couldn't seem to break through into the majors—my game was suffering. I wasn't myself, and my temper was flaring. So I went to counseling. I lucked out and got a good counselor. He even came and saw me in the hospital, and then we did sessions over the phone and online.

"I'm telling you all this because while it might seem like my decision to buy the store is a last-minute one, it isn't." For some reason, discussing his struggle to keep his emotions under control was making him emotional. *Add another checkmark in the irony column.* He swallowed the lump in his throat.

"We had no idea," Mom said, tears in her eyes. "If you were struggling so much, why didn't you tell us?"

"You did a good job of hiding it," Dad added.

"Because I didn't want to have this conversation. I didn't want to worry you. And I'm a grown-up. I take care of my own problems. I learned that from you." He smiled, relieved that his secret was out in the open now. But that didn't mean he wanted to derail the topic at hand. "Enough of all this emotional talk."

"Now you sound like your father," Mom mumbled. Then she touched Hayden's arm. "I'm so proud of you, Hayden. I didn't think we could be any prouder than we were when you realized your dream of making it to the majors." A tear slipped down her cheek. "But we are. Right, Harrison?"

Dad sniffed. "Yes," he said, turning to Hayden. "Very proud."

Hayden appreciated the support they had always given him without hesitation. Yet as much as that meant to him, there was something else he needed even more.

"Mom, Dad, are you willing to sell Price's Hardware to me?"

Chapter 12

A nd here's where you and the Bosom Buddies will have your knit and crochet nights." Riley gestured to the middle of the store. Bins and small shelving units stuffed with yarn crowded the area.

Her grandmother rested her forearms on the wheelchair's armrests. This morning the doctor said Mimi needed to use the chair for one more week because he was concerned that moving her to crutches too soon might cause more problems. Her grandmother wasn't happy with the decision, but she didn't give the doctor too much trouble about it.

"Do you think there will be enough room here?" she asked. "At least this week, since I'm still stuck in this chair."

"Once we clear out everything there will be plenty of room." Riley pulled over the Man Chair and sat in front of Mimi. "Right now all the inventory is out on display. It's overwhelming." She flipped open her sketchbook, making sure she moved quickly past Hayden's portrait. She should have torn it out, but she couldn't bring herself to do it. In fact, she had done more work on it this week. "I've also designed some storage ideas for the back room. Instead of putting everything on the floor, we limit the merchandise to a few skeins, and when customers want more of a particular yarn, we can go in the back and fetch it for them."

Mimi nodded. "I've just always done what my mother and grandmother did. They had fewer yarn options and more customers, so the inventory turned over quickly." She surveyed the shop. "You're right. All my friends are right. I let the shop get out of control."

"Don't worry, Mimi. It won't take too much work to rein it back in." Riley smiled.

"There it is again." Mimi beamed. "That beautiful smile. If redoing this shop will keep that smile on your face, let's do it!"

"Don't forget about your house," Riley said. "I have plans for that too."

"I'm sure you do." Mimi tilted her head. "I'm worried you've bitten off more than you can chew. It's going to take time to do all that work, even with Hayden's help."

"I know."

"What about your job in New York? I'm sure Melody is ready for her roommate to return."

Riley explained about Charlie, and how the rent was covered at least for the next month. "As for my job . . ." She touched the sketch in her lap. "Let's just say the New York art world won't miss me for a little while longer."

Mimi shook her head. "I'm sure that's not true.

I thought you told me you had several shows recently, although I'll admit my memory ain't what it used to be."

Inhaling a deep breath, Riley admitted, "They weren't exactly shows. More like sales." Her cheeks heated and she knew she finally had to be honest. "As in flea market sales."

"Oh." Surprise flashed across Mimi's face, then she nodded. "There's nothing wrong with that. Were your customers satisfied with their purchases?"

"I think so." Riley remembered one young woman who had moved to the city from South Carolina and was picking up furniture and décor from the flea market to furnish her new apartment. *"It's tiny,"* she'd said in a sweet, Carolinian accent. *"But it's all mine, and this picture will be perfect for the wall above my sleeper sofa."*

Riley had remembered being just like her when she first arrived in New York—full of excitement and anticipation, ready to take on the city and make her mark. Fortunately this woman had a business degree and wouldn't end up another failed artist like Riley. For some reason, the thought didn't carry the sting it had in the past. She also didn't want to think about New York. She wanted to focus on her work here.

"I have an idea," Mimi said. "Once everything is finished, how about I commission a few pieces of original Riley McAllister art to decorate the walls?"

"Well, I was thinking about doing one anyway." *Before I leave.*

"That would be jim-dandy. You can use materials here in the shop for inspiration." Her smile was warm. "I've always loved your work, even if I'm a little biased. I think it will also help sell the store when the time comes."

Riley paused as unexpected sadness washed over her, and this wasn't the first time her emotions were out of whack since supper with Hayden last night. She'd been kicking herself for being so abrupt with him, but if she hadn't, she would have ended up kissing him, and that would have made a complicated situation worse. Before she fell asleep last night, she thought about Hayden's passion for his hometown and about all the work she was putting into Knots and Tangles to improve it, only for it to be sold. *That's what I want, though. Right?*

"Riley? Is that idea okay with you?"

She turned to Mimi, seeing her expectant look. "I'd love to create art for the store," she said, tamping down her sadness and trying to be as enthusiastic as her grandmother.

"Wonderful! Now you're really going to be busy! Let me know what you need. Money, supplies. I can even get a couple of the BBs to help do some things around here. Myrtle should be back from her trip next week, and she's going to pass out from shock that I'm actually letting all this happen."

Riley laughed. "That sounds good. We need to settle on a budget."

Mimi waved off the idea. "I can afford anything you need."

"But a budget is always a good idea." Despite her lack of money, she'd always had a budget that she tried to follow to the letter. Tracey had never had enough money, not even for food sometimes. Riley always made sure that even if she was flat broke, she had enough to keep a roof over her head and something in her stomach.

"All right. I'm coming to realize you know best." She lifted her chin and looked at Riley. "How about we go to the diner and get some lunch? You can tell me all about these storage plans for the back room."

A short time later, they were in the diner, which was half empty even though it was lunchtime. Mimi wheeled her chair on the opposite side of a table that had bench seating on one side.

"Oh shoot," she said. "We should have invited Hayden to join us."

Butterflies danced in Riley's stomach at the mention of his name. She'd managed not to think about him while going over her plans with Mimi, but she should have known the distraction wouldn't last long.

"Next time we'll invite him," Mimi said.

Anita came over and offered them menus. She had gotten a haircut since the last time Riley saw her—a cute pixie style with caramel highlights throughout her auburn hair. She looked adorable.

"Hi, Riley," she said, then added, "How are you feeling, Ms. McAllister?"

"I'm feeling like some sweet tea, sugar. Extra sweet, please." She grinned. "I'm also doing well, thanks. Next week I'll get my crutches, and then there'll be no stopping me."

Anita laughed. "I'm so glad. We miss you on the team. Myrtle too." She pulled a notepad from her apron, then wrote down the drink order. "What would you like, Riley?"

"I'll have water, thanks." Before Anita could leave, she added, "I like your hair."

She blushed and touched the back of her head. "Thank you. I got it done yesterday after my shift." She checked the kitchen before turning to Riley again. "You're the first one to notice." She jotted down their orders. "A water and a super-sweet, sweet tea. Got it. Be back in a jiff."

As Anita walked away, Mimi leaned over. "She's such a darling girl, but I feel bad for her."

Riley frowned. "Why?"

"That uniform she and the other waitresses have to wear. It's *hideous*."

Anita had disappeared into the kitchen, but another waitress Riley didn't recognize was taking a customer's order on the other side of the diner. Riley had to admit her grandmother was right. The uniform was a throwback to the diners of the fifties, even though this diner hadn't been updated since the seventies. The dresses were short-sleeved with white trim and a white collar, along with a hemline that hit above the knee. All of which was fine, but the rest of the dress was a bright shade of Pepto-Bismol-pink.

"Talk about something that needs to be updated. This entire place could use an overhaul." Mimi sat back in her chair, a catty expression on her face. Then she started observing the room. "I'll be right back," she said as she started to roll away from the table.

"Where are you going?"

"To talk to Jasper Mathis. He's lookin' a little lonely over there all by himself." She went over to the old man who was at a small table with only two seats. Riley watched as Mimi rolled right up to him. He seemed more annoyed than glad for Mimi's company.

Anita arrived with the drinks, then pointed her thumb at Mimi and Jasper. "I wonder if there's something going on with those two," she said.

Riley straightened. "Why?"

"Oh, I don't know. It might be the romantic in me, but I think they make a cute couple."

At that moment Jasper frowned at Mimi.

"Ms. McAllister always makes sure to stop by

to say hello to Mr. Mathis if he's sitting alone."

"He doesn't seem all that happy to see her," Riley said.

"I think he's hiding his true feelings." Anita sighed. "Wouldn't it be adorable if they got together?"

"No," Riley blurted. "My grandmother hasn't been interested in anyone since Poppy died thirty years ago."

"Are you sure?"

"She would tell me." Riley was positive her grandmother wouldn't keep a secret like this from her. *Or would she?*

Anita nodded. "Like I said, I'm just overly romantic." She glanced over her shoulder again as Tanner walked out from the kitchen to the counter where the cash register was, a white kitchen towel slung over his shoulder, his long hair pulled back and secured in a hair net. He crouched and disappeared behind the counter for a second, then stood back up, having retrieved a large silver baking tray, and went back into the kitchen.

Riley would have sworn she heard Anita sigh again.

Mimi was heading back to the table, and Anita stepped aside to let her in her spot across from Riley. "What a delightful man," Mimi said, her words dripping with sarcasm. "All I did was tell him hello, and you would have thought I'd asked him to solve world peace while standing on his head and juggling beach balls."

Mimi took a sip of tea. "Perfect as always, Anita."

"I do my best."

Riley and Mimi gave her their orders—a grilled cheese for Riley and a patty melt for Mimi. As soon as Anita left, Riley whispered, "What's going on between you and Jasper?"

Mimi's eyes widened. "What are you talking about? I just went over there to say hello."

"He was frowning at you."

"I know. He finds me irritating, although I have no idea why." She moved the tea glass over an inch. "Me and Jasper . . . Hoo boy. Oh well, never mind." She looked at Riley, her expression sobering. "There was only one man for me, Riley. No one can replace your Poppy."

Riley nodded. She never knew her grandfather, since he passed away from cancer before Riley was born. But Mimi had made sure Riley knew about him. When she was little, they would pore over photo albums, and Riley would listen to endless stories about Maple Falls back in the fifties and sixties and how Mimi and Poppy had been friends since they were children. The night of their senior prom, Poppy asked her to marry him. Although Riley wasn't big on romance, she had to admit her grandparents' relationship was a romantic one.

While waiting for their food, Riley and Mimi continued discussing the renovations of the house, and Riley mentioned she'd given a budget to Hayden already. "He reminded me that he would give us a discount on supplies if we bought them from Price's," Riley said.

"How nice. And unsurprising. The Prices are good people."

Especially Hayden. The unbidden thought popped into her mind. She couldn't stop thinking about him for more than five minutes, apparently.

Anita soon returned with their lunch, then hurried back to the kitchen. Mimi took a bite of the patty melt and her eyes lit up with delight.

"That Tanner is a good cook," she said around a mouthful. After swallowing, she asked, "When do you want to start work on the house?"

"As soon as possible. You'll have to pick out paint colors—"

"You can do that."

"Okay. Hayden said last night that you need to choose what kind of roof shingles you'd like too."

"Last night?" Mimi's eyebrows shot up faster than a lightning bolt.

Uh-oh. "We, um, kind of had dinner last night. So we could talk about the renovation. Just as friends. I mean, business friends. Business acquaintances." The longer she talked the less convincing she sounded, and she steeled herself for Mimi's inevitable onslaught of questions.

But all she said was, "I'll go with whatever you two recommend."

Riley was surprised, but she wasn't about to ask why she wasn't being nosy. *Just be grateful.*

They finished their lunch and Mimi ordered a slice of coconut cream pie for dessert, declaring, "Mabel makes a mean coconut cream pie." Riley wasn't sure who Mabel was, but she had to be one of the cooks. She ended up splitting the pie with Mimi. After last night's dinner and today's lunch, she definitely needed to go for a run tonight.

As they made their way back to Knots and Tangles, Riley pushing Mimi's wheelchair, clouds filling the sky and giving everyone a slight respite from the heat, she saw Hayden putting a sandwich board in front of Price's. When he finished, he waved in their direction, then walked over.

"Good morning," he said to Mimi first, then looked at Riley. "Or afternoon, I guess."

"Close enough," Mimi said. Then she grabbed her wheels and started to roll away.

"Mimi—"

"I'll meet you at the shop." She raised one hand and waved it at Riley and Hayden. "I need the exercise." She continued rolling herself down the sidewalk.

"I better go after her," Riley said.

"She'll be okay for a few minutes."

Riley turned to him, and when their gazes met, her toes tingled. Which was so corny but true.

"Are you free tonight?" he asked.

She hesitated. They just had supper together last night, and now he wanted to see her again tonight. He'd insisted that they were just friends, but did friends spend this much time together? She realized she didn't have any idea, and that saddened her. She had missed out on more than she'd thought.

"I was going to go for a run tonight. Mimi and I had some of Mabel's coconut cream pie. The calories were worth it, but I don't need my waistline getting any bigger than it is."

His gaze traveled down to her toes, then back up. "Everything about you is perfect to me."

She shivered, despite the balmy temperature. She'd never had a man gaze at her with so much appreciation before. Then she remembered that he had the exact same expression last night when he picked her up at Knots and Tangles. *Oh my* . . .

He took a step back. "Mind if I run with you?"

That brought her back to reality. "I'm really slow."

"I don't mind. I just need to talk to you about something important, and it can't wait. I'd tell you now, but it will take some explaining."

She was intrigued. "All right."

"How about the old trail near the high school?"

"The one by the woods? I haven't been on that trail in forever."

"It's not in great shape, but then again . . ." He shrugged. "We both know that's par for the course in Maple Falls. I'll meet you there around six, okay?"

"Sure."

He grinned. "Thanks, Riley." He turned and jogged across Main Street to the hardware store, then went inside.

Riley walked back to the shop, and it didn't take her long to catch up with Mimi. Her grandmother was a few feet from the door and Riley opened it for her.

"Whew," Mimi said, pushing herself inside. "That was a workout. But I'm glad I did it. Being in this wheelchair has made me lazy."

Riley nodded, still thinking about Hayden. Despite trying to keep her emotions in check around him, she was looking forward to seeing him, and not only because she was curious about what he wanted to discuss. Had he talked to his parents already?

"How's Hayden doing?" Mimi asked, picking up a skein of yarn and examining it as if she'd never seen it before, which was a good possibility.

"He's fine." A pause. "We're going for a run tonight."

"That's nice, dear." Mimi put the yarn back,

then moved to a bin beside the counter. "I think I'll go through the yarn in this one first."

Riley moved over to her, bewildered by her apathy. "You don't sound surprised. Or even interested."

Mimi set a skein of neon-pink-and-purple yarn on the counter and wrinkled her nose. "What was I thinking buying this stuff?" Then she turned to Riley. "I *am* interested, sugar. But I also want to respect your privacy. You have no idea how much I want to pepper you with questions about you and Hayden, but I won't."

"Even if I want to talk about it?"

The skein of horrendous yarn fell out of her hand. "You do?"

"Maybe. A little." She picked up the yarn off the floor and handed it to Mimi, then leaned against the counter. "I'm so confused."

"About Hayden?" When Riley nodded, Mimi said, "Men can be confusing creatures, that's for sure."

"You didn't seem confused about Poppy."

"No, but then again I knew him all my life. We had the same goals and dreams. He didn't mind that I ran the yarn shop, and I was fine with him working at the soft drink factory. All we wanted was to raise a family . . ."

Riley heard the catch in her grandmother's throat. "We don't have to talk about this."

"No, I'm fine." Mimi smiled, but there was a

sheen of tears in her eyes. "Things didn't work out the way we hoped, and that happens. It happens to everyone. But the years I had with your Poppy were the best ones of my life."

"When did you know you were in love with him?"

Mimi touched the yarn in her lap. "Oh, probably fifth grade."

"Fifth grade?" Riley was incredulous. "How can you be in love with someone when you're that young? I mean, really in love."

"I was always precocious for my age."

Riley laughed. "I'm serious, though."

"I know. Back then it was puppy love, obviously. But even when he was a boy, he had a kind soul. He tried to hide it, of course, especially when he became a man. Showing tenderness wasn't a manly thing back then. Yet when we were together, he dropped the tough guy act. He'd pick wildflowers for me from his parents' backyard because he knew I liked them. If he had a candy bar, he always gave me half without me even asking. One day he started carrying my books at school, and then he was doing it every day. Gestures like that showed me he cared, and as we grew older, he continued to do things that made me smile. How could I not love him?"

The bell above the shop door rang, but it was the postman. Mimi talked to him for a few minutes while Riley absorbed what her grandmother had said. It was a good story, but it didn't clear up her feelings for Hayden. She shouldn't have expected it to, but she did like seeing the love in Mimi's eyes when she talked about Poppy.

As soon as the mailman left, Mimi turned to Riley. "Now, tell me why you're confused about Hayden. And don't even think about putting me off, or I'll never give you peace about this again." Her tone was teasing, but the expression in her eyes was serious.

Riley sat on the stool behind the counter and touched one of the keys on the cash register. "I've never had a boyfriend, Mimi."

"That's okay—"

"At eighteen, maybe. Not at twenty-eight." She sighed. "I don't understand relationships or my feelings or how I'm supposed to act around other people."

"Oh, Riley." Mimi rolled her chair around to the back of the counter and held her hand. "I'm so sorry. I should have taught you all those things."

"Tracey should have taught them to me." She pulled her hand from her grandmother's, her heart growing hard as it did when she thought about her mother.

"You're right. She should have." Mimi paused. "What are you feeling about Hayden?"

"I like him. A lot."

Mimi smiled. "There's a lot to like in that young man. He reminds me some of your Poppy. Not in the looks department, although your grandfather was handsome. And sexy—"

"Mimi," Riley warned. "I don't need that level of detail."

"Right. Ahem. Anyway, Hayden is a terrific kid. I don't blame you for liking him. But one of the important things to know about relationships is that it takes time to get to know someone. Focus on getting to know Hayden better, if that's what you want to do. Which I imagine is the case, since you two are going running tonight, you insane people."

Riley chuckled, feeling less pressure. Much like revealing a bit of her past to Hayden helped make her feel better, admitting that she had feelings for him to Mimi was a relief. She was so used to keeping everything inside, she hadn't known how good it felt to share parts of herself with other people she trusted.

"Remember what I said before. I want you to relax and enjoy yourself while you're here. That includes the time you spend with other people, like Hayden and Harper and the other girls. Don't worry beyond that. Okay, sugar?"

"All right." She smiled and took her grandmother's hand. "Thank you, Mimi."

They spent the rest of the afternoon sorting through yarn, and Mimi found more to donate. Most of the skeins and yarn hanks were pretty, and whoever was the recipient would be pleased.

Riley also noticed that Mimi had kept the purple-and-pink yarn.

When they got home later, Mimi settled in her recliner for the evening news with a bowl of SpaghettiOs, which had always been one of her favorite meals. Riley changed into her one pair of clean shorts and a fresh T-shirt. She ate a protein bar on the way to the trail Hayden had mentioned and remembered it was more of a hiking trail than a running one, although Riley had jogged on it when she was younger. When she pulled into the vacant lot by the woods, Hayden was already there, dressed in red shorts and a plain white T-shirt.

Riley's nerves kicked up as she got out of the car, but then she reminded herself of what Mimi had said. *Enjoy yourself.* Still, she wanted to give Hayden another warning.

"Remember, I'm slow."

"You keep saying that, and I'm going to keep telling you that I don't care." He grinned and walked over to her. "Nice evening for a run. What do you think?"

I think you're sexy. Yikes, she almost said that out loud. It was bad enough she was trying not to be obvious about checking him out. She didn't need to enjoy herself that much.

"It's very nice," she managed to say, tucking her thoughts back in her brain.

They started to jog at a slow pace, neither

saying anything. The canopy of trees provided good shade as they jogged. She could feel herself getting breathless, but it felt good. She missed running in beautiful places like this.

Soon Hayden spoke. "Aren't you interested in what I wanted to talk to you about?"

She nodded, ducking under a low tree branch. "I am, but I was waiting for you to start."

"You really aren't pushy, are you?"

"Nope." She glanced at him. "Sorry to disappoint."

"Hardly. That's one of the things I like about you. You give me space. Lately I think I'm the one who's been kinda smothering." Before she could ask him what he meant by that, he said, "This morning I told my parents I want to buy the store."

Riley halted, her chest heaving slightly. "You really went through with it. What did they say?"

"At first they were surprised, of course. Then they told me about their other buyer, which I already knew about. Dad said he and Mom would talk it over." He frowned. "It wasn't the answer I was hoping for. How about we walk the rest of the way?"

Riley smirked. "Don't tell me you're wimping out now. We're only halfway through the trail."

He flashed a grin and dashed off. She laughed and headed after him. It didn't take long to catch up to him, mostly because he wasn't running that fast, and she was running at close to her top speed. Then they were even and started to match pace again.

"I'm surprised your parents even have to think about it," Riley said as they fell into a rhythm.

"See it from their side. All three of their sons had established careers. No one expected me to come back to Maple Falls, much less want to buy the store. They had been making plans for a couple of years now, working slowly toward retiring. Once my brothers and I had decided on our own paths, they knew the store would eventually have to be sold. I'm still not crazy about them not telling me, but I understand."

A thought occurred to her. "I know you said last night that you want to buy the store, but are you sure it's not because you're feeling pressured to?"

"Because of the other buyer?" She nodded, and he said, "Not even a smidge. I'm fully committed to doing this."

The woods led to a small meadow, and the trail wound around the edge of it. When they hit the clearing, Riley looked at the horizon and halted. Some of the clouds that covered the sky earlier in the day were spread around the sunset, and the view was stunning, the warm rays lighting up the wild, green meadow grass. Tiny wildflowers carpeted the field, and the beauty of the scene reached into her soul.

Hayden stood beside her and didn't say

anything for a moment. "What are you thinking about?"

"My grandparents. Wildflowers. The sunset." She sighed and whispered to herself, "Good things."

He took her hand, and it seemed like the most natural thing in the world. They both remained silent, taking in the sunset together.

"We'd probably better head back," he said after a few minutes. "I ran on this trail in the dark once and nearly broke an ankle when I tripped over a tree root." He let go of her hand and moved away.

That was a first. Usually she was the one leaving him. But she didn't mind. She glanced at the meadow one more time before following him.

They finished their run, and when they reached their cars, Hayden opened the back passenger-side door and pulled two water bottles out of a small insulated cooler. Riley had her own water bottle, but she accepted his. After they took a long drink, she said, "I'm not sure why you wanted to tell me about the hardware store tonight and not when I saw you this afternoon. It didn't take you that long to explain what happened."

He tugged on his collar. "I, uh, wanted to see you again."

Riley huffed, then moved closer to him. "Sneaky, Hayden Price."

"A little. You have to admit we both had a good run and a nice talk."

She couldn't help but smile. "Yes, we did. But . . ."

"But what?"

"There has to be a consequence for your action."

He started to back away, half grinning. "I don't like the sound of this."

Before he could get out of reach, she stood on her tiptoes and dumped the rest of her water on top of his head.

"Whoa!" His eyes grew wide. "That's cold!" Then he grinned and took a step toward her. "And refreshing."

The teasing glint in his eyes told her she was next. "No, you don't," she said, turning to dash off.

But he grabbed her around the waist, holding the water bottle above her head. Then he stilled. Droplets dripped from his hair, running down the side of his face and cheeks. One landed on the top of his lip, and she couldn't resist wiping it away.

He held her close to him, water poised above her head, for what seemed like forever. At any moment he would dump the water on her. Her heart slammed in her chest. Why didn't he? She was leaning back from him, which meant he was supporting a good bit of her body weight, but he didn't seem to struggle with it at all.

"Hayden," she whispered.

"Yes?" His eyes didn't leave hers.

The attraction, the desire she saw in his eyes stirred her. Was this part of getting to know Hayden better? She knew it wasn't, not in the casual way she and Mimi had discussed.

No, there was nothing casual about this moment.

Even if she wanted to stop herself, she couldn't . . . and she absolutely did not want to stop. She slid her arms around his neck, threaded her fingers through the damp ends of his hair, and tilted her face to his.

Then she kissed him.

Chapter 13

Hayden couldn't think. He threw the water bottle to the side and pressed Riley against him, accepting the gift of her kiss while trying to hold himself back. It wasn't easy, but he managed, letting her take the lead as she explored his mouth with hers. Heaven. This was pure heaven.

When she eventually pulled away, he searched her face, unsure what to expect. Her kissing him hadn't even been on his radar. He told her the truth about using the talk with his parents about the store as a ruse to see her again, and he'd intended their run to be relaxed and friendly. But holding her in his arms, reeling from a kiss he hadn't wanted to end . . . He had no idea how to react.

"Riley," he murmured.

"I . . ." Her eyes were wide with shock, but she didn't move away. He could also see the satisfaction on her face.

That boosted his ego. "What?" he asked, running the back of his fingers over her hot cheek.

"I'm all sweaty and stinky and—"

"I don't care."

She couldn't face him. "I don't know why I did that." When she started to squirm in his arms, he reluctantly let her go.

"I hope it was because you wanted to." He held his breath, because there was a chance she could devastate him now and not even realize it. When Riley had her guard up, she couldn't be budged.

But that guard was nowhere to be seen. "I don't like being confused. I don't like not understanding how to act or react. But I do like how I feel with you." She shook her head. "You probably think I'm crazy or silly. Or both."

"How about neither? This is new territory for me, too, Riley. I've never felt this way about anyone before."

"Then you're not confused like I am."

"I didn't say that." He put his hands on his waist. "How about we stop analyzing this and just live in the moment? Why don't we just enjoy the time we spend together, without worrying about what comes next?"

She shook her head. "I thought I . . . I'm not sure if I can. Not when I feel this way."

He dropped his hands and went to her, tilting her chin so he could meet her gaze. "Do you want to try?"

To his surprise, she put her hand on his but didn't move it away. "Yes. I do."

Hayden kissed her forehead, then looked at her again. "Thank you."

"For what?"

He smiled. "For being you."

She scoffed. "Yes, because I'm such a prize."

"You are to me." He hoped she wouldn't think the words were too much, but he meant what he'd said. They couldn't keep going around in circles like this. They both liked each other and wanted to spend time together. It shouldn't be that complicated.

Her gaze softened. "Thank you." Then she surprised him again. "Come over for supper Saturday night after the softball game."

"To talk about the house?" When she nodded, he felt the sting of disappointment. It disappeared when she added, "Maybe we could play cards or something too."

"That sounds great." He grinned, then walked over and picked up his discarded water bottle. "I'll be over as soon as I shower and change after the game."

Riley nodded, and then got into her car. He waited until she drove away before he started grinning like an idiot. Saturday evening couldn't get there fast enough.

As soon as Riley pulled out of the parking lot, she put in her earphones and called Melody. "You won't believe this," she said as soon as her friend picked up.

"And hello to you too. Hang on. Let me turn

283

down the TV." A few seconds later, she said, "All right, lay it on me."

"I kissed Hayden."

Silence. "Who's Hayden?"

Riley had been so caught up in her excitement about him that she'd forgotten she never told Melody about him. She quickly got her friend up to speed.

"And you kissed him," Melody said.

"Yes." Riley grinned with pride.

"Have you never kissed a guy before, Riley?" she asked, her tone tinted with shock.

"I've *been* kissed." Even by Hayden, but she wasn't going to mention that or her friend would be even more confused, not to mention offended that she was only hearing about all this now. "But *I've* never kissed anyone. Until now."

"If you weren't the one telling me this, I would find that hard to believe."

"What is that supposed to mean? That was kind of insulting."

"It wasn't meant to be. I'm glad you let loose enough to kiss him." She chuckled. "Was it good?"

"Very. And that's all I'm saying."

Melody laughed again. "I haven't had a conversation like this since junior high. And no, that's not an insult either."

Riley turned down her grandmother's street. "I just needed to tell someone—someone who doesn't live in Maple Falls. If I told anyone here, it would be in the newspaper by morning." She remembered how Harper said she and the girls wanted a full report. She'd tell them something the next time she saw them, but she wasn't ready for them to know about this. She'd done more gut spilling in the last few days than she had in her entire life, and she wasn't used to it.

"Then you like this guy, huh?" Melody asked.

"Yes." Now that she was allowing herself to feel the emotions Hayden brought out in her, she was filled with happiness.

"Do you think it might be going somewhere?"

Melody's question tempered her joy. "I don't know. Right now I don't care." She pulled into Mimi's driveway. "I just want to be happy, you know?"

"Yes, I do. I'm glad you're finally letting yourself enjoy life."

Riley sat in the car and talked to Melody for the next twenty minutes as they caught each other up on what was going on in their lives. Melody had an audition for an off-off-Broadway play that she felt good about, and she and Charlie were still getting along as roommates.

"I miss you," Melody said. "But if being back in Maple Falls is what it takes to make you happy, then I'm glad you're there."

Riley opened her mouth to correct her but decided against it. In spite of what had just happened, she hadn't changed her mind about going back to New York, but she didn't want to think about leaving right now. She remembered what Hayden had said about living in the moment. That idea was foreign to her. She usually spent so much time thinking about the future and how what she did in the present affected that future, that she didn't take time to enjoy anything. Now that she knew what it was like to slow down, set aside her worries, and have a good time, she was willing to try.

Not just for Hayden, but for herself as well.

For the next three weeks, Riley put in ten-hour days between working at the yarn store and helping Hayden rehab Mimi's house. By the middle of June, Knots and Tangles looked like a completely different store. The walls were painted crisp white, as were the wooden shelving units and cubbies. The shelves lined the two walls and were filled with a colorful array of hanks, skeins, and balls of yarn. Riley had repainted the checkout counter a soft sage green, and next to it she'd installed a pegboard, painted it the same color as the walls, and hung a variety of packages containing knitting needles, crochet hooks, stitch markers, and other yarnish novelties.

She was most proud of the center of the shop. She'd gone to a variety of local thrift and antique stores and hit a couple of flea markets with Bea. She found four mismatched armchairs upholstered in various shades of light purple that somehow all went together. An oval, wood-topped coffee table with a brass pedestal sat atop a faded sage-green area rug with off-white curlicues, completing the gathering space she had envisioned. The Man Chair had to stay, of course, and was positioned by one of the picture windows. She'd set up a table near it where shoppers could help themselves to coffee and water. Riley wanted to get rid of the lime-green couch, but Mimi put her foot down. They compromised by keeping the couch in the back room.

While the shop was in the rehab process the last three Thursdays, the Bosom Buddies had met at different houses. Tonight, however, they would see the finished results of Riley's hard work, and she couldn't wait.

This would be the second Thursday BB gathering she'd attended since returning to Maple Falls. Being surrounded by all the yarn and knitting and crochet supplies made her want to pick up the hobby again. She'd been thinking of ways she could incorporate different motifs into the art Mimi had commissioned.

Riley was putting out a tray of mini cheesecakes on the front counter, specially ordered from a bakery in Malvern, when Bea and Myrtle walked into the shop fifteen minutes early.

"Oh my." Bea pressed her pudgy hands against both her plump cheeks. "Riley, you have outdone yourself."

"Is this Knots and Tangles?" Myrtle marveled as her gaze traveled over the store. "It's beautiful. When I came back from my cruise two weeks ago, I thought you had performed a miracle in this place, but now . . ." She went to Riley and gave her a warm hug, much like she had when she saw Riley for the first time after returning from vacation.

"Isn't it?" Mimi came out from the back, limping with her cane. She'd only needed the crutches for less than a week before switching to the electric-blue cane she now used.

Riley was thankful her grandmother was almost healed, but it also signaled that her departure wasn't too far away. She refused to think about that now. Instead, she was going to enjoy the happiness and camaraderie of the Bosom Buddies tonight, a lesson she had learned not only from her grandmother and each of these women, but also from her budding friendships with Harper, Olivia, and Anita, whom she always met for lunch after church on Sunday.

Harper and her mother had a strained relationship, Anita was hopelessly in love with Tanner, who didn't seem to know she existed, and Olivia was working on her second master's, this one in American Southern literature. Riley still played her emotions close to her chest and hadn't mentioned Hayden too much. She also made sure not to sit with him at church, and he'd agreed. Neither wanted to inspire any small-town gossip.

As each of the BBs entered the shop, they all expressed their amazement. Even Madge, whom Riley had learned was extremely picky and critical about almost everything.

"This is stunning, Riley." Madge looked around the store as the rest of the women sat down, their project bags in hand. "So fresh and tidy and welcoming."

Riley blushed. "Thank you. That's what we were going for."

"We? This is all you, sugar," Mimi said, beaming with pride from her seat across the room. "I just approved the colors."

"And gave me the inspiration." She smiled and walked over to the group, then put her hand on Mimi's shoulder. Mimi covered Riley's with her own.

Tonight's group project was knitting and crocheting hats for chemo patients at the various hospitals in central Arkansas. Riley was pleased to see that the patterns weren't plain but had creative touches that made them special. As the women started to work, she joined them with a crochet hook and started her hat. Riley had grown to appreciate her grandmother's friends' loyalty and support, and not just as a member of a needle group. These women were Mimi's family, and Riley's by extension.

"I'm impressed with what you've done with the outside too," Peg said, her needles flying fast as she knitted with, surprisingly, the neon-pink-and-purple yarn Mimi had saved from the donation bin. "I love the blue you painted the facade."

"Hayden helped with that," Riley said, crocheting four chains with her flax-colored yarn.

The women stopped and looked at her.

"He did, did he?" Bea asked, pursing her lips.

"Now, you gals don't start." Mimi pointed her crochet hook at each of them. "Hayden is also working on my house. He's a very talented young man."

"We all knew that." Viola grinned. "We just didn't know he was so chummy with you and Riley."

"We're friends," Riley said quickly, then pulled too tight on the magic ring and had to undo it.

"Friends," Gwen said, winking at Mimi.

Mimi shook her crochet hook at them. "Y'all are incorrigible."

"Why yes, we are." Bea grinned. "And you love us in spite of it."

The women laughed and then began to discuss the upcoming Fourth of July picnic at church.

Hayden had been dropping hints to the mayor about restarting the Too Dang Hot Parade next year, but Riley didn't think he'd been taken seriously yet. He wasn't going to give up, though. They'd talked about it the other night as they sanded down the shutters he'd taken off the front of Mimi's house.

"Since I'm still in negotiations for the hardware store, I haven't had time to press the issue," he'd said.

His father had accepted the initial offer for the store, so they were working with Henry to figure out how to get out of the deal by compensating the buyer. So far nothing had worked, but Hayden remained optimistic. *"I can't imagine we won't come to an agreement at some point,"* he'd said. *"I'm not one to back away from a challenge."*

Riley smiled to herself as she continued to crochet. She knew firsthand how stubborn and persistent Hayden could be.

The next two hours she concentrated on her work, chiming in occasionally when one of the BBs asked her a question or drew her into their conversation. She was half finished with her pattern when the evening ended. Bea offered to take Mimi home when Riley said she wanted to stay awhile longer and do some straightening up.

As soon as everyone had left, Hayden opened the back door and poked his head in.

"Is it safe?" he asked, his gaze darting dramatically around the empty shop.

"If you're asking if the BBs left, they did."

He walked into the store, and as usual Riley

took time to watch him. Even the simple act of walking showed off his athletic grace, coupled with his fit body. She still had difficulty keeping her eyes off him. Tonight a lightness was also in his steps, and when she met his eyes, she saw excitement.

"You're happy," she said as she moved toward him from behind the counter.

"I'm always happy to see you." He stopped close to her, and she anticipated the light kiss he always gave her when he was sure they were alone. Instead, he leaned against the counter and stared at her, still grinning.

"I get the feeling there's something else going on."

"You would be right about that." Suddenly he picked her up and whirled her around before setting her lightly on her feet. "I'm now the proud, and happy, owner of Price's Hardware store."

Riley squealed. "They let the store go?"

He nodded. "Finally." He took her hand. "Let's celebrate. I bought a bottle of champagne when my parents agreed to let me buy the store, and it's been sitting in the fridge at home. I also want to show you something else—"

The bell above the door jingled. Hayden dropped her hand, and they both turned to see who had come in.

"We're closed," Riley said, then froze.

"Even to me?"

A sickening feeling jolted in her stomach. *After all these years* . . .

"Riley?" Hayden whispered, searching her face. "Are you okay? You turned kind of pale."

Riley couldn't move, couldn't speak. All she could do was stand there and stare at the woman she hadn't seen since she was thirteen years old. The woman she'd hoped never to see again. Tracey. *My mother.*

Chapter 14

R iley?" Hayden grabbed Riley's shoulders, then glanced at the woman who had walked into the store. He had no idea who she was, but her presence clearly unnerved Riley. He turned to Riley again. "Talk to me, honey."

"Hey, Riley."

Riley stiffened and her complexion drained completely.

"You lookin' good, baby. New York must be treatin' you real well."

Riley came to life and brushed past Hayden as she stormed toward the woman.

"What are you doing here?" Her voice shook. "You said you'd never come back when you took off with your boyfriend of the week. Remember? Because I do. I will never forget you sayin' that was the last time I'd ever see you again."

The woman flinched and licked her cracked lips. Her expression turned impassive. "I suppose I deserve that."

"You *suppose?*" Riley's tone turned tight. "That's all you have to say?"

Hayden could see Riley was losing her composure. He moved to stand next to her. To his surprise, she gripped his hand.

The woman flipped her nearly waist-length

brown hair, which was on the thin side, over her slim shoulder. Now that he was closer to her, Hayden could see that she'd lived a rough life. Her leathery skin was full of wrinkles, especially around her mouth. There were uneven streaks of gray in her hair, and she reeked of cigarette smoke. But there was something he recognized about her too. Her eyes. They were just like Riley's.

"I'll come back when you can be civil to me," the woman said, leveling her gaze at Riley.

"Go ahead and leave. That's what you do best, isn't it?" Riley snarled.

The woman shot out of the store, the door clicking shut behind her.

Riley's entire body began to shake as she let go of Hayden's hand. When she started to hyperventilate, Hayden hurried to lock the door and turn off the lights. The back storeroom gave off enough illumination, and he guided her there. He didn't want any passersby—or even worse, a busybody—to see her in distress.

"I'm sorry," she said in between gulps of air. "I—"

"Don't apologize." He took in a deep breath, knowing he had to be careful with what he said while she was in such a fragile state. "Was that your mother?"

Her eyes filled with confused vulnerability. "That was Tracey. Calling her *mother* is a big stretch." She shook her head and slumped onto one of the three chairs in the storeroom. "I can't believe she came back. After all this time . . ."

He sat next to her, staying silent. What could he say? She hadn't mentioned her past since the last time they were right here in the back room of Knots and Tangles, when she had talked a little bit about her mother. Since then, their conversations had stayed firmly planted in the present, although he was itching to talk to her about the future— their future—at some point. Definitely not now.

"She looks awful, doesn't she?" Riley shook her head. "Hard to believe she's only forty-three."

That shocked him. "Really?"

Riley nodded. "She had me when she was fifteen. She had already dropped out of high school by then, and Mimi sent her to live with Mimi's older sister when she was pregnant. I always assumed it was because she was impossible to deal with." She hugged her arms and leaned forward. "I never knew who my dad was. I'm not sure Tracey even knows."

Hayden nodded, rubbing his palms back and forth over the hem of his cargo shorts. But for Riley not to know who her father was . . . He couldn't imagine how she felt about that.

"Why did she come back?" Riley shook her head. "Never mind. I don't want to know. I cut her out of my life when she cut me out of hers."

She seemed to be speaking to an invisible

person in front of her instead of Hayden. When she shot out a string of curse words, he reached for her hand. He'd never heard her curse before.

"I'll take you home," he said.

"I've got Mimi's car." She yanked her hand out of his grip.

Dread filled him. Her walls were flying back up. "I'm still taking you home."

Riley shook her head and sat up straight. "I'm fine. I can drive."

Hayden knelt in front of her. "I know you can. I also know that you aren't fine right now, and that's why I'm taking you home."

"I guess arguing with you would be pointless?"

"Totally. I've learned from the best." He hoped to get at least a partial smile, but all he got was a hard glare.

She stood, her legs unsteady as she got her purse and turned out the back-room lights. They walked to the small parking lot behind the building, and he held out his hand for her keys. Soon they were on the road back to Erma's.

After pulling in the driveway, he cut off the engine. "I can stay if you want."

Riley shook her head, hands clenched in her lap. "Mimi and I have to talk. I'm sure Tracey will show up on her doorstep soon. Probably with both hands out." She turned to Hayden. "How will you get home?"

"I'll take your car and pick you up in the morning before the store opens."

"Right. That makes sense. Sorry, I'm not thinking clearly."

"Don't worry about it." He started to get out and open the door for her, like she'd always let him since their supper at the steakhouse. But she had the door open before he could move.

Then she leaned over and kissed him. Soft, yearning. He could taste her pain. After she pulled away, she scrambled out of the car and ran into the house.

Hayden touched his mouth, stunned and devastated by her kiss. They had kissed a few times since their run on the trail three weeks ago. With that time being the exception, he was always the initiator. Her kiss tonight held a sense of finality, and that scared him.

He stayed until she went inside. Then he leaned back against the driver's seat. This evening hadn't turned out like he'd hoped. He'd envisioned them breaking open the champagne and enjoying some time together. But it wasn't toasting his success that he'd anticipated. It was the place where they would've had the toast that would have made the moment special.

He blew out a long breath. That would have to wait, and for once he was fine with waiting. He was more concerned about Riley right now. He was glad she intended to talk to Erma about

Tracey showing up out of nowhere. That was a step in the right direction, instead of her usual tendency to clam up.

He'd seen changes in Riley over the last couple weeks, changes that made her even more desirable to him than before—and she'd been very desirable then. It was as if he'd been witnessing the blossoming of Riley McAllister. He prayed her mother's appearance wouldn't shut her down permanently.

Riley halted in the small alcove after walking through Mimi's front door and tried to catch her breath. She'd never been knocked sideways so hard before. Seeing her mother after fifteen years . . . She still couldn't comprehend it fully. One question kept hammering her brain: *Why now?*

"Riley?" Mimi called from the living room. "Is that you? Because if it isn't, I've got two baseball bats in my hands, and I'll beat the living daylights out of whoever you are."

"It's me." Riley stepped into the living room.

"Oh, thank the Lord. Not that anyone's ever broke into this house in sixty years, but there's always that one chance." She glanced at the baseball bat leaning against the wall by her recliner. Riley had never seen it moved out of that position. "I'd hate to have to back up my threat."

Riley nodded, knowing her grandmother was

half joking. She should probably have a talk with her about installing a home security system at some point. Wow, she just saw Tracey and she was thinking about security systems? How messed up was that?

"Riley, sugar." Mimi pulled the lever on the side of her recliner and the footrest snapped shut. "You look like you've seen a ghost."

She sat on the couch and hugged her arms again. How was she supposed to tell Mimi that her wayward daughter had returned? Then again, Mimi had always appreciated straightforwardness. "Tracey's in town."

Mimi's eyes grew wide, and she sucked in a breath. "When? How?"

"She stopped by Knots after you left." Riley explained what had happened, including Hayden's presence. "I couldn't believe it, Mimi."

Her grandmother's lips pressed into a thin line. "I can't either. Did she say where she was staying? How long she would be here?"

"No, and I didn't ask her." She squeezed her arms tightly. "I don't care either."

They sat in silence for the next few moments. "There's nothing we can do about it tonight," Mimi said, her expression still hard.

"Do you think she'll stop by here?"

"I don't know. When it comes to her, I never know." She stood and grabbed her cane. "Thanks for giving me the heads-up. I'm going to bed."

301

Riley nodded as she looked at Mimi again. She hadn't seen her grandmother this upset since the last time Tracey was around.

She wished she had the strength to comfort her, but right now she couldn't do anything but sit here and try to balance her own emotions, and she was failing at that too. Every bit of anxiety and anger and depression she'd experienced when she lived with her mother bubbled to the surface. After only a few seconds around Tracey, she was that scared, helpless little girl again, the one she had tried so hard to keep tucked inside.

Now she threatened to break through the surface—and Riley had no idea how to stop her.

Erma sat at the edge of the bed, frozen. She didn't want to believe what Riley had told her, but she knew her granddaughter was speaking the truth. The only thing that would upset Riley this much was seeing her mother again.

She pressed her lips together. She couldn't believe Tracey had gone back on her word. Then again, why should she be surprised? Her daughter had been a source of heartache almost since the day she came into Erma's life. She and Gus thought they knew what they were in for when they'd adopted her at nine months old after discovering they couldn't have children of their own. They were warned that she had attachment issues due to her neglectful birth mother, but they'd thought they could overcome all that with enough love, care, attention, and prayer. As it turned out, they couldn't.

Tracey had done one good thing in her life—having Riley. Somehow, despite her erratic childhood, Riley had turned out amazing. Erma loved her with all her heart.

She still loved Tracey too.

Erma got up and limped to the window, pulling the curtains to the side. It was dark in her backyard, but she could see the shadows of the stack of mulch Hayden brought over two days ago in preparation for him and Riley to redo the flower beds on Saturday since they had a bye week in the softball league. The season was almost over, and the team was at .500, thanks to another team forfeiting a game a week ago, but from all accounts the players had enjoyed playing, and the church members had been faithful in attending the games, include Erma.

She leaned her forehead against the warm window. *Tracey, honey. What are you doing?* Was it too much to hope that her daughter might have finally straightened out her life? That her return meant she was ready to settle down and become a functioning member of society? Had she at least gotten clean from the drugs and alcohol that had plagued her since she was thirteen?

"How many times have I hoped for that?" Erma

whispered. "How many times have I prayed she would be whole?"

Those prayers had multiplied during the past month when Tracey had contacted her twice by phone, wanting to reestablish their relationship. Erma had been firm about her boundaries—Tracey had to prove she was not only clean but also willing to change. Until then she wasn't welcome back in her home. *Maybe my prayers have finally been answered.*

Erma wasn't sure how long she stood at the window, but her leg started to ache, and that was the sign that she needed to get off it and prop it up. She dressed in her pajamas and eased into bed, foregoing her nightly devotional reading, and instead turning off the light and closing her eyes. She knew sleep would be elusive tonight, and it wasn't just because Tracey was here.

What if she tells Riley the truth? Will my granddaughter ever forgive me?

Chapter 15

Hayden arrived at Erma's the next morning and knocked on the back door, knowing Riley and Erma ate breakfast together in the kitchen every morning. When he didn't hear anyone answer, he knocked again, then turned the doorknob. The door opened, and he walked inside. The kitchen was empty, the coffee pot too. He frowned. He would have to remind the women that they needed to lock their doors at night. But now wouldn't be the time.

He paused, wondering what he should do. Then he decided he could at least make coffee. By the time it finished brewing, Erma had limped into the kitchen with her cane, looking bleary-eyed and more than a little surprised to see him sitting at the table.

"Hello," she said, frowning. "Did Riley let you in?"

"Um, no." Now he questioned whether he'd done the right thing or not. "The door was unlocked."

"Ah. I guess I forgot to lock it last night."

At least he knew she did usually lock the doors. "Hope you don't mind that I made coffee."

"Mind? I'm grateful." She hobbled over to the counter and hooked her cane over the edge, then pulled two mugs from the cabinet. "I'm assuming you want some?"

"Please."

A few minutes later, she had joined Hayden at the table, and steaming mugs of fresh brew sat in front of them. "Thank you for bringing Riley home last night. I wouldn't have wanted her to drive after seeing Tracey. Her relationship with her mother is complicated."

"I got that impression." He took a sip of coffee but didn't inquire further. Usually Erma was a chatterbox, but her drawn, worried expression concerned him.

"Has she told you anything about Tracey?" Erma asked.

Hayden shook his head. "Not much, other than they moved around a lot when she was little."

"That's putting it mildly." Erma sighed. "My daughter has issues. I'm thankful she hasn't passed them down to Riley. But Tracey's inconsistent parenting has influenced her. It was unavoidable." She pushed away her mug. "I also made a lot of mistakes. Mistakes that have turned into regrets."

While he couldn't relate to what Erma was saying, since he'd never been a parent, he did remember what Doug, his counselor, had said when Hayden was down on himself.

"'We can only do our best with what we have to work with at the time,'" Hayden said.

Erma's head jerked up and she smirked. "That's quite profound. Did you read that on the internets?"

"Nope. A wise person told me. Over and over and over." He lifted his mug and tilted it a bit toward her. "It's pretty set in my noggin."

"I need to set it in mine."

Riley came shuffling into the kitchen, her hair wild around her face, as if she'd spent the night tossing and turning. The tank top and shorts she was wearing left little to the imagination—which got his imagination shifting gears and humming. He averted his gaze.

"Ahem," Erma said. "Hayden's here."

Riley's eyes widened. She glanced down at herself, then at Hayden, her cheeks heating. "Be right back." She dashed out of the kitchen, and he could hear her running up the stairs.

"Anyway, you were saying?" Erma lifted the mug to her lips.

"I, uh." What had he been saying?

Erma chuckled, sounding a little more like her usual self. "At least you had the good grace to look away. What a polite young man you are, Hayden Price."

"I try to be." Now if he could just get the image of Riley in a thin tank top out of his mind, his thoughts would be polite too.

A few minutes later, Riley entered the kitchen again, this time fully dressed in a red T-shirt and shorts. She was pulling her hair into a ponytail as she joined them at the table.

"Sorry," she mumbled, dark circles under her eyes.

"I'll start breakfast," Erma said.

"I'll do it." Riley started to stand.

"You stay right there, sugar. It's my turn to cook this morning, remember?"

Riley nodded, then asked Hayden, "How long have you been here?"

"Long enough for coffee." He paused. "How did you sleep last night?"

"Horribly, no surprise." She leaned her forearms against the table.

"I filled the car with gas on my way over here," Hayden said.

"Thank you." Erma pulled out a cast-iron frying pan from the lower cabinet next to the stove. "Do you like bacon and eggs, Hayden?"

"Of course."

"I'd whip up some homemade biscuits, but I don't want you to be late for work." The pan clanged as she placed it on the stovetop.

"I'll take a biscuit rain check, then."

While Erma started cooking, Riley got up and fixed herself a cup of coffee and set it on the table. Without asking, she picked up Hayden's and refilled it, too, then set it down in front of him.

"Thanks," he said, reaching for the sugar bowl on the table.

She nodded, but he could see she was deep in her own thoughts. She refilled Erma's cup, too, then sat back down, the faraway expression still in her eyes.

The bacon and eggs didn't take long for Erma to prepare, and soon Hayden was presented with a delicious breakfast. They ate in silence, both women in their own worlds. For some reason Hayden wasn't uncomfortable with the silence. He wished he knew how to help them, as he had grown to care deeply about Erma too. But this was something he couldn't fix, or even attempt to. All he could do was be there for them when they needed him.

"Go on to work, Riley," Erma said when they finished eating. "I'll clean up."

She nodded. "Let me brush my teeth and I'll be right back down."

After Riley left, Erma turned to Hayden. "I can't tell you how much it means to me that she has you," she said, tears shining in her eyes. "Especially now."

He nodded. "I'm not going anywhere, Erma. Whatever she needs, I'm here."

Erma smiled and patted his hand. "Thank you," she whispered.

Riley returned, and a short while later they pulled into the parking lot behind the yarn store. Much like last night, Hayden cut the engine and turned to her.

"If you need me, just holler," he said. "I'm right across the street."

She turned to him and nodded. "Thank you, Hayden."

He gave her the keys, and then they both got out of the car and he waited until she unlocked the shop and walked inside. He didn't want to leave her, but he had to admit she seemed much better today than she'd been last night, which gave him a bit of freedom to focus on his job. His father was ready to transition the store to him, and Hayden wanted to start today.

His store. He still couldn't believe it. He was so thrilled to be the owner. He was more excited about the future than he'd ever been while playing ball. Then again, his future had always been uncertain when he was a ballplayer, despite how hard he worked and how dedicated he was. He still had the work ethic and dedication, and now he could transfer it to something stable. Stability had become important to him, and he was starting to see it was also something Riley needed, even if she didn't know it.

Maybe one day she'd allow him to give that to her.

Riley turned the sign on the yarn shop door to Open, then went back to the counter. She had decided when she woke up that morning, exhausted from a rough night's sleep, that she had to put Tracey out of her mind. Surely her mother had gotten the message that Riley didn't want her around. Even if Tracey had decided to come back to Maple Falls permanently, it wouldn't last. How many times had Riley heard the same thing from her mother, that this would be their forever home? Forever only lasted two weeks, or maybe a month. One special time it meant half a year, but nothing more than that. Tracey never stuck to her promises. Now wouldn't be any different.

Business was slow this morning and, desperate for a distraction, she thought about the back storeroom, then remembered Lorri, the customer who came in a few weeks ago who owned a yarn store in Malvern. She'd talked about her yarn-dyeing business, and Riley had considered it off and on while she was redoing the shop. She had also been pondering the art pieces she promised her grandmother. Dyeing her own fiber would not only be fun but would also make her art more unique. She decided to call Lorri that afternoon and arrange a time to visit her and learn about the process.

Later that morning, two women Riley wasn't familiar with walked into the store. Their reactions bolstered her mood.

"I haven't been here in years," one told Riley as she paid for several hundred dollars of yarn for various projects. "I just happened to mention to Susan that it was time to check out this place again. We live in Hot Springs Village, so it's not that far to travel." She looked around the shop again. "It's so different from what I remembered."

"We just remodeled."

"Oh. Are you the new owner?"

Riley paused, a tiny bit of disappointment tugging at her heart. "No. I'm her granddaughter, but I'm helping run the shop for a little while."

"Well, you're doing a wonderful job." The woman smiled, revealing shiny white teeth that were either dentures or veneers. From her advanced age, Riley thought they were the former. "Have you thought about advertising in our Village paper? We have two groups of knitters and crocheters that meet periodically. I know they would love to check out the changes here." Her friend nodded, pushing her fluffy gray hair back with her tortoiseshell reading glasses.

"That's a good idea. I'll check into it."

After they left, Riley wrote herself a note to talk to Mimi about advertising. That led her to the idea of having a grand reopening, maybe later this summer. Then in the fall they could—

She wouldn't be here in the fall. The shop might not be either if Mimi had been serious about her desire to sell the place. The renovations on her house were nearly done. The roofer had finished up last week, and all she and Hayden had left were some cosmetic touches. The job that had seemed overwhelming at first had gone smoothly and quickly, thanks to Hayden, who not only knew a lot about rehabbing a house but was also organized and precise.

A wave of sadness consumed her, nearly taking her breath away. The reality of leaving slammed into her. She had talked to Melody a few times over the past three weeks, and her friend was expecting her to come back. Charlie had found a new apartment and would be moving sometime this month. Riley wouldn't leave her roommate high and dry.

But the thought of leaving Mimi tore at her heart. They had gotten so close, even closer than they'd been before. Their relationship was different now that Riley was an adult, and while she still saw Mimi as her grandmother, she also saw her as her best friend. She'd also grown closer to Harper and Anita and Olivia and the Bosom Buddies and even had friendly interactions with the softball players. While she still wasn't the assistant coach, she was the chief water girl, making sure everyone had enough to drink during and after the games.

Then there was Hayden. Her chest squeezed even harder. She would have to leave him too. He had just bought his father's store, and he had grand plans for revitalizing Maple Falls. She wouldn't even think of asking him to go with her. He wouldn't agree to it anyway. They were friends, with a few romantic benefits. Not boyfriend and girlfriend. Not lovers, although she often dreamed that they were. They hadn't even gone public with their relationship.

She would leave Hayden behind, like she would leave the others. Her home, her life, was in New York. More importantly, New York was safe. She had no connections, no ties other than Melody. *No chances of getting hurt.*

Another customer arrived, and Riley turned her attention to work, spending the rest of the day helping the few customers who visited the shop and discovering she was a halfway decent salesperson when she wasn't trying to sell her own work.

But when she was alone, she was a wreck.

"I'm right across the street." Hayden's words echoed in her mind, and more than once she nearly went to him, knowing he would give her the comfort she denied herself. But she forced herself to stay put. Riley McAllister had always handled her own personal business. This time wasn't any different.

As soon as five o'clock arrived, she closed up and hurried to Mimi's car. When she got behind the wheel, she turned on the engine and waited for the air conditioner to kick in as her shoulders relaxed. She hadn't realized how tense she was all day. How every time the bell rang over the door, she expected Tracey to walk in again. But she hadn't, and Riley took that as a sign that her mother had left Maple Falls again. Soon it would be her turn.

Her cell phone started to ring as she pulled out of the parking lot. She glanced at the screen. Hayden. She knew she should answer it, but she couldn't talk to him right now. Just seeing his name made her reconsider leaving, and she couldn't afford to do that. She tossed the phone on the passenger seat and headed home.

That Sunday Hayden sat in his usual seat at church—fifth pew from the front, right side, at the end of the row near the middle aisle. He tried to focus on the upcoming service, but all he'd been able to think about was Riley. She'd been distant, first ignoring his calls on Friday, then barely saying anything Saturday when they worked on the flower beds together. When he offered to take her out to dinner that evening, she declined, saying she had to work on one of the art pieces she'd promised Erma. He left Erma's deeply disappointed.

The disappointment hadn't abated much, but he tried tempering it with logic. She was still reeling about her mother, and he needed to remember that. He'd already suspected she might close in on herself anyway, so he shouldn't be surprised that she had. His receding well of patience would have to suffice until she worked through this. One thing was for sure, he wasn't going to give up. Hayden Price never threw in the towel on anything unless forced to, like his baseball career, and that had turned into a positive.

The only way Riley was going to get rid of him was if she pushed him too far away—and he was worried she might do just that.

He glanced behind him, relieved to see her sitting there with the Three Musketeers, as he called Olivia, Harper, and Anita. At least she had come to church, which was a good thing. Erma was with her BBs, which was also good. He was glad they had people in their lives to support them.

Tanner slid next to him on the pew. Hayden glanced at him and noticed his ponytail tied up in a bun and white gauges gleaming in his ears. That edgy style contrasted with the red-and-white gingham shirt and khaki pants he wore.

"Anyone sitting here?" he asked.

Hayden shook his head and scooted over.

"Good." Tanner settled in the seat. "I thought maybe, you know."

"Know what?"

"You were saving this seat for Riley."

Hayden pointed his thumb in the direction behind him. "She sits there."

"Oh. It's been a while since I've been in church. Didn't realize there was assigned seating."

Smirking, Hayden shook his head. "Technically there isn't, but everyone knows there really is."

Tanner leaned over and whispered, "So, you and Riley. What's going on there?"

"We're friends." He stared straight ahead. Tanner normally wasn't so nosy.

"Just friends?"

"Yes." Hayden clenched his jaw.

"Good. So you won't mind if I ask her out?"

Hayden shot him a deadly look.

Tanner chuckled and held up his hands. "I'm kidding, I'm kidding. I also got close to the truth, apparently."

Jesse started playing guitar, and Hayden was glad for the interruption because he was ready to throttle Tanner, which was not appropriate church behavior. Tanner was still grinning when Jesse finished the worship song. He was about to start another when a low murmuring started in the crowd.

Tanner glanced around. "What's going on?" he asked Hayden, as everyone focused their gazes at the back of the church.

"I don't know." But when Hayden twisted around in his seat, his stomach dropped. Walking into church, head held high, was Tracey McAllister.

Hayden spun around and saw Riley staring straight ahead, iciness returning to her eyes.

Uh-oh. He glanced at Erma, who was gripping Bea's arm. Double uh-oh. If he were a cursing man, he would have been thinking much worse.

Riley forced herself not to let her mother bother her. Tracey had walked straight to the front row and sat down, passing everyone else in the church, some who might have recognized her, despite her hard life having erased any semblance of the youth she had when she left Maple Falls. She crossed her legs and set her purse next to her, as if she were as much of a fixture on Sunday mornings as the Bosom Buddies were.

Gripping the edge of the pew, Riley yanked her gaze from her. Tracey was doing this on purpose, disturbing the service and drawing attention to herself in the most dramatic way possible. Riley didn't know why, and she didn't care what her reasons were. She wasn't going to give her mother the satisfaction of bothering her. But as soon as the service was over, she was getting out of this building.

Before Jared could say amen to the final prayer, Riley slid out of the pew and dashed outside, heading straight for Mimi's car. Her stomach churned. Being outside in the hot, sticky air contributed to her nausea. But she'd rather be out here than inside with her.

She turned her back to the church, fishing for the key in her purse. She found it and opened the driver's side door, then got inside, put the air conditioner on full blast, and slammed the door. As soon as she started to put the car in reverse, she saw Hayden rush out of the church and run toward her.

She gripped the gear shift. She'd been an absolute jerk to him yesterday and had outright ignored him the day before. Which was wrong. But she couldn't help it. Her mother showing up reminded her of how this would end. The same as everything ended—with Riley getting hurt.

Hayden tapped on the window. She hesitated before pressing the button and rolling it down. "What?"

He blinked. "Let's go."

She frowned. "Go where?"

"I'll tell you." He rounded the car and got into the passenger's seat. "Drive."

"Where—"

"Just trust me, okay?"

She put the car in Reverse, and they left. Then she gasped. "Mimi! I left her at church."

"Don't worry about her," Hayden said. "She's a grown woman. She'll find a ride home."

Knowing her grandmother had her pick of personal taxi drivers, she followed Hayden's directions until they came to a dirt road right at the edge of Maple Falls. She trusted him, but she was annoyed that he wouldn't leave her alone.

"Where are we?" she snapped, wishing she'd

driven off as soon as she saw him coming out of the church.

"You'll see in about half a mile."

Her hands ached from gripping the steering wheel so hard as she continued driving. Finally he told her to slow down, then to stop in front of a house and small barn that were both leaning in an alarming way.

She threw the car into Park and turned to him. "All right, Hayden. What's going on?"

He looked at her, but his characteristic twinkle and cheerful expression were missing. "I saw Tracey walk into church."

She crossed her arms. "So did everyone else."

"I figured you'd want to get away. This was as good a place as any."

"Which is?"

He stared straight ahead at the questionable buildings in front of him. "My house." He opened the passenger door. "Come on, I'll show you around."

She paused as he got out of the car. This was the place he'd assured her he could fix up by himself? He was the most optimistic person she'd ever known, but clearly he had bitten off more than he should have. All she wanted to do was go back to Mimi's and be alone. But what if Tracey showed up there too? Hayden was right about coming here. Tracey would have no idea where they were.

"It's three bedrooms," he said, gesturing to the front of the house, partially hidden by tall weeds and intermittent grass. "But I'm planning to add a fourth. I'm going to raze the barn, though. There might be some wood to reclaim, but I won't be sure until I get in there and take it apart."

He started to talk about the kitchen, then the living room, and the bedrooms as they walked around to the back of the property. "See that huge elm tree? I thought that would be a good place for a tire swing."

"Uh-huh." How could he act like a real estate agent when her life was in pieces? She had no choice but to humor him.

He turned to her, a bead of sweat dripping down his face. The day was unbearably hot, even more than usual for early July. "If I'm boring you, please tell me."

His words, along with the hurt expression on his face, softened her heart a bit. "It's not boring. I'm just . . ."

"I know. You're upset about Tracey." He moved toward her, his arms open. "It will be okay."

"No, it won't." She backed away from him. "It's never okay when it comes to her."

"All right." His arms went to his side.

"I want to go back to Mimi's." She turned around and started to leave.

"Riley, don't—"

"Don't what?" she whirled around and faced

him. "Don't be upset? Don't close myself off? Too bad, Hayden, because that's what I do." Her throat closed as she hit her fist on her chest. "This is *me*. The real *me*. And I know how this ends."

He shook his head, his expression bewildered. "How what ends? I have no idea what you're talking about."

She backed away, unable to stop the tears. "I end up getting hurt."

He hurried to her. "I'm not going to hurt you, Riley."

"You will. You'll get tired of my issues, tired of my pity parties, tired of me wanting more than I deserve."

He held his hands out to her. "Where is this coming from? I won't get tired of you, Riley. Everyone has issues, including me. Especially me. Are you saying you'll get tired of me?"

Without realizing it, he was giving her an out. She lifted her chin. "That's exactly what I'm saying. I don't need anyone's extra baggage."

"Wow," he said, flinching.

She continued her onslaught. "I'm going back to New York, Hayden. Mimi's fine, the shop is in good shape, and the house is finished. There's no reason for me to stay."

"No reason at all?" He scowled. "Not a single one you can think of?"

She fought to keep her chin from trembling. "Not a single one."

He stood still. "Then I guess you'd better get packing."

His words pierced her. He was giving up that easily? *Of course he is.* They all did, even Mimi at one time. Where was her grandmother when Tracey was dragging Riley all over the state, even into Oklahoma and Missouri, when Riley was a child? Why had she only agreed to let Riley live with her when she was a teenager?

Hayden pulled out his cell phone, then turned his back on Riley. "Tanner. Hey. Can you pick me up? Cool. Here's the address."

Riley stared at Hayden's back. The calm way he was talking to Tanner drove the spear deeper into her heart. So much for all his words about patience and never leaving. It didn't take much time—what, four or five weeks?—before he gave up on her. That had to be a record. At least Tracey and Mimi had kept her around for years.

Her heart burned as she got into the car and sped out on the dirt road. The tears fell, cool on her hot cheeks. Anger filled her. This was all her fault. She never should have let Hayden get close to her, but she'd ignored all the alarm bells in her brain. She wouldn't be feeling this intense pain if she had kept her distance and blocked him out of her heart. But he had been so persistent. So charming. So wonderful. So perfect and everything she had ever wanted . . . but knew she could never have.

She wiped the tears from her cheek with the palm of her hand and let out a bitter laugh. What a fool she'd been to think life could be any different. That he was different. *But I'm the one pushing him away.*

She had to admit to her part in it, but better she cut ties now than later. Because she had been well on her way to falling in love with him. And if she was hurting this much now, she would have been fractured into a million pieces if she'd admitted she loved him. There would have been no way she could put herself back together then.

Hayden had to force himself not to throw his phone across the field. A smashed phone wouldn't fix his and Riley's relationship. Correction, ex-relationship. Instead, he shoved it in the pocket of his khaki pants, feeling a seam in the fabric rip. He didn't care. The fury inside him took over his innate ability to gather his emotions and set them aside. His greatest fear had come true.

All this time he thought he was making headway with Riley. That she felt the same about him as he did about her. That they might have a future together some day. Of course he knew he had his work cut out for him, and she was not only worth it, but he'd hoped he was getting closer to her heart. Then she wrecked that hope with a few choice words. She was going to leave Maple Falls the same way she'd arrived—closed, distant, self-protected. The only thing left for him to do was piece his heart back together.

He paused, wiping the sweat off his brow with the back of his hand. Not all of his perspiration was due to the heat and humidity. He took in a couple deep breaths and counted to ten. That settled him a bit, cleared the red flames of anger in his brain so he could sort out his thoughts. He pulled out his phone again and texted Doug. He used his personal number only in emergency situations.

Having a bad time. Can we set up an appointment this week? Hayden

He stared at his cell phone, not expecting an answer right away. Just reaching out to his counselor calmed him enough that he was able to see how much Riley was hurting. And what had he done? Piled on the hurt. He'd seen the pain in her eyes before she left, which was why he turned his back to her. He didn't want to cave in. Not this time. It was time for him to face reality. He'd wanted to earn her trust, but how could he do that when she refused to give him a chance? She wasn't the only one who was in pain.

His phone pinged and a text popped up.

Sure. I'm free tomorrow morning at 8.

Hayden responded, then set a reminder of the appointment in his phone and another to tell his father he would be going to work late. He probably didn't need the reminders. How could he forget any of this happened? But he was used to doing it for his counseling appointments, and old habits died hard with him. He put his phone back in his pocket and waited for Tanner, who showed up a short while later in his Jeep. Fortunately his friend didn't say anything as he drove him back to the church and parked next to his Subaru.

"Hey, dude, if you need me, give me a call," Tanner said.

Hayden turned to him and nodded. "Thanks." Then he got out of the vehicle and opened his own car door. Instead of leaving right away, he turned on the air and sat there, letting it cool his skin.

He knew Riley would follow through on her promise to leave. She probably had one foot out the door the moment Tracey showed up. He believed love could overcome a lot of things, but not if the other person wasn't at least willing to meet partway. Riley obviously couldn't. Or wouldn't. Either way it didn't matter.

"Maybe it's for the best," he muttered as he shifted into gear and left the church. Cutting the cord now would save a lot of heartache.

He couldn't imagine his heart hurting more than it did right now.

Chapter 16

E rma faced her daughter for the first time in fifteen years. She sat on one side of the kitchen table, Tracey on the other. Riley was right: her daughter looked awful.

If she was sober, it was a recent sobriety. Erma could see the drug scars on her arms that she tried to hide with a too thin burgundy sweater that was obviously secondhand, if not third. Her heart started to break, but then she shored it back up again. Tracey had made her own decisions, and she had to face the consequences.

Still, a mother's heart could never be completely hardened toward a child, and that was why Erma had agreed to talk to her after the service today, despite the doubtful looks of the BBs, who had surrounded her the moment the service ended.

"How is Riley doing?" Tracey asked, pressing her fingers against the vinyl tablecloth.

Erma noticed her short, dirty nails and wondered when her daughter last had a real bath or shower. It was hard to tell from the scent of smoke wafting from her clothing.

"Riley is well. At least she was until you showed up."

"You didn't tell me she was here the last time I called. I thought she was still in New York," Tracey said.

"How did you know she was there?"

Tracey put her hands in her lap. "I have ways of keeping tabs on *my* daughter. Not everyone in this town has turned their back on me."

Guilt and manipulation. Erma was used to it, but it never failed to rile her. She calmed her emotions, briefly wondering who in Maple Falls was still in touch with Tracey. Then she realized she didn't want to know.

"I'm glad to hear that you have some support," she said, meaning it.

Tracey averted her gaze, her thin shoulders slumping. "That's more than you ever gave me." She wandered around the kitchen. The walls were bright and fresh, thanks to Riley, who had spent Friday night after work applying the light, bright-yellow paint to the walls. "House looks nice. So does the shop. Obviously you're putting a lot of money into both places."

Erma steeled herself for what was coming. Tracey couldn't get through to her on the phone, so now she was here to manipulate her in person.

"What do you want, Tracey?" Erma knew the answer to the question already. Her daughter wanted money. Money that she would probably blow on drink, drugs, and men. She'd done it enough while raising Riley, leaving the child to her own devices. Erma's heart pinched. *I should have acted sooner.* "I've already given you plenty of money."

"You mean my inheritance?" Tracey met her gaze, some of the steel returning to her eyes. "It wasn't that much."

"It was a *large* sum of money." Erma clenched her jaw.

"And it's been fifteen years. How did you expect me to live off a few thousand dollars?"

"It was more than a few, and I expected you to get a job so you could support yourself." She fought for composure. "You still haven't told me what you want."

"Believe it or not, Mother, I don't want anything from you. I came here to tell you that I'm living in a halfway house in Hot Springs."

Erma nodded. She'd heard this before, too, more than once. "I see."

"I promise I'm going to get clean this time. I swear." When Erma didn't respond, she scoffed. "You don't believe me. You never do."

"How can I? You've lied to me too many times to count. Not to mention how your choices and behavior affected your father."

Tracey pulled on her fingers, not looking at Erma. "I should have known you'd bring him up again."

"He was your father—"

"I never knew my *real* father. Or my real

329

mother. But I'll admit, Dad was the better parent."

An arrow straight to the heart. Gus had always had a soft spot for Tracey, and there were a few times when she was growing up that their relationship had been decent—when Erma was the stricter disciplinarian. Then Gus had died, and that affected Tracey deeply. Which was the only reason Erma didn't tell her to leave right now. Her daughter truly believed Gus was the better parent. In hindsight, maybe he was. Maybe things would have been different if he were still here. *I wish you were, my love.*

Tracey rubbed her nose. "Look, I didn't have to tell you what was going on with me."

"No, you didn't. So why are you now? And why were you calling me before?"

"Because I need some help."

Erma leaned back against her chair, her leg aching more than it had in weeks. For a short moment she actually thought Tracey might have changed. That her daughter was here to reestablish their relationship, not to ask for more money.

"Just a few bucks," Tracey continued, leaning so far against the table Erma heard the legs of the chair scrape against the wooden floor.

"The halfway house should cover your needs," Erma said, keeping her voice as emotionless as if she were talking to a piece of wood.

"It's not enough." Tracey shot up from the chair and started to pace, rubbing her stubby fingers together faster. "I have court fees to pay. Restitution to some people I stole checks from."

Erma shook her head. She couldn't handle hearing a list of her daughter's most recent crimes. Not right now. "Tracey, did the court order you to the halfway house?"

She nodded. "It was either that or jail. If I don't go, then it will be jail. But if I pay off my debts and have a solid place to live, then they might let me go free."

Her daughter looked so forlorn that Erma almost lost her senses and got up and hugged her. But she had to be firm, just like she was fifteen years ago. "Then go to the halfway house. Get clean. Get a job. Then you can pay back the court fees."

Tracey threw up her hands. "I can't believe you're so selfish! You're rich and you can't spare anything else for me, your only daughter."

"I gave you what you asked for!" Erma sprang up from the chair, a blast of pain shooting down her leg. She ignored it. "I gave you the money you wanted, and you promised me you would never come back for Riley. You swore you would never see her again."

"What?"

Erma spun around, horrified to see Riley standing there. *Oh God.* "Riley . . . Sweetheart."

She moved toward her granddaughter. "Let me explain—"

"She paid me off." Tracey walked over to Riley, smiling fully for the first time, revealing several gaping holes where teeth used to be. "She said she would give me the money they had set aside for my college fund, plus some of Dad's inheritance, if I left you with her and never came back."

"Is that true?" Riley's eyes filled with shock as she turned to Erma.

"Yes, but there were reasons—"

"She thinks I'm a bad influence." Tracey laughed. "And she's right." Then she moved closer to Riley. "But I'm getting straight now. I need a little help. You're an artist, right? Living in New York—that has to be expensive. I've never been to New York, but it sounds exciting. We could get an apartment together. Hang out. You can show your old mother the sights." She kept smiling. "We could get to know each other again."

Riley recoiled. "No."

Tracey's smile turned into an ugly straight line. "Eh, I can't cross the state line anyway." She turned and looked at Erma. "Are you gonna help me or not?"

Tears welled in Erma's eyes. "No, Tracey. The only person who can help you, is you."

She kept her hard gaze on Erma for so long, Erma thought her daughter was trying to stab her with her eyes. Before she could stop her, Tracey turned to Riley.

"Did she ever tell you the truth?"

Riley's eyes, so much like Tracey's, turned to stone. "About the money? No."

"I'm not talking about money. It was mine anyway. She owed that to me." Tracey shot a vicious look at Erma again. "I'm talking about how she and Gus weren't my biological parents."

"What?" Riley's expression morphed into confusion.

"That's right. They adopted me." She laughed, and it sounded unhinged. "I guess you've been lied to twice. Not a very *parental* thing to do, is it?" Then she turned to Erma. "If something bad happens to me, it's your fault. You understand? It will be on your head, *Mother*." She stormed out the back door.

Erma stared at the door, flinching as it slammed shut. She closed her eyes, trying to get her bearings. She was too old for this. She had gone through it too many times. Then the reality of what just happened hit her like a stone to her chest.

"Riley, let me explain—"

"I heard enough." Riley backed away. "You didn't want her to see me anymore. She wanted money. You made a deal with your *adopted* daughter."

"I love you, Riley. I was happy to have you here with me at long last."

"Then why didn't you come get me before? And why didn't you tell the truth about Tracey?" Riley cried. "If you wanted me here so badly, why didn't you . . ." She gasped. "Why didn't you save me?"

Erma started to cry. "I wanted to. More than anything. And I should have. I should have gotten you sooner. But she had the courts on her side. I hired a lawyer, paid thousands in legal fees, only to have them tell me that you weren't in physical danger, and that if I took Tracey to court, she would win. I didn't want to put you through that."

"You should have." Riley's voice turned cold. "Just because she didn't hit me doesn't mean I wasn't abused."

Her granddaughter might as well have stabbed her in the heart, her words hurt so much. "I know, sugar. I know. And I'll live with that for the rest of my life. But you must believe me. Tracey's adopted, yes, but that didn't mean your Poppy and I loved her any less. She had problems . . . lots of problems. We tried to deal with them the best we could, but we failed. Then when Tracey showed up with you on my doorstep, it was an answer to prayer, not a deal or a payoff. Not to me." She started to sob. "It was a miracle."

Riley's heart didn't budge. She had shut it down almost completely after she left Hayden, intending to come here and go straight to her room to start packing. She'd even searched on her phone for an available flight, only to find out they were full until Tuesday. She would have to wait until then, but she would at least have her bags packed. If they were, she wouldn't be tempted to change her mind and stay in Maple Falls.

Then she'd overheard her mother and grandmother arguing, and her world crashed around her again. Mimi, the one person she thought she could trust in this entire world, had betrayed her.

A part of her wasn't surprised Tracey was adopted. That explained a lot of things, especially the fact that Tracey wasn't anything like Mimi, in looks or personality. But there had been plenty of opportunities for Mimi to tell Riley the truth. Not just about the adoption, but about the money.

A volcano of emotions erupted inside her. The memories of the times she'd cried alone in strange places, wishing her grandmother would rescue her, only to be disappointed again and again. This was just another in a long list of disappointments and pain. That she could feel anything at all right now was a marvel.

Then suddenly everything shut off inside until she was numb. She looked at Mimi, who was leaning against the table, pain evident on her face.

"I'm leaving Tuesday," Riley said, the chill back in her tone. "I already booked my flight."

"Riley, please." Mimi held her hands together,

almost begging. "Sit down. We need to talk this through."

"No, we don't." She turned and went upstairs, quickly packed her things, and came back down. Mimi was in the living room, wincing and limping more than usual as she made her way to the recliner. She practically fell into it.

Seeing her grandmother suffering almost stopped Riley. But she firmed up her resolve.

"Where are you going?" Mimi asked.

"I don't know." She opened the door. "I'll figure it out."

"Riley—"

She let the door shut as she walked out.

Her eyes were dry as she walked down the road, the suitcase dragging behind her. As she made her way down her grandmother's road in the muggy heat, her mind began to clear a bit. Where was she going to go? She still had to figure out how to get to the airport, although that would be solved easily with an Uber. But her flight wasn't until Tuesday. And she was almost back to where she'd been financially when she arrived in Maple Falls. She'd only received two paychecks from Mimi and was slated to get a third this week. Most of that had gone to buying an airline ticket on short notice, and she had put a little bit more into buying art supplies and canvases for the artwork she was going to make for the store. That was never going to happen now.

She walked at least another mile, until she was so hot and sweaty and thirsty she had to stop. She couldn't walk aimlessly around Maple Falls for the next two days. She pulled out her phone and dialed.

"Riley?" Bea's confused voice came out of the speaker.

"Can I stay with you tonight?" She'd figure out where she would land tomorrow night later.

"Is something wrong with Erma?"

"No." What was one more lie in a lifetime of lies?

A pause. "Well, of course you can."

"Would you mind picking me up?" She gave Bea her location.

"I'll be right there, honey. Won't take me but a jiff to jump in the car."

"Thanks." She turned off her phone and stuck it in her pocket. Emotionless, she moved to a shade tree on the side of the street and waited for Bea. Her heart had been so filled with pain after pushing Hayden away. It was empty now.

She felt . . . nothing.

The next morning, Riley woke to a huge breakfast spread, more than she could possibly eat. Bacon, eggs, sausage, fresh biscuits slathered in butter, orange juice, coffee, milk, apple turnovers, and blueberry muffins.

"I fixed you a little something," Bea said,

plopping a platter of hotcakes on the table.

"I see." Riley blanched, still full from the huge meal Bea made last night. One thing she had forgotten about Bea was that the woman cooked when she was upset or nervous. Riley's suspicion was confirmed when Billy, Bea's husband, who had somehow stayed thin and wiry for the fifty-three years he and Bea had been married, walked into the kitchen and put his arm around her plump shoulders.

"Looks good, honey." He kissed her round cheek, then sat down at the table. "Doesn't it, Riley?"

"Very good." She didn't know how she was going to force down even a fraction of this food, but she wasn't going to reject it either. "Thank you, Bea."

"You're welcome." She sat down and mopped her brow with one of the napkins on the table. "Now, let's say grace, and then we'll eat."

Riley bowed her head, but her mind was as empty as her heart. When the prayer was over, she saw Bea piling food on a plate. She handed it to Billy, who promptly dove in as she began adding food to another plate, then gave it to Riley.

"There's pure maple syrup for those hotcakes." Bea's extra-wide grin had a nervous edge to it.

Guilt broke through her numbness. Obviously, her presence upset Bea, even though she was trying to hide it under Southern hospitality and rich cooking. Riley cut into the eggs, both scrambled and sunny side.

She'd made plans to stay with Harper tonight, and Harper had also agreed to take her to the airport. Funny that out of the group of three friends, Riley had formed a bond with the one who couldn't be more opposite from her. But since the first time they met, Harper was the one to reach out to her. They had clicked somehow, and while she liked Anita and Olivia, too, she would miss Harper the most. She also knew Harper would probably ask her a million questions, but she would handle them when they came. Right now she needed to focus on eating enough food to make Bea happy.

"Remember, honey, today's the day I have lunch with Pastor Jared and the men's ministry," Billy said, already half finished with his meal fit for two.

"Oh good, because I have plans for lunch too." Bea poured syrup on her hotcakes. "I've already got a ham cooking in the oven."

Riley blanched. "Harper's picking me up at eleven," she said. "I'm staying with her tonight."

Bea set the syrup on the table with careful, slow motions. "I see."

"But I appreciate you letting me stay last night and the wonderful meals."

Bea nodded, but she still wasn't looking

at Riley. Instead, she was slowly cutting her hotcakes into tiny pieces.

"When I get back to New York, I can send you some money for the food and lodging," Riley said.

"Uh-oh." Billy wiped his mouth with his napkin. "That's my cue to leave." He got up and kissed Bea again. "Go easy on her, dear."

Riley looked at Billy, then at Bea. Her stomach sank at the sight of Bea's red face and narrowed eyes. After Billy left, she said, "Bea, I—"

"Now you listen to me, young lady. First of all, I take offense that you think I would accept a single penny from you for keeping you here and feeding you. Do you think Erma paid me when you stayed over all those times?"

"I—"

"No, she did not. And secondly"—she held up two plump fingers—"you are part of my lunch plans today. Call Harper and reschedule."

"But . . ." Riley didn't have the strength to argue with her. Besides, Bea kept her attention on her food and didn't spare a glance for Riley, even when she finished her meal and got up from the table. "Can I help with the dishes?" Riley asked meekly.

"No."

Riley shot up from the chair and went to brush her teeth in the spare bathroom, which was next to the spare bedroom down the hallway. She ran her fingers through her hair, then sighed as she peered at her reflection in the mirror. She looked nearly as bad as Tracey, minus the almost emaciated frame and missing teeth. But the dark circles beneath her eyes and her pale complexion revealed that all was not well within her. And it wasn't. Not by a long shot.

She holed up in the guest bedroom, not wanting to risk Bea's wrath, for the rest of the morning. Harper had been fine with picking her up later that day. All Riley had to do was kill a couple of hours, have lunch with Bea, and then head back with Harper. By tomorrow evening she would be back in New York, where she belonged.

It wasn't long before she grew bored, and she pulled the sketchbook out of her duffel bag. She quickly moved past her drawings of the shop, ignoring the pang in her chest, and the renderings of what would have been her first piece of original art for Knots and Tangles.

Then she landed on Hayden's portrait. It was almost finished, and he'd even posed for her, in a joking way, one time. She touched the corner of the page, ready to rip it out. But she couldn't bring herself to do it. The drawing wasn't a masterpiece, but the subject was as close as anyone could get to being one. Riley felt a tightness in her chest, and she slammed the book shut, shoving it back into her bag. She spent the rest of the time playing pointless games on her phone until Bea called her into the kitchen.

When she entered, she had expected the expansive meal taking up almost every inch of table space—and Bea didn't have a small table. What she had not expected was Peg, Madge, Viola, Myrtle, and Gwen sitting around it, all with their arms across their chests as if they had choreographed the position. Their furious expressions could burn a block of ice. Behind them were Harper, Anita, and Olivia, who appeared just as upset.

She froze. She was in big trouble now.

Chapter 17

S it down, Riley Jean."

Riley nodded at Myrtle's command and sat in the lone empty chair on the other side of the table from the women. She folded her hands in her lap, unable to bring herself to look at any of the Bosom Buddies.

Bea started to get up. "Let me get you some tea—"

Gwen put her hand on Bea's forearm and shook her head. Bea remained in her chair.

Finding her steel, Riley lifted her chin. "I guess Mimi called you all and blabbed everything. Say what you have to say, and I'll move on."

"You will move on when we tell you to, young lady." Madge's razor-sharp tone could've sliced through diamonds. "And for your information, Erma didn't call any of us."

"I called her." Bea fidgeted with the butter knife next to her plate. "I knew something had to be seriously wrong for you to want to stay here. But she refused to talk to me. That's when I called everyone else."

Crossing her arms over her chest, Riley stared at them. Her friends hadn't said a word, but they were still watching her with a mix of incredulity and betrayal. Riley hoped she came across as cool on the outside, because inside she was a shaky mess.

"How can you treat your grandmother this way?" Viola burst into tears. "She's the sweetest, kindest, most loving, most sacrificing, saintly person I know."

"You're laying it on a little thick," Peg whispered.

It wasn't empty flattery to Riley. Her grandmother was all those things, despite the hurt and anger coursing through her.

"You're breaking her heart." Viola sniffed. "After everything she's done for you."

"I never said I was staying here permanently." Riley hated the tremor in her voice, but she couldn't stop it. "She always knew I was going back to New York."

Harper's jaw dropped. "I didn't know that."

"Me either," Anita added, her eyes growing wide.

"Why didn't you tell us?" Olivia said, holding out her palms.

Riley couldn't face any of them right now. She was the one who was hurt, but they were making her feel like the bad guy.

"We saw Tracey at church yesterday," Myrtle said. "We know she's a part of what happened between you and Erma."

Riley glanced away. "I'm not gonna talk about her." For some unknown reason she again slipped into the Southern accent she'd tried so hard to get rid of when she moved east.

"That's good, because we're not discussing her either. She's done enough damage to you and Erma over the years." Gwen's words were strong, but her tone held compassion. "And I'm sorry about that."

"Me too," the BBs all said in unison.

"It doesn't matter," Riley said. "The past is the past."

"If that's the case, then why aren't you leaving it there?"

Riley glowered at Peg, who had removed her bright-red-framed glasses. Riley could see tears in her eyes too.

"Why are you punishing your grandmother?" Bea moaned.

"Whatever happened, it wasn't her fault," Viola mumbled. "I'm sure Tracey boxed her into it. She's always made trouble for Erma, even though Erma always tried her best."

"Shh," the BBs chastised.

"Right. No Tracey talk."

The ever-present shame Riley tried to keep at a distance her entire life was filling her once again. Suddenly she burst into sobs—deep, soul-crushing sobs, as every bit of her inner strength left her.

"Oh, honey." Bea got up and put her arms around Riley, who in turn wrapped her arms around Bea's thick waist. "It's all gonna be okay."

Riley barely heard her as she cried oceans of tears that had been trapped inside far too long. Painful memories surfaced, things she had witnessed in childhood and never told anyone. The horrible things Tracey would say to her when she was drunk or high. The times she wondered if she'd ever eat again. The prayers she'd said over and over that Mimi, or anyone, would take her away from her mother forever—and the guilt she felt every time she'd uttered that prayer.

Soon all the BBs were crowding around her. One stroked her hair. Another patted her back. Yet another grasped the fingers of one of her hands on the back of Bea's waist. Myrtle cooed that they were there for her and Mimi, that they wouldn't let Tracey hurt them again. The love she had craved for so long from her mother, but never received, was being poured into her by these lively Southern ladies, and Riley suddenly realized that they were her family too. She saw her own buddies, all three of them, standing behind Erma's friends, nodding in agreement.

When she didn't have a tear left to shed, she lifted her head. "Can I have a tissue?"

"Of course, honey." Peg snatched a napkin off the table. "Use this."

Riley blew her nose as they all returned to their seats. She knew she needed to apologize, but all she could say was, "Thank you."

"Anytime, Riley." Bea smiled, her double chin quaking. "We're here for you."

"And Erma," Madge added.

"We're here for both of you," Harper said. "You need to remember that."

She looked at each of the women as she gripped the napkin, now damp from her tears. "I'm sorry," she said. "All of you are right." Then she realized the full extent of what she'd done to her grandmother and wanted to crawl into a hole. "I hurt Mimi, and I shouldn't have."

They all nodded, and then Myrtle said, "You know what you need to do, then."

"Yes," Riley said, starting to get up from the table. "I have to talk to her."

"You should have a bite to eat first," Bea said.

"Bea!" all the Bosom Buddies said in unison.

Riley held Bea's hand. "Thank you, but this can't wait."

"I'll drive you over," Myrtle said, rising from her chair.

"I'll drive her," Harper said.

"We'll go with you." Anita grabbed her purse off the one vacant space on Bea's counter and put the short double strap on her arm. Olivia also stood.

Riley nodded, overwhelmed with emotions she'd never felt before, but that her soul desperately needed.

"I'll get my stuff." Before she left the kitchen,

she paused, looking at each woman in front of her, old and young. "I love you all," she said, her voice thick.

They all smiled. "We love you too."

Although she was defying her doctor's orders by not resting and elevating her leg, Erma continued pacing back and forth in the living room. She hadn't slept a wink last night, and even though she knew Riley was safe and well taken care of at Bea's, it didn't ease her mind. Despite Riley's upbringing and her habit of separating herself from others to keep from getting hurt, she had never been rebellious. In fact, Erma had never had a bit of trouble from her, other than the typical teenage pouting and moodiness, a welcome respite from the difficulties she and Gus experienced raising Tracey. She'd hoped Riley would find her place in Maple Falls, but she couldn't blame her that she hadn't. Some obstacles were too difficult to overcome, and she had to acknowledge that she was a part of them. If she had been honest with Riley to begin with, they might not be in this situation now.

Erma pressed her hand to her heart. Her ticker was fine, but the pain she felt in her chest was almost too much to bear. Riley had the right to be angry, considering what Tracey had put her through, and Erma only knew about a few things. She was sure her granddaughter had witnessed and endured many awful things that she hadn't said a word about, not even to the counselor Erma had taken her to when she first started living with her. When Riley turned fourteen and said she didn't want to see the counselor, Erma had acquiesced. Over the years she questioned that decision, along with so many others.

Her leg was on the verge of giving out and she finally sat down. Her thoughts raced. Would she ever see Riley again? Had she committed an unpardonable sin? Perhaps she had. But she couldn't change that now, just as she couldn't change Tracey. Riley was an adult. Erma had to respect her decision, and part of that respect was not chasing her down and begging her to come back.

She closed her eyes, nearly breathless from the ache in her heart. How could she go on without Riley?

A knock sounded at the door, but Erma ignored it. She knew it had to be Bea. Or possibly the whole BB group. She didn't want to see them right now. At some point she would apologize to Bea for being rude last night, but not now. The only person she wanted to see was Riley.

The front door opened, and Erma steeled herself for the onslaught of her friends, who always meant well. Instead, Riley walked through the door, her duffel bag over her shoulder.

Erma jumped up from the chair, hiding the

shooting pain in her leg. She wanted to run and take her granddaughter in her arms, but she held her ground.

"Hi," she said softly.

Riley stayed in the shadows of the alcove. "Can I come in?"

"Of course." Erma wished she'd grabbed her cane to hold on to, because she could feel herself starting to sway.

Riley walked into the living room but kept her distance from Erma. "I'm sorry, Mimi," she said. "I shouldn't have left you like that."

Relief flooded Erma, nearly knocking her over. "It's all right, sugar," she said. "I understand why you did."

"But I don't." She set her duffel bag on the floor, walked over to Erma, and hugged her. "I don't understand anything anymore."

"Oh, sugar." Erma held her tight. "That's my fault." It would be easy to lay all the blame at her daughter's feet, but she couldn't do that. "I should have done things differently." She smoothed back Riley's mussed hair. "I should have told you the truth about everything. I should have let you know Tracey was adopted. I never should have listened to that lawyer. I should have held my ground and taken you out of Tracey's care years before I did. I was a lot stronger when your Poppy was alive."

"You're the strongest woman I know."

"Not strong enough. Not then." She reached for Riley's hand. "I'll answer any questions you have, but I need to tell you everything first." She explained the circumstances around adopting Tracey, the difficulty she and Gus had raising her, and then about the money. "Tracey was right about one thing. The money I gave her was hers. Your Poppy had always been frugal, and I was never one to need very much in the way of material things. Not only had he left me well taken care of, but he'd also put aside a good amount for Tracey.

"I kept that money from her for years, thinking I would give it to her when she was well enough to handle it. When you were thirteen, I thought that day had arrived. She had gotten sober, remember?"

Riley nodded. "It didn't last long."

"No, it didn't. But when she was off the booze, I told her about her inheritance. Shortly after, she stopped by with you." Erma took a breath. "There wasn't a deal. If there hadn't been any money involved, I would have told her the same thing—she wasn't welcome to come back here. Not until she straightened herself out for good. I've stuck to that promise to this day." She gripped Riley's hand. "As you can see, she still hasn't done that, even after all these years. I'm not sure if she ever will, and it breaks my heart. I still love her, despite everything."

Riley nodded, her eyes filling with understanding. "I can't believe I'm saying this, but I do too. Chalk that up as another thing I don't understand."

Erma stood on tiptoes and kissed Riley's cheek. "You might not be my blood kin, Riley, but you are my granddaughter. You are my real family. Don't ever, ever doubt that." She wiped away the tears that had spilled down her darling girl's cheek. "We have a lot to work through, you and I. Eventually I'm sure we can figure it all out."

Riley clasped Erma's hand with her own. "Together." She touched her forehead to Erma's.

"Together."

On Tuesday afternoon, Hayden was still in the back office of Price's Hardware. He'd spent yesterday and most of today going through all the paperwork, procedures, and anything else he could find to keep himself occupied so he didn't have to deal with customers. Fortunately he had the excuse of wanting to go over every single thing in his father's desk and filing cabinets. He would have done it anyway eventually. Right now he just couldn't fake enthusiasm about nuts or bolts or paint or anything else—inside the store or out.

His father and mother must have sensed something was wrong, because both had expressed concern about his mood since he'd returned home Sunday afternoon. When he snapped at them that he was fine, they kept their distance. He wasn't fooling anyone, especially not them.

He tried to focus on the stack of paperwork in front of him, but all he could see was Riley's face, and all he could do was kick himself for being such a jerk. So much for earning her trust. For being patient. For not pushing. He'd even argued with himself for falling for someone who clearly had a lot of stuff in her past. *Pot, meet kettle.*

Hayden sat back in the creaky, green office chair that had seen better days and sighed, then leaned forward and pounded his fist on the desk in frustration.

"Yep. You're fine all right."

Hayden turned and looked at his father, who was standing in the doorway. "Sorry," he said, then started nonchalantly shuffling the papers as if he hadn't used the desk as a punching bag.

His father walked into the office, picked up the folding chair that was leaning against the wall, and brought it over to Hayden. He flipped it open, then sat down. "Start talking."

"There's nothing to talk about."

"Right. Because you're fine."

Hayden grimaced, then turned to him. "I'm a little bothered, that's all."

"A little?"

"Fine. A lot. Now will you leave me alone?" He closed his eyes. "Sorry. Again. I didn't mean that."

"Apology accepted. And no, I'm not leaving you alone. Not until you tell me what's going on. I haven't seen you this upset since you were a kid."

"I guess I'm acting like one too."

"That depends. What's got you so hot under the collar?"

Hayden ended up telling his father everything but leaving out anything personal about Riley. "I thought she was the one for me, Dad. I really did."

His father sat back in the chair and stroked the short beard he'd started growing recently. "And now you think she isn't?"

"She made that decision for me."

"Hmm. I see."

"See what?"

Dad leaned forward. "Son, I don't want you to take this the wrong way, but this might be the first time something didn't come easy to you."

Hayden looked at him, incredulous. "Are you kidding me? Do you think playing ball was easy? That getting rejected by the majors over and over was a picnic?" He clenched his jaw. "That losing my career was *fun?*"

"Not at all." His father's tone was even. "But you have to admit, Hayden, you're a gifted athlete. You've always worked hard, but you had something ninety-nine percent of people don't have: superior speed, incredible coordination, intense discipline. Those things aren't taught. And they've given you a leg up."

"All right." Hayden spun around in the chair and faced his father. "I'll give you that. I've got some talent."

"Some?"

"A lot." He threw up one hand. "But that doesn't negate all the hard work I've done in my life. And not just at my sport. I kept up my grades, worked here at the store—"

"And now you own this store."

"Not without a fight."

Dad scoffed. "Three weeks of negotiations is not a fight. Hayden, listen to me. Along with strong discipline, you tend to be impatient. You're used to getting what you want."

Hayden was dumbfounded. No one had ever said that to him before. He'd been told he was intense. Competitive. Not a quitter. *But I quit Riley, didn't I?*

"There are higher stakes in the world than a career," Dad continued. He looked around at the office. "I wasn't ready to give all this up."

That surprised Hayden. "What?"

"It's going to be hard for me to walk away. I've worked in this store since I was seven. My dad and grandpop had me unpacking boxes and filling shelves as soon as I was able to do it without knocking things over. I love this store." His gaze turned contemplative. "I would have worked here until my last day, I think."

"Then why are you walking away?"

"For your mother. For years she's come in second. Actually, third sometimes, because of you boys. She's spent her entire married life supporting me and you kids, and I finally realized two years ago that she needed to be first for once. She wants to travel. To see the country and maybe some parts of the world. I want to give that dream to her." He smiled. "It's my turn to sacrifice."

"Harry." Jasper poked his head inside the door. He was wearing a Price's Hardware shirt Hayden had given him. The man spent so much time at the store and was so helpful, Hayden thought he needed to make Jasper an official, if somewhat sporadic, employee. "Someone wants to know if you have Allen wrenches."

Dad laughed. "We're a hardware store. We have every wrench you can think of."

"That's what I told her, but darned if I can find any of them. Did you move them, Hayden?"

When Hayden shook his head, Dad said, "I'll be right out." After Jasper left, Dad got up from the chair. "Now, that's a switch. Usually Jasper is helping me." He looked at Hayden. "I'm sure you'll figure this out, son. Just don't take as long as I did."

Hayden stared at the empty doorway. Sacrifice. He always thought he'd sacrificed a lot in his life. The future had always held uncertainty, until he came back to Maple Falls. Then he'd known what he wanted—to work in the store, to rehab an old home, to live in his hometown for the rest of his life, and recently, to revitalize it. It wouldn't be easy and would take some time, but he was confident he could get it done with a lot of dedication and persistence.

Then there was Riley. He'd thought dedication and persistence would have gotten through to her, but he'd been wrong. Now that she wasn't going along with his timetable, he'd decided to move on. He'd been so deep in his own hurt pride and impatience that he forgot the most important thing—she meant everything to him.

Somehow he would find the patience he needed. He would swallow his pride. He would make sure to match her rhythm, not force her to go along with his. He'd always been a leader, a team captain. The star of his family, the town, his own life. Now he would have to let that go and put someone else first . . . if she would let him.

He'd have to try.

He shot up from the chair and went to the front of the store. His father was busy with the wrench customer, so Hayden told Jasper to let him know that he would be gone for the rest of the day. Jasper agreed, and Hayden went to the back parking lot and jumped into his car.

Then he stilled. Riley was probably back in New York by now, but on the off chance she wasn't . . . He got out of his car and headed to Knots and Tangles.

Erma sat behind the front counter and worked on another chemo hat, this one teal and cream, interspersed with speckles of pink and pale-gold. She was using a smaller hook and thinner yarn than the pattern required because the hat would be for a child or teenage cancer patient. She smiled as she lifted her gaze and looked around the shop. What would her mother and grandmother think of how everything had turned out? *They'd be happier than a pig in a muddy wallow.* She was sure of that.

The bell rang and Hayden dashed into the store. Erma set her crocheting down and got up from the chair with the help of her cane and plenty of ibuprofen. Her leg was hurting from lack of care the past two days, but she intended to slow down from now on until it fully healed.

"Hi, Hayden," she said, surprised to see him.

"Has Riley left?"

Erma shook her head. "Not yet. But she has a flight scheduled for Friday." She would have sworn Hayden almost swayed at the news.

"Where is she now?"

"In the back." Erma walked to him. "She's very tender right now. I don't know what happened between you two, but whatever you say to her, be extra careful. She's had a rough time."

He nodded, his expression as serious as she'd ever seen it. "I understand."

"I hope so." Erma narrowed her gaze. "I won't stand for her getting hurt."

"Me either."

She watched him go to the back room and prayed he meant those words.

Chapter 18

R iley looked at the canvas in front of her, then at the selection of yarn she'd chosen from the Knots and Tangles inventory. The colors were a wild variety of cool aqua, deep purple, fiery red, and lemon yellow, along with a few lighter neutrals she would intertwine sparingly. She separated the fibers of the aqua yarn and placed a few of them on the canvas, the vision for this art piece slowly coming together. Hopefully not too slowly, since she wanted to finish it before she left on Friday.

When she heard footsteps coming into the room, she turned, then froze. Hayden. Despite everything, she still marveled at how sexy he looked in a hardware store uniform. *Extremely sexy.*

"Hey," he said, stopping a few feet from her.

"Hi." She set the fibers on the table and shifted on her stool.

His gaze went to the blank canvas. "Are you working on something?"

"Yes." She couldn't keep her eyes off him.

"Uh, a new art piece?"

"Yes." Her heartbeat started to kick into gear.

Hayden moved closer to her. "Can I ask what it is?"

"No."

"Okay." He threaded his fingers through his thick hair. "Artist privilege?"

"Yes." Wow, did he smell good. Fresh soap, the outdoors, and a scent that was pure Hayden.

He glanced away and shoved his hands in his pockets. Then he looked at her again. "Can we, uh, talk?"

"No." She got up from the stool, unable to resist him anymore. She went to him and put her arms around his neck. "I don't want to talk."

"But—"

Riley kissed him, this time not holding back. She murmured against his mouth when he drew her against him, his hands wrapping around her waist, then grazing her back and finally cupping the back of her head. Perfection. This was where she belonged. In his arms. In his life.

Finally he pulled away. "Riley," he breathed. "What's going on? Erma said you're leaving."

"I am." She rested her hands on his shoulders. "Friday."

"And this kiss?"

"I thought it might be the start of the apology I owe you."

He laughed but still looked dumbfounded. "It's the best apology I've ever had."

She led him over to the thrift store couch she'd purchased last week before her world came crashing down. Now she was building it back up, the bricks fresh and new, the foundation solid. She and Mimi had talked for hours, opening their hearts and their pain to each other, strengthening their already tight bond. Hayden, she hoped, would be next.

"I don't want you to leave," he said as soon as his backside hit the couch. When she started to speak, he added, "But if you do go, I'll respect that."

He sounded so formal, and now she was questioning her boldness. But she wasn't going to back down now. She had thought about him almost nonstop since she and Mimi finished their marathon talk session, and she had to stop denying how she felt about him. She almost laughed, seeing him here in the shop right now. She had planned to seek him out after work today. In fact, it had taken all her self-control not to run over to the hardware store and beg for his forgiveness.

"I shouldn't have let Tracey get between us."

Hayden frowned. "I didn't realize she was."

"She always is, at least for me. I've let my past take over my present." She was afraid to say the next words but knew she had to. "I'm scared, Hayden. I've always been scared. Of getting too close to people and being rejected. I've always made sure I'm in control of my life and my feelings. I thought keeping my distance from people would silence the fear. And it did for a while.

"Then I came back here. And you came into my life, and the Bosom Buddies, and Harper, Anita, and Olivia—

"The Three Musketeers." At her questioning look he added, "That's what I call them."

"Yes, them. And finally this shop, even this town. It all beckoned me, which made the fear return. It exploded when Tracey showed up."

Hayden's eyes were filled with sympathy as he took her hand and remained quiet.

"I can't keep running away from the past. I have to face it. I'm not sure what that involves right now, other than getting some counseling. Mimi said she will too."

"That's good. It's helped me out a lot."

She wondered about that, but now wasn't the time to ask. "I'm telling you all this because . . ." Her breath started to hitch. "Because . . ."

"You don't have to say anything else, Riley. I'm in the wrong here too. I told you I would be patient and earn your trust. Then at the first sign of hardship I rushed you and flipped out. I'm so sorry about that."

"It's okay."

"No, it's not." He ran his thumb over her cheek. "I still have some stuff to work out, things I thought I'd conquered, and a couple issues I didn't know I had. I talked to my counselor,

Doug, on Monday, and he helped me, but I think seeing him on a regular basis for a while would be good for me."

Riley nodded. "I'm glad to hear that. Hopefully I can find someone who can help me."

Hayden removed his hand from her face. "In New York?"

He sounded so forlorn that she wanted to hug him again. "No. Here. In Maple Falls."

His eyes widened. "You're staying?"

"Yes. But I have to go back to New York and settle things with Melody and wait until we find her another roommate. As soon as that happens, I'll be back."

"And I'll be waiting."

She smiled, her heart full. "I was hoping you'd say that."

He tugged her into his lap, then gave her a long, lingering kiss. When they parted, she laid her head on his shoulder.

"Can I take you to the airport at least?" he asked, playing with a strand of her hair.

"Absolutely. You can pick me up, too, when I come back." She raised her head from his shoulder. "If that's not too much trouble."

"Never." He cupped her face. "I'm hooked on you, Riley McAllister."

She chuckled. "I see what you did there."

He mock-frowned, then grinned. "Oh, I get it. Hook. Knots and Tangles." Then he turned serious. "I mean it, though. I'm here for the long run. No matter what."

Riley leaned against him again, fully trusting in his words.

Epilogue

THREE MONTHS LATER

R iley adjusted the sign in front of Knots and Tangles. Grand Reopening. It was surprisingly cool for a mid-September morning in Arkansas, and since business was usually best on Saturdays, she expected today to go well.

She admired the display of brightly colored yarn in the windows. Not only had Mimi decided not to sell the business, but she also said she would wait until Riley came back to relaunch the store. Riley caught a glimpse of her reflection in the front-door glass and tugged on the hem of her thin, wheat-colored sweater, layered over a plain white T-shirt. She'd half expected Harper to comment on her reopening day outfit, which included jeans and brown slip-ons, but it seemed her friend had finally accepted Riley's comfortable style.

Her grandmother kept the store open while Riley was in New York and pulled out all the stops for the event this weekend—advertising in the local paper and those of nearby towns, offering special sales, and providing snacks in the back room. Hayden had applied his rehabbing skills and turned the area into a half-workroom, half-storage area. And of course the Bosom Buddies and the Three Musketeers were out in full force. Olivia disliked the nickname. "It's too cliché," she'd said more than once, but they hadn't come up with anything else they could all agree on yet. They were all inside, ready to support Mimi and Riley on their new adventure, starting in about fifteen minutes.

Riley had hoped to return to Maple Falls sooner, but two weeks after she returned to New York, she received a call from one of the small art galleries she'd contacted three years prior about showing her work. She couldn't believe the owner remembered her, but the woman invited Riley to showcase one of her artworks in an amateur art show she was promoting the following month. Riley had not only finished the mixed media project for Mimi's store, but she'd also gotten several interested offers for the piece. She'd turned them down. That work of art was for Knots and Tangles and was prominently displayed right above Riley's new line of dyed yarns. She'd learned the process from Lorri and perfected the technique during her time in New York. She had also decided she would sell some of her art online and in the store when she returned home.

Home. She was finally home.

She moved off the front step, then turned to

inspect the store entrance, making sure it was warm and welcoming. Satisfied that it was, she'd started to go inside when she heard Hayden's low whistle. She turned from the door and faced him, smiling.

"Hello, beautiful." He joined her on the shop's stoop. "Ready for today?"

"Definitely." Like her, his dress was casual—jeans, white T-shirt, black-and-gray plaid shirt—and she nodded her approval. He looked amazing, as usual. She had a few extra minutes before the shop opened, so she sat back down on the stoop, patting the empty space next to her. "You didn't have to take off work for it, though."

"But bosses can do that, you know." He smiled as he sat down, close enough that their legs touched. "I figured I'd stick around and see what it's like to work in a yarn store."

"You've decided to learn how to knit?"

He shook his head.

"Crochet?"

"Nope."

"Dye yarn?"

"Tempting, but no."

She frowned. "Hayden, I think you're going to be bored out of your mind. I'm sure there's something you'd rather be doing than hanging out here."

"I can't think of anything I'd rather do, because you're here."

She could barely breathe. She'd only been back in Maple Falls for two weeks, although she and Hayden had talked on the phone every day she was in New York, and he'd taken a weekend to spend with her in the city. Seeing the city through his eyes had been fun, and although they had spent time apart, their relationship was stronger than ever. As he'd promised, he didn't push her. He was patient and gave her the confidence and trust she needed.

Melody had approved, of course, and although she was sad that Riley was moving, she was also happy for her.

"Couldn't happen to a better roomie," she said, hugging Riley before she got on the plane back to Arkansas.

"Come visit me as soon as you can." Riley fought the tears in her eyes.

"I will." Melody hugged her again.

"Oh wait." Riley dug into her purse and handed Melody several bills. "I keep forgetting to give you this."

Melody took the cash. "What for?"

"The curse jar. I had a bit of a relapse back in July."

Melody laughed, then waved as Riley headed for the gate. "Invite me to the wedding!" she called out.

The wedding. At the time she had laughed at Melody's words, thinking they were a lighthearted joke. But lately she thought about it more often, in a fantasy kind of way.

Yet as she sat there with Hayden, on the stoop of the shop she loved, the people she loved on the other side of the door, she realized something that should have been so clear before. "I love you, Hayden."

His eyes lit up, then closed, and she wondered what he was thinking. When he opened them again, there was a slight sheen to them. "I've been waiting to hear you say those words," he whispered, "from the moment we met."

"At the airport?"

He shook his head, giving her a smile she knew was only for her. "Tenth grade."

Riley laughed. "Yeah, right."

His brow went up as he took her hand. "Are you mocking fifteen-year-old me?"

She paused, her mouth partly open as she searched for the teasing glint she expected to see in his eyes. "You're not kidding."

Hayden squeezed her hand. "No, I'm not. Fifteen-year-old me wasn't the sharpest tool in the box, though. If I had been, I would have asked you out back then. But the feelings were there."

His honesty touched her. "They were there for me too. I think we had to go through everything we went through, both good and bad, to get to this point."

He put his arm around her shoulders, and she leaned against him. "See, I was thinking about how many years I wasted being apart from you, but your explanation is better." He pressed his lips against her hair. "By the way, I love you too."

A thought popped into her head, and she didn't think twice about it. "Now that we have that settled, let's get married," she said, surprising herself with the proposal, but she didn't regret saying it.

"Wait, what?" His arm dropped from her shoulders and he faced her, his handsome face filled with shock.

"Married. Your house is almost done. The store is open, the hardware store is doing well. The chamber of commerce is willing to look at your revitalization ideas. Mimi is back to her usual self."

"That all sounds so logical," he said flatly.

"It does? Well, I can change that." She grinned and put her arms around him, kissing him soundly. From inside the store she could hear the Bosom Buddies applauding and a few shrill whistles from Anita, who had killer whistling skills. Riley laughed as she pulled away from him, still smiling.

"Wow, you're serious, aren't you?" he said, looking bewildered. "You want to get married."

"Yes. I do." Then she paused, doubt filling her. She was springing the idea on him right before she would have to spend the day dealing with what she hoped would be a barrage of customers. That wasn't exactly fair. "If you want to wait, though, that's fine too—"

He helped her to her feet, threw open the door, and gently pulled her inside Knots and Tangles.

"Guess what?" he said to the nosy women who were crowded together only a few feet from the windows. "We're getting married!"

Erma gasped, her gaze darting from him to Riley. "What?"

Hayden turned to Riley. "We should make it official."

She leaned toward him, lowering her voice. "I thought it was, since I proposed to you already."

"I can't help that I'm old-fashioned." He dropped to one knee. "Riley, will you—"

"Wait, wait, wait." Harper strolled over to them, wearing a casual outfit of kitten heels, white slim pants, and a purple checkered blouse. "You can't propose without a ring."

"Yes, he *can*," Riley pointed out.

"Harper's right." Anita appeared next to her, the bangs from her pixie cut touching her brown eyebrows. "Where's the ring?"

Hayden, still kneeling, said, "I haven't gotten that far yet."

Olivia crossed her arms and peered down at him. "So, you're doing this backward? What kind of proposal is that?"

"Help," he squeaked, raising his desperate gaze to Riley.

"Oh, for goodness' sake." Erma grabbed a skein of Riley's brand of hot-pink yarn, then walked back to the counter. A few minutes later, she handed a strand of it to Hayden. "Use this."

He took the yarn from her and tied it on Riley's left ring finger. "Will you marry me, Riley?"

"Yes." She leaned down and took his face in her hands, kissing him until he nearly fell over as applause filled the store.

"It's about time!" Bea said.

"Oh, we have a wedding to plan!" Viola clapped.

"This is so exciting!" Peg bounced on her tiptoes.

The women gathered together, all abuzz, the grand reopening of the shop forgotten. Riley met her grandmother's gaze. Mimi nodded and smiled, then joined her Bosom Buddies and the younger women. The two generations hugged each other.

Hayden slipped his arms around Riley's waist. "There's no backing out now," he said. "If we did, we'd have the BBs and Musketeers after us."

Riley leaned against him, her heart filled with love as she visually embraced the women who had all become surrogate mothers to her and sisters to Mimi. They, along with Riley's new girlfriends, were the family she had always longed for.

She glanced at the bow on her finger, then turned to Hayden and matched his smile with one of her own. Soon he would be the husband she'd always dreamed, but never dared hope, she'd have. *Happy endings are true after all.*

A Note from the Author

Dear Readers,

The Maple Falls series was first inspired by a visit to Arkansas Yarn Co, located in Malvern, AR. After I visited Lorri Helberg's store (yes, she's the Lorri in the story!) the idea of *Hooked on You* was born.

I'm an avid crocheter—some might say addicted, and I'm okay with that—and I love to collect yarn and patterns. I discussed the idea of developing a yarn colorway and a pattern to go along with the book with Lorri, and thanks to her and two fabulous pattern designers, Cheryl Ham (knitting) and Tamara Kelly (crochet), I'm excited to announce an exclusive yarn colorway called *Hooked on You* and a hat pattern, The Riley Hat, available in both knit and crochet!

To find out more about the yarn and patterns, visit my blog: kathleenfuller.com/books-and -hooks-blog. There you will find everything you need to knit or crochet one of these hats with the beautiful *Hooked on You* yarn. If you make The Riley Hat, make sure to tag me and the artists on Instagram: Kathleen Fuller (@kf_booksandhooks), Arkansas Yarn Co (@ArkansasYarnCo), Tamara (@mooglyblog), and Cheryl (@hypnoUcyarn) so we can see your creations!

Thank you so much for reading *Hooked on You*. I hope you enjoyed visiting Maple Falls and reading Riley and Hayden's story. Look for Tanner and Anita's story next, along with another exclusive yarn colorway and patterns. God bless you and yours.

Kathleen

Acknowledgments

I have so many people to thank for helping me write *Hooked on You*. A huge thank you to my agent, Natasha Kern, for helping me get through the writing process during the toughest year of my life. To the editors who worked alongside me on this book: Becky Monds, who helped me talk through the book and series ideas; Karli Jackson, who did an amazing job showing me the potential of Riley and Hayden's story; Jodi Hughes, who made sure all the details were exactly right (I'm not a detail person!); and Laura Wheeler, who managed the project so beautifully. A big thank you also to my good friend Laura Larimore, who introduced me to the real-life Lorri and her wonderful yarn shop, which sparked the idea for Erma, Riley, and the rest of the citizens of Maple Falls.

I especially want to thank the Books & Hooks Facebook group for all their input and help in coming up with the business names in Maple Falls. It was so much fun getting your ideas and voting on favorite names, and they were all perfect for this small Arkansas town.

And of course, a big hug and thank you to you, dear reader. I hope you enjoyed visiting Maple Falls. There are more stories to be told in this small town, so stay tuned!

Discussion Questions

1. Riley moved away from Maple Falls to become an artist and escape a painful past, only to find success and healing when she returned home. Do you think it was necessary for her to leave Maple Falls and Erma? Why or why not?

2. Hayden has to restart his life and his career after a devastating injury. Discuss a time in your life when you had to regroup after a life-changing event. What helped you move forward?

3. Riley and Hayden both had secret crushes on each other in high school. Have you ever had a secret crush?

4. When Riley returns to Maple Falls, she closes herself off to everyone except for Mimi, believing that keeping herself separate will spare her from getting hurt. Can you identify with Riley's decision?

5. When Hayden finds out his father is selling the hardware store, he feels betrayed. Do you agree with his parents' reasons for not telling him?

6. Maple Falls is experiencing a plight that many small towns are dealing with in real life—businesses are closing, people are

leaving, traditions are disappearing. What are some ways Maple Falls and other small towns can be revitalized?

7. The Bosom Buddies and Harper, Anita, and Olivia are true friends to Erma and Riley. Do you have a friend or group of friends that are your "bosom buddies"?

8. Tracey has caused Erma and Riley a lot of pain. What advice would you give them if Tracey returns to Maple Falls in the future?

9. Hayden is used to things going his way, and he learns to put Riley's needs first in order to continue their relationship. What do you think Hayden needs from Riley?

10. Who is your favorite character in *Hooked on You*? Why did you choose that character as your favorite?

About the Author

With over a million copies sold, Kathleen Fuller is the author of several bestselling novels, including the Hearts of Middlefield novels, the Middlefield Family novels, the Amish of Birch Creek series, and the Amish Letters series as well as a middle-grade Amish series, the Mysteries of Middlefield.

Visit her online at KathleenFuller.com
Facebook: @WriterKathleenFuller
Twitter: @TheKatJam
Instagram: @kf_booksandhooks

Center Point Large Print
600 Brooks Road / PO Box 1
Thorndike, ME 04986-0001 USA

(207) 568-3717

US & Canada:
1 800 929-9108
www.centerpointlargeprint.com